"I take it ours wasn't a long courtship,"

Ash said.

Josephine swallowed hard. "What makes you say that?"

"Your sister had never met me before."

He was watching her face as she answered, and she couldn't help but avoid his probing eyes. She hated lying. If there were any other way, she would have taken it. "It was kind of a whirlwind thing."

"I swept you off your feet, hmm?"

"Something like that."

"Wined you and dined you until you couldn't resist me?"

"God, no. Wining and dining would bore me to tears!" Her answer was spontaneous—and honest.

He leaned forward in his chair. "Then what? What kinds of things did we do together, Josephine?"

Dear Reader,

What better way to start off this month—or any month—than with a new book by *New York Times* bestselling author Nora Roberts? And when that book is the latest installment in her popular Night Tales series, the good news gets even better. I think you'll love every word of *Night Smoke* (which is also this month's American Hero title), so all that remains is for you to sit back and enjoy.

With *Left at the Altar,* award-winning author Justine Davis continues our highly popular Romantic Traditions program—and also brings back Sean Holt, a character many of you have suggested should have his own book. *Annie and the Outlaw,* by Sharon Sala, is another special book. This one boasts the Spellbound flash to tell you it's a little bit unusual—and as soon as you meet hero Gabriel Donner and discover his predicament, you'll know exactly what I mean. Our successful Premiere program continues this month, too, introducing one new author in each line. Try Kia Cochrane's *Married by a Thread* for a deeply emotional reading experience. And don't forget Maggie Shayne—back with *Forgotten Vows...?*— and Cathryn Clare, who checks in with *The Angel and the Renegade*. All in all, it's another wonderful month here at Intimate Moments.

I hope you enjoy all our books—this and every month—and that you'll always feel free to write to me with your thoughts.

Enjoy!

Leslie J. Wainger
Senior Editor and Editorial Coordinator

Please address questions and book requests to:
Silhouette Reader Service
U.S.: 3010 Walden Ave., P.O. Box 1325, Buffalo, NY 14269
Canadian: P.O. Box 609, Fort Erie, Ont. L2A 5X3

FORGOTTEN VOWS...?

Maggie Shayne

Silhouette®
INTIMATE™MOMENTS®
Published by Silhouette Books
America's Publisher of Contemporary Romance

SILHOUETTE BOOKS

ISBN 0-373-07598-7

FORGOTTEN VOWS...?

Copyright © 1994 by Margaret Benson

Printed in U.S.A.

Books by Maggie Shayne

Silhouette Intimate Moments

Reckless Angel #522
Miranda's Viking #568
Forgotten Vows...? #598

Silhouette Shadows

*Twilight Phantasies #18
*Twilight Memories #30
Kiss of the Shadow Man #38

*Wings In The Night

MAGGIE SHAYNE

lives in a rural community in central New York with her husband and five daughters. She's currently serving as president of the Central New York chapter of the Romance Writers of America and has been invited to join the National League of American Pen Women. Maggie's first novel, *Reckless Angel,* appeared on the Waldenbooks bestseller list for series romance, and her second book, *Twilight Phantasies,* landed on the Waldenbooks mass market romance bestseller list, also receiving an award and acclaim from critics. In her spare time, Maggie enjoys speaking about writing at local schools and conducting a romance writing workshop at a local community college.

This is for Jessica,
my special heroine,
who has a heart as big as
the moon and a smile as
bright as the sun.
I love you.

Chapter 1

He was the key.

She shifted in the hard little chair and studied him. It was the first time she'd seen him...with her eyes. Everything was the same, though. The square, cruel jawline, the thick, dark lashes that tried to soften its effect, the tiny, crescent-shaped scar amid the curling black hairs at his wrist. His hair seemed blue black against the stiff, white linens. The only difference was that, at present, he was breathing. Even his scent was exactly as she recalled it. A blend of blatant male virility and some spicy shaving cream. Such a potent mix was a pleasant distraction from the disinfectant aroma, and that of the floor wax they were constantly slopping on, in hospitals the world over.

His eyes opened, blinked into focus and narrowed as he studied her. Beyond the curious expression she saw nothing. They were empty, those deep brown eyes. Vacant, just as the doctors had warned her they would be. It was cruel, what she had to do to him. And even then, it might not work. She'd been warned not to attempt to alter what was preordained. But what choice did she have, really? She'd foreseen her own sister's murder. It was going to happen right after the murder of the man in the bed.

"Do I know you?" He sat up slightly as he spoke and the sheet slipped down to his waist. He wore no hospital gown. The sight of his tanned skin, stretched taut over a broad chest and liberally sprinkled with dark, springy curls, shook her. In answer to his question, she nodded. He shook his head, frustration showing in the way his gaze intensified. "Bad enough I couldn't remember my own name. I can't believe any blow on the head would make me forget *you,* lady."

She felt a flush creep up her neck, and yet another round of doubt attacked her. She wasn't certain whether his finding her attractive would make this easier or harder. Especially since the feeling was mutual. She'd prepared herself for the sexual magnetism this man held for her. She'd sensed it before she'd ever come here. She'd decided she could handle it. But if it were a two-way street, traveling it might get damned complicated. For a moment she seriously considered getting out of her chair, walking out the door and never turning back. Then she glimpsed his chest again, and in a flash that left her dizzy she saw it bloodied. She saw the paleness of the skin between the splashes of crimson. She felt the stillness of once-powerful lungs, and the deadening silence of a magnificent heart.

"Hey. Are you okay?"

She forced her white-knuckled grip on the chair arms to ease and dragged her gaze from his chest, back up to his milk-chocolate eyes. Numbly she nodded. She shifted in the chair, leather creaking against vinyl.

"You going to tell me who you are, or am I supposed to guess?" The dark brows were still drawn together in concern and curiosity.

"You'd never guess in a million years," she said softly to the man she'd never met until today. "I'm your wife."

"My...*what?*"

"Your wife."

He shook his head slowly and she could tell by the shrinking of his pupils that it ached. A white bandage at the back of his skull stood like a banner of surrender amid the soft, sooty hair. The car accident that had put him here had caused no other injury. Only that one blow to the head, and the resulting memory loss. For Joey's purposes, it was the perfect opportunity to intervene in a deadly situation.

"My wife." He closed his eyes briefly, then opened them again, studying her with poorly disguised skepticism.

"You don't believe me."

He shrugged, eyes narrow, almost mocking. What had happened to the emptiness? Her mind was wide open. The problem was, she had no control over what she "picked up," and what she didn't. The images, the feelings, were random. God knew there were some things she'd rather not feel at all. Sickening, horrible things.

"I don't believe much of anything unless I see proof," he told her. "That's just the way I am."

She frowned. "And just how do you know *what* way you are?"

The sardonic smile died and the clouds returned to his eyes. "I don't know. That just came out." He shook his head slowly. Joey felt a rush of sympathy for him, followed quickly by a rush of guilt. Her presence here wouldn't make things any easier.

"It must be pretty lousy, forgetting your entire life." Worse yet, with what she was doing to him.

He searched her face. "I've talked to the people I work with—"

"At the *Chronicle,*" she inserted, just to show him she knew.

He nodded, his gaze intensifying, never wavering from hers. "They filled in a lot of the blanks for me. But no one mentioned a wife. How do you explain that?"

She wasn't unprepared. She'd known which bases would need covering, and she'd covered them. He had no family, or none she'd been able to trace. There would be no doubting in-laws to contend with. She called to mind the lines she'd rehearsed for this moment and cleared her throat. "Did they tell you about your weekend in Vegas?"

He nodded, his face wary. "I went there to follow up a lead on...a story I was working on."

"The Syracuse Slasher." His eyes widened, but he hid his surprise quickly. "Your lead was a dead end. But the trip wasn't entirely wasted." She licked her lips, reached down to the backpack on the floor beside her and pulled out the rolled, ribboned document. The scent of fresh ink worried her, but she doubted he'd notice that. She handed it to him, hurrying on as he unrolled it. "When you asked me to go along, I had no idea what you were planning, Ash."

He frowned over the marriage certificate that proclaimed Ashville Allan Coye and Josephine Belinda Bradshaw were husband and wife. He would find no flaw, she was certain. The forger she'd hired was one of the best.

Finally he shook his head. "So I have a wife. It's so odd. It's like I've never seen you before in my life. I hope that doesn't hurt your feelings too badly."

"I knew what to expect when I came here." She swallowed, failing to remove the hard lump in her throat.

"So we were just married on Saturday? And no one else knew about it?"

"That's right. We arrived back on Sunday night. I went to my house and you went back to your apartment...to pack a few things, you said. When you didn't come back I didn't know what to think."

"And now that you know?"

She drew a bracing breath and steadied her tingling nerves. It was necessary, she reminded herself. If she let him out of her sight for a minute, it could mean disaster. And this was the only way. She couldn't very well go to the police. They'd laugh her right out of the building. They'd never believe her. Very few people ever had. It was sickeningly ironic that she could get people to accept lies more easily than the truth. The super at the building where Ash lived, for example. He'd bought this same story, hook, line and sinker, and unlocked the apartment for her. If she'd told him the truth he'd have called the "guys in white." It was always that way.

Except with her father. He'd never doubted her gift. He'd never accused her of having an overactive imagination. And he'd always known when she was lying. But he was nothing to her now. Less than nothing.

"Well?" Ash prompted, reminding her he'd asked a question.

She straightened her spine, met his velvety brown gaze. "I imagine we'll pick up where we left off." She let her eyes search his face, tried to put longing into her expression. It was easier than it ought to be. "At least, I hope so."

Ashville felt his brows leap up. She wanted to play house with him. Well, that would require some serious consideration. He studied her again. Her hair was a mixture of pale brown and honey gold and strawberry blond. It was wild and long. She reminded him of a calico kitten with all those swirling colors in one head of thick, crazy hair. The feline image stayed with him when his gaze lingered on her exotically slanted, emerald green eyes and the black velvet forest surrounding them. She was small, no more than five feet tall, and she had incredible legs. No contour was hidden beneath the skintight leather pants she wore. The rest of her shape was concealed by the matching black jacket, unfortunately. She smelled of fresh air and leather, and she looked at him as if trying to see right through him.

"Can we do that, Ash?"

He licked his lips. "I'm thinking." Who the hell was she, anyway? What was her game?

She rose, scooping her backpack up and dropping it on the chair. She turned her back to him and bent over it. He heard the rasp of the zipper. Then she rummaged inside. Watching the subtle movements of her black-leather-encased, perfectly squeezable little backside, he felt himself inclined to go along with her scheme, whatever it was.

When she turned she held a pair of jeans—*his jeans*—and a button-down dress shirt of pale gray. The cat had been in his apartment.

"These are for when you're released." She opened the narrow closet opposite the bed and busied herself hanging the clothes. She'd brought socks, too, underwear, his cross trainers. She licked her lips again, and he noticed that her hands trembled just slightly as she stowed each item in the closet. "I wasn't sure what kind of shape your other clothes were in, after the accident."

He just watched her prattling on, nervous, seemingly making things up as she went along. She couldn't seem to hold his gaze or sit still or stop filling the tense silences with inane chatter. "Is there anything else I can bring you? Magazines or books or—"

"No." He was baffled. "Look, um..." He glanced down at the marriage certificate in his hand. "Josephine—" She grimaced and her nose wrinkled. Damn. When she wasn't outrageously sexy, she was unbearably cute.

"It's Joey, and I'll only forgive that mistake once, amnesia or no amnesia."

He couldn't help but smile as he tapped the paper in his hand. "That's not what it says here. Josephine Belinda Bradshaw."

"Well, regardless of what it says there, my name is Joey." Her lashes lowered over those green eyes and she added, "Joey Coye."

He shook his head. He'd have to resist the cries of his body that were telling him to go along with her scam, whatever it was, just long enough to exercise a few husbandly prerogatives. He reminded himself that women like her were a dime a dozen. This was a serious game she was playing. She was up to something.

"Okay. Joey, then. Do you mind me asking how you got into my apartment?"

Her eyes focused on his, filled with enough innocence to fool the devil himself. "You gave me a key, Ash."

"Oh."

The investigative reporter inside jumped with questions. His libido was making noises of surrender. Loud noises. But the still-small voice of self-preservation squeaked its dissent.

Because, after all, the accident had been no accident. Someone was trying very hard to kill him.

Then again, forewarned was said to be forearmed, right? And what better way to beard the cat than in her den? She certainly looked harmless enough.

"Ash. Is anything wrong?"

He sighed. "No. As a matter of fact, you couldn't have come at a better time. I'm getting sprung today."

Her eyes doubled in size at that instant. "T-today?"

"Yeah. So if you'll hand me those clothes, I'll be ready to leave in just a minute."

"Leave?"

"You are taking me home, aren't you?" He was enjoying her panic, but he was careful not to show it. He kept his expression blank, trusting.

"Home? I don't—"

"No." He stopped her before she could say anything else. Eyes downcast, he bit his lower lip to keep from grinning. "It's okay, I understand. I thought when you said you wanted to pick up where we left off..." He swallowed an imaginary lump. "It's all right. What kind of a husband would I be, like this?"

He'd called her bluff. He'd watched her squirm, and now he was giving her a way out. Obviously whatever scam she was pulling wasn't meant to extend beyond this hospital room. He could wait until later to do a background check on her, figure out what this fiasco had been all about.

But wait a minute. She was tugging the clothes from the hangers, bringing them to the bed. She set them down and perched on the mattress, and her hands were gripping his shoulders. Her eyes stabbed into his with unmistakable sincerity.

"Don't ever let me hear you talk that way again. Look, I was just taken by surprise. I didn't realize they'd let you go so soon. With a head injury this serious, I figured..." She shook her head fast and her crazy curls swung back and forth over her face. "Of course I'm taking you home. I wouldn't have it any other way."

He frowned and searched her face. "Are you sure—?"

Her shoulders squared and her spine stiffened. Determination lit her eyes. "Get dressed, Ash. I'll go and see about getting your release forms and we'll get out of here."

He nodded and watched the sway of her hips, as mesmerizing as a hypnotist's pocket watch, as she turned and left. When the door closed, he shook himself. He got out of the bed, went to the door and cracked it, just to be sure she wasn't standing outside. Then he grabbed the phone.

When he heard the city editor's voice on the line, he didn't waste time with preamble. "There's a drop-dead gorgeous little cat here claiming to be my wife, Radley. She wants to take me home. I'm going."

Radley Ketchum chortled. "Wake up, Ash. You're still dreamin'. No, wait a minute, you can't be. You might dream about going home with her, but you'd never dream you'd married her. What's going on?"

"Look, I'm serious." Ash darted a glance toward the door and rushed on. "She has a certificate that says I married her in Vegas on Saturday."

"And she expects you to buy it? You? The most dedicated bachelor in the state of New York?"

"Well, she probably figures I don't know that, don't you think?"

Radley was silent for a long moment. "Look, you better not go with her. This whole deal was supposed to keep you alive, not get you killed."

He thought about the look in her eyes when he'd pretended emotional agony. "I don't think it's her."

"Oh, no? What makes you so sure?"

Ash shook his head. "I don't know. Gut feeling, maybe."

"Does she smoke?"

"How the hell do I know if she smokes? Look, I'll let you know where I am when I get there, okay?"

"She lights up a cigarette, my friend, you get the hell out. You have any urge to stick around, you just think about those butts with the coral-frost lipstick stains on them that the cops found at the scenes of all three murders."

"Yeah. Don't worry, I'm not suicidal."

"One more thing. You get her address on record some-where before you leave that hospital, just in case you can't call with it later. Phone number, too. Give me her name right now and I'll see what I can find out about her."

"Her name, she says, is Mrs. Ashville Coye."

"Very funny."

"The marriage certificate reads Josephine Belinda Brad-shaw. Calls herself Joey."

"Got it. Take care of yourself, pal, and, Ash?"

"Yeah?"

"Just in case she *is* our slasher, you be real careful not to let on that the amnesia is just a cover."

He hung up the phone and got dressed just in time. She was back at the speed of sound and, moments later, leading him into the corridor. She seemed nervous. Her glittering emerald gaze darted around, seemingly watching everyone. Ash veered toward the desk, taking her with him. She had a death grip on his forearm, but he didn't think she was quite aware of it. He asked the nurse on duty for a pad and a pen and turned toward his "wife."

"What's your address?"

"Eight twenty-nine Gaskin, in Clay. Why?"

He jotted it down. "Just in case anyone tries to reach me here, I want to let them know where I am."

Her eyes widened. She reached past him to rip the top page from the notepad and then crumpled it in her fist. "I don't think that's such a good idea."

Ash leaned negligently against the desk, eyeing her. There was a heightened color to her cheeks. Her full lips were parted slightly in agitation. She was one hell of an attractive woman. "Why not?"

"I just don't like my home address being so readily avail-able to any nut case who happens to ask for it. That's all."

She tugged the pen from his hand, leaned over the pad and wrote something down. She shoved it across the desk to the nurse. "If anyone tries to reach Mis—my husband, give them this number."

"So during my sentence, will I be allowed visitors?"

She whirled to face him, her hair flying. God, she was jumpy. He smiled so she'd know he was kidding. He wasn't, but it wouldn't pay to let too much show. His "wife's" expression eased slightly, and she picked up a large zippered bag from the desk. She offered him a shaky smile in return, turned her back to him and started for the elevators.

Ash caught up within a second or two. "What's that?"

"What?" She thumped the down arrow repeatedly, gaze raking the halls.

"The bag...honey."

Her brows lifted, but she handed him the bag. "Your personal effects. The stuff they took off you when you were admitted. You know, wallet, loose change." She averted her eyes. "Wedding ring."

Oh, man, she didn't miss a trick, this jumpy, long-haired cat of his.

"Wouldn't want to go too long not wearing that," he muttered. "Feel naked without it."

"Are you being sarcastic or making a joke?" She searched his face, her own worried, wary. He shrugged. The doors slid open and she shot a nervous glance at the people inside. It took her a minute, as if she had to study each face individually, before she made up her mind. About what, he had no idea. Ash caught the doors before they slid closed again.

"We're holding people up, Joey. Is something wrong?"

She blinked, met his eyes and gave her head a small shake. She stepped into the elevator. She stood very close to him, he noticed. Her attitude was damned strange. Not like some woman who was pulling a scam just to get him in the sack. God knew, it wasn't necessary. He'd have obliged her in a New York minute if she'd simply asked. One time and one time only, of course. Women like her were not the kind he had any real use for. Well, okay, one real use for. He knew her type. He'd sifted through enough of them in his search for "Miss Right." There were so many that seemed to fit the role he'd written for the woman who would be his life mate. But usually, when he got them home after an evening of wining and dining, they readily agreed to hop into bed with him. And that ended that. Qualification number one for the future Mrs. Ashville Coye was that she not be promiscuous enough to have sex on the first date. He'd prefer she not be promiscuous at all.

Which is why he figured he'd have known this little cat was no wife of his even if the amnesia had been real. She had "loose" written all over her.

It was in those bedroom eyes that seemed to look right through to your hidden fantasies. And it was in those luscious lips, so full and moist looking they made a man want to taste them.

He scoffed at his own train of thought. Probably collagen.

The doors slid open and she was the first to step out. She gave a quick glance around the lobby, following it with one over her shoulder to be sure he was right behind her. Then she started for the exit, her hips swaying enticingly. No less than seven male heads turned as she passed, he noted.

She didn't seem to notice.

Ha, she knows damn well the show she's putting on, he thought. Feigned indifference is all part of the game. Peaks their interest quicker. Makes her seem like a challenge. He almost laughed. The guy that would find jumping her a challenge hadn't been born yet.

She strode purposefully across the parking lot and Ash followed. The July sun rebounded from the pavement, making the asphalt feel like an oven. Not even a hint of a breeze to put in an appearance, and the air was heavy and stifling. She stopped beside a monster-size, glistening black motorcycle. Grabbing a black helmet with an angular, tinted face shield, she pulled it over her head. When he stopped right behind her, she held out one that matched.

"You're kidding, right?"

She thumbed her visor back, tilted her head to one side. "You're right. God, if I'd known you were being released today, I'd have brought the car."

"That's not what I—"

"Look, why don't you go back to that coffee shop off the lobby? I'll ride home and get the car." She looked him up and down, frowning. "I hate to leave you alone, though." She snapped her fingers. "I know, we'll call a cab and leave the bike—"

"You talk too much, you know that?" He grabbed the helmet and pulled it on, wincing as it slid past the bandaged wound on his head. The amnesia might be phony, but the damned concussion was real enough. "I'm fine. I was just wondering about you." He looked doubtfully at the bike as he fastened the strap under his chin. "Looks like a lot for a little thing like you to handle. Mind if I drive?"

"The last time you drove, you wound up in the back of an ambulance." She flipped her visor back down with a snap and swung one leg over the seat. Well, he'd managed to tweak her temper. He'd been wondering if her concern for his health and happiness would have any bounds. The Harley was low slung despite its size. Still, her feet barely reached the pavement. She kicked the motor to life and revved it. Ashville caught a whiff of gasoline and exhaust. He sighed in resignation and climbed on behind her. His crotch slid forward on the slanting seat until he was pressed to her backside. Putting his arms around her waist, he decided he might not mind the ride so much.

She caught his hands in hers and moved them until they just rested on her sides, above her hips. Again the visor was thumbed up. She twisted her head and shouted above the roar of the motor. "Move 'em and lose 'em . . . darling."

He thumbed his visor back, too, and tried for a pained expression. "I'm sorry."

Her anger vanished. Her huge eyes softened and she almost pouted. "It's just less distracting this way, Ash. That's all."

He nodded, a little surprised at how easily he could skirt her anger by acting hurt. A con artist with loose morals and a heart. He could hardly wait to find out what she was up to . . .

And whether it had anything to do with the Slasher murders.

He pushed his visor down. She did likewise. A second later they lurched forward and shot into traffic.

Chapter 2

She'd done her research on him. In fact, she'd done little else for the three days since she'd heard of his highly publicized accident. She knew him well enough to pull this off. She told herself that over and over again as she leaned into curves without easing her speed, and finally veered right, into the parking lot of the Three Rivers Inn. The bike dipped suddenly into the sunken lot, leaving her stomach somewhere in the region of her throat—God, she loved that sensation!—and zipped out the other side, onto Gaskin Road.

His hands tightened on her waist. She ignored the warmth that settled somewhere under her skin where he touched her, and smiled. He must be hating this. Aside from being a confirmed bachelor and a notorious playboy, he was a die-hard conservative. It must be killing him to ride on the back of a Harley driven by a woman.

But she couldn't take any pleasure in his discomfort. The man was in a terrible situation. More than likely, he didn't even remember his political leanings. Even so, his remark about her letting him drive had rankled. Still did.

She swung right again, into the long dirt driveway, emerged onto the strip of pavement and pulled to a stop at the front patio. Killing the motor, she heeled the kickstand down and leaned the bike onto it. Then she tugged the helmet from her head and shook her hair loose. She glanced over her shoulder to see he'd already removed his. He was looking at the big, white split-level and shaking his head.

"This is yours?" He seemed skeptical. "What are you, independently wealthy?"

"It's no mansion." She swung her leg up in front of her and over the seat, landing with a little hop on the sizzling blacktop. She smelled the river and a hint of rain in the sultry air.

He got off, as well, following her around the side of the house, over the well-worn path and to the back door. "Your backyard's as big as a football field... and it's riverfront." He shaded his eyes with one hand and looked over the smooth green lawn to the narrow brown river at its edge, some sixty yards away.

"Half a football field at best." She unlocked the back door and swung it wide, preceding him in.

"You don't want to tell me, is that it?"

She faced him and saw his suspicious eyes, and the persistence suggested by his set jaw. Uneasiness crept up her spine. But he was asking about the house, the property. Not her lies.

Necessary lies. Necessary to keep him alive. And Caroline.

"Ash, there's nothing I won't tell you. Just ask."

"How does a woman your age afford a prime hunk of real estate like this?"

She shook her head. The man was like a dog with a bone, and she wasn't certain she was ready to tell him about her business. If she told him a little, he was liable to go snooping around and find out more. He was just the type who'd write her off as a lunatic and count himself lucky to escape with his hide intact.

"My age? Ash, I'm thirty, not exactly fresh from the cradle. Besides, I grew up in this house," she told him truthfully. "When Mom and Dad decided to move to a retirement village in Miami, I didn't want to see it go. Parents are very understanding as mortgage holders, you know." She slipped out of her jacket and hung it on a hook near the door.

"What do you do for a living, Joey?" His tone said he wouldn't give it up.

"I'm an independent consultant."

"To whom?"

She wished he would drop it. "Businesses, mostly." To change the subject, she waved a hand to indicate the room they were in, a sparse area with cement floors and white walls littered with exercise equipment. "This is my torture chamber, as you can see. There's a bathroom through here, and that other door leads to the basement '

His gaze lingered on the weight bench and narrowed. "You pump iron?"

"You disapprove?"

"It's unfeminine."

"The results aren't."

He looked her over thoroughly, his gaze traveling a deliberately slow path over her. For the first time in her life, Joey felt uncomfortable in skintight pants and a skimpy bustier. "I'll let you know," he quipped.

A small, hot shiver zapped up her spine, like an electric charge.

"Why'd we come in this way, instead of through the sliding doors at the front?" He was glancing around with something a bit more intense than curiosity.

"Habit. Mom was vigilant about her carpeting. It wouldn't have mattered if the president had come to the door, she'd have told him to go around back."

He chuckled at that, and the sound was so comfortable she relaxed a bit. "Come on, I'll show you the rest." He followed her up the shallow stairs, emerging into the small kitchen. A doorway at each end led into the L-shaped living room. He moved around, eyes seeming to take in everything at once.

It occurred to her that maybe he was looking for something familiar, something that would jog his elusive memory. She felt a twinge of conscience. "Ash, you really didn't spend much time here. Your own apartment will probably seem more familiar to you, though. We'll spend some time there later on, if you want. See if it stirs up the past for you."

He frowned at her. "Why would you want to do that?"

She frowned right back. "Why wouldn't I?"

"Now there is an interesting question." Before she could form a reply, he was walking away from her. She swallowed. He must suspect that she wasn't being honest about their... relationship. She'd have to watch herself. He'd stepped into the living room and was looking up the stairs.

"Three bedrooms and a bath up there. Go ahead, look around. I want you to feel at home here." She meant it, she realized. She wanted this to be as easy on him as possible. The man was going through what was probably one of the worst things any human could experience. Loss of his own identity. And to make things worse, she was giving him a false one to latch on to.

He started up the stairs, but the sound of a horn blasting out front stopped him. He joined her in peering through the sliding-glass door with the broom handle in its tracks to prevent it being opened. He gave it a closer look, and shot her a puzzled glance.

"Habit again. Same broom handle has been there since I was a kid. I told you, nobody comes in the front door."

His smile was real, and for a moment it distracted her. Then she returned her gaze to the car outside. In the driveway, Caroline and the girls spilled from their station wagon and trooped over the path, waving gaily.

Joey felt the bottom fall out of her stomach as she realized the implications of her sister's untimely visit. She hadn't been prepared to begin this thing so soon. She'd expected to have time to figure out a way to talk to Caroline.

"What's the matter?" He said it as if he already knew and was poking fun at her. "You're so pale all of a sudden. Who is that?"

"My...sister, Caroline." She closed her eyes. Think! "Ash, I...I haven't told her about you...about us." She felt sick.

"You didn't tell your own sister you ran off and got married?" His dark brows made surprised arches over his brown eyes and he shook his head, tsking repeatedly. "Shame on you, Joey."

There was no time to beg him to keep his mouth shut. There was no knocking among family...not in this house. Never had been. In a fraction of a second, two blond, giggling girls were racing up the stairs and hurling themselves into Joey's arms.

"Aunt Joey, we came for a picnic!"

"Can we go fishing?"

"We'll throw them back, we promise."

"Yes, please?"

"Slow down, you two. Easy." Joey hugged her nieces, feeling the surge of affection they always inspired in her. She adored them, and she knew part of it was probably the unlikelihood of her ever having children of her own. "Go on to the kitchen. There's candy in the lazy Susan. Go on now."

They peeled themselves from her and raced back into the kitchen. Their mother, dressed as always in baggy sweats and an oversize T-shirt, which she thought hid the fact that her figure had suffered a bit from carrying the two girls, stood behind them. Her hair, so like Joey's in length, texture and coloring, was pulled into a bouncy ponytail, and her smile was bright.

"Hi, Joe." She saw Ash standing there and frowned. "Sorry we didn't call first. I never guessed you'd have company. We can go if—"

"Oh, I'm not company." Ash stepped forward, extending a hand. "My name's Ashville Coye. You must be Caroline. You're more beautiful than your sister told me you were."

Oh, his amnesia hadn't made him forget how to ooze charm. Stunned, Caroline shook his hand weakly. Her gaze jumped from Joey to Ash and back again, and then she blinked. "Ashville Coye—you're the reporter who's doing the series on the Slasher killings, aren't you?"

He shot Joey a quick glance. "I guess that would be me."

"Well, what a coincidence! It's nice to meet you." She seemed a bit confused. "I heard about your accident. I hope you're... better now."

"Your sister is helping me through."

Caroline smiled brightly, then glanced apologetically at Joey again. "Look, the girls and I will go to the park instead. I'm really sorry I—"

"I think you'd better stay," Ashville said in a deep, steady voice. "Joey and I have some news."

Joey swallowed hard, feeling as if a fist had just punched her in the solar plexus.

"News? Joey, what does he mean?" Caroline's voice went a shade higher. "Is anything wrong, honey? You're not sick are you?" A hand immediately went to her sister's forehead, then her cheek. Why was that always the pattern with mothers? Any mother, anywhere in the world, would do it in exactly the same manner. Palm to forehead, then to cheek. And not just to her own brood, but to anyone, friend or foe, who showed signs of having a fever.

Joey shook her head. "Nothing's wrong. I'm not sick, Caro."

"It's this Slasher thing, isn't it? You've gotten yourself into some kind of tr—"

"No, Caroline." Joey glanced up—because he was at least a foot taller than her—into Ashville Coye's stern face and knew there was no way out of this. Next she looked into her sister's blue eyes and felt her own sting. Caroline might never forgive her for this when she learned the truth, but it would be worth it to save her life. There was no one in this world closer to her than Caroline.

"I... that is, Ash and I..."

She couldn't go on. Her mouth felt as though she'd rinsed it with ashes. Caroline would never believe this. She knew her too well.

She felt Ashville's hand close on hers and lift it. "I think this says it all."

Frowning, Joey glanced down to see the simple gold band she'd bought and placed on her left hand. It was a prop. Nothing but a prop.

Caroline's eyes widened. "This is a joke, right? It has to be a joke. Look, Mr. Coye, no one knows how much my sister detests the institution of marriage better than I. You can't be seriously standing here and trying to tell me that she . . . that you . . . Oh, my God, you're not kidding. Are you?"

When he saw the tears pooling in Joey's eyes, Ash thought maybe he'd taken his challenge a bit too far. He didn't have a clue why Joey wanted him to believe she was his wife. He'd thought she would cut the act if forced. He'd been wrong. Whatever was going on in her head, she must be damned serious about it. Otherwise, she never would have continued the charade in front of her sister. It was pretty obvious how close they were.

It was also increasingly and uncomfortably obvious that Joey had some kind of involvement in the murders. He'd wondered about that from the beginning, and her sister's cryptic comment about the killings added credence to his suspicion. But, damn, it was tough to look at her and suspect her of being a brutal serial killer.

A moment later he found himself enveloped in a hesitant but genuine hug. Then Caroline hugged Joey, harder. Fiercely, really. And she was crying, too. She sniffed and straightened. "I never thought it would happen." She sobbed some more. "Joey, honey, didn't you even have a wedding?"

"It was a . . . sort of a . . . spur-of-the-moment decision."

Caroline frowned, this time at both of them, finally settling her gaze on Ash. "Did you get my sister pregnant? Is that what this is—?"

"Caroline, please!" Joey diverted the woman's attention. "Look, you've been after me to settle down for years. You ought to be happy for me."

Her lips thinned as her gaze moved downward to Joey's admirably flat belly. "I'm sorry. It's just that it's so sudden. I'm in shock, that's all." She took Joey's hands in hers and stared into her sister's eyes. "Are you happy, Joey? Because if you are, then that's all that matters."

Joey kept a remarkably straight face. The tears were a nice touch. "Yes, I'm very, very happy, Caro."

Caroline swallowed. Without releasing Joey's hands or even turning her head she called, "Girls, come in here. I want you to meet your new uncle."

The incessant stream of high-pitched chatter died abruptly. Two angelic blond faces peered into the room, quieter than they'd been since they'd arrived.

"Ashville, these are my daughters. Bethany is seven, and Brittany is six. Girls, this is your Uncle Ashville...Aunt Joey's new husband."

Two pairs of blue eyes rounded. "Husband?"

"Uncle?"

The older one came forward, and Ashville, feeling more guilty by the minute, dropped down to one knee. He felt a new anger at his make-believe wife. Playing head games with him was bad enough, but to start in with a couple of helpless kids, and, in effect, to force him to play along, that was too much.

One pair of eyes probed his. "Are you going to turn Aunt Joey into a boring-Suzy-Homemaker-baby-machine?"

That question, coming from such a pint-size spokesperson, almost made him laugh out loud. "A what?"

The second one, Brittany, joined her sister. "That's what happens when you get married," she explained seriously. "You never get to have any fun anymore. You have to stay home and do laundry and have babies."

"And husbands boss you around and tell you what to do."

"We're never getting married."

"Never."

Both girls stood before him, pudgy arms crossed, jewel blue eyes hostile, pale golden brows furrowed. They could have passed for twins.

"Just who told you all that?" he asked, amused.

"Aunt Joey," they chorused.

All eyes turned to her, and she shrugged helplessly.

"Well, you see, when your Aunt Joey met me she decided it wouldn't be so bad to do laundry and have babies, after all."

"The hell I did." She clapped a hand over her mouth, but her eyes shot daggers at him.

The little girls studied him, tilting their golden heads to one side.

"Look, we'd better go." Caroline tugged at the girls. "I want to have you over for dinner. Soon. I'll call you, Joey. *We'll talk.*" She paused at the stairway, glanced at her sister and frowned hard. "Is everything all right?"

"Yeah. Stop worrying."

Caroline nodded, hugged her sister once more and opened the back door.

"He's very handsome, Mommy." He thought that was Brittany. It was hard to be sure. They were dressed alike in denim bib overalls with little pink bows down the seams. The only difference in them that he could detect was that Brittany was about an inch shorter. And they wore different colored hair ribbons.

"Will he make Aunt Joey stop riding the motorcycle?" That was the yellow ribbon. Bethany, he thought.

"Will she still get to take us sp'lunkin' when we're big enough?" And that was the red—wait a minute. Sp'lunkin'?

That was all he heard, because the door was closed and the girls hustled outside. He cocked a brow at Joey. *"Sp'lunkin'?"*

"Caving." If looks could kill, Ash figured he'd better start on his last will and testament.

"Caving?"

Her glare was ferocious. "How could you do that? Just stand there and blurt out that we were married? I could kill you!"

Interesting choice of words, considering that someone had so recently tried. "Well, what was I supposed to do? You *are* my wife. Aren't you?"

She shook her head fast. "I wanted to tell her in my own way. She's going to think I've lost my mind!"

"No doubt, seeing your views on marriage. Boring Suzy Homemaker baby machine?"

Her eyes narrowed. "It's accurate. Look at Caroline. She used to be crazy, fun, confident. Lately Ted's turning her into a..." She bit her lip, stopping herself.

"Go on, into a what?"

She shook her head. "Doesn't matter. It's a whole different situation. You're nothing like Ted."

"Are you sure?" He really wanted to hear more about her feministic views of male domination. Caroline looked perfectly content to him. Obviously loved her girls. Then again, who wouldn't? They were heart grabbers, those two. And some women enjoyed being Suzy Homemaker. He was sure of it... though he had yet to meet one of those.

She glanced up at him from beneath her lashes. "That you're nothing like Ted? The day you prove otherwise, you're out the door, pal."

He shrugged. "So what's for dinner?"

She held her anger for a moment longer. Then it dissolved and she laughed. It was a small laugh, but a laugh all the same. For a second he was insanely glad he'd managed to douse her blazing anger and make her smile. Just because she wasn't the type of woman he'd spent most of his life looking for didn't mean she had to be his enemy.

But if she were plotting something, like his murder, for example, she definitely was.

"I'm not much of a cook. And I don't aspire to be. There are more exciting ways to kill time, you know."

Figured. Not only did she dress almost as provocatively as his mother had, she didn't cook, either. A sudden suspicion hit him. Maybe that was why she wouldn't tell him what she did for a living. If she were a business consultant, then he was a brain surgeon. Maybe she was a whore.

He searched her face and glanced again at the surroundings. It certainly didn't look like the kind of place where men trooped in and out at all hours. The kind of place where a young boy would huddle in the darkness, afraid of the sounds coming from his mother's room, afraid of the harsh, deep voices of strangers.

"Is anything wrong?"

He shook his head, dousing the surge of memory with a supreme and practiced act of will. "If you don't cook, then what do you eat?"

"You have anything against pizza?"

"Nope."

She frowned, tilting her head to one side. "What is it, Ash?" She took a step nearer, searching his face with those sparkling green eyes that seemed to exude laser beams. "You remembered something, didn't you?"

He shook his head. "No. I was trying to remember, but no luck." Actually, his childhood with his sex-for-hire mother was something he wished he could forget. "So are you going to call for that pizza, or am I? I'm starving."

* * *

Something was bothering him, she was certain of that much. But if he wouldn't say, she sure wasn't going to press him. It wasn't as if she had any right to. She wasn't *really* his wife.

Still, the preoccupied look in his dark, shadowy eyes remained throughout dinner and right up to the late news.

"I take it ours wasn't a long courtship."

She swallowed hard and faced him across the room. He was in the forest green recliner, but not tipped back. She sat curled with her legs under her on the matching sofa. "What makes you say that?"

"Your sister has never met me."

He was watching her face as she answered, and she couldn't help but avoid his probing eyes. She hated lying. If there were any other way, she'd have taken it. "It was kind of a whirlwind thing."

"I swept you off your feet, hmm?"

"Something like that."

"Wined you and dined you until you couldn't resist me?"

"God, no. Wining and dining would bore me to tears!" Her answer was spontaneous, and honest.

He leaned forward in his chair. "Then what? What kinds of things did we do together?"

She pressed her lips tightly. She'd rather say nothing than spin blatant lies. Best to stick as near the truth as possible. She could tell him the kinds of things she liked doing, even though she'd never done any of them with him.

"I have an aversion to all things boring, but sometimes a night vegetating in front of the TV is just what the doctor ordered."

"And when we weren't vegging?" He was just a little pale, and there were lines of tension in his face, like he was just barely restraining himself from grimacing. She felt a dull throbbing in her head, and knew it was his, not her own.

"Sometimes we'd jump on the bike and ride south till we'd see more cows then people. Then we'd find a likely patch of wilderness and do a little poking around. Sometimes we'd just stay home and laze in the backyard. Especially on a warm, clear night, with the river sloshing along and the crickets raising a ruckus. I'm a die-hard stargazer, you know."

"No. I didn't know."

She felt a little uncomfortable under his intense gaze. "No, how could you?"

He shifted in the chair, elbows on his knees. "No nightclubs? No dance parties?"

"Do I look like a party animal to you?"

He nodded.

She couldn't hide her surprise. "Really? Well, I'm not. I like excitement, but that doesn't do it for me."

"What does? Sp'lunkin'?"

She nodded hard. "Ever tried it?"

"I don't know. Have I?"

She could have slapped herself for making a slip like that. "Like I said, we haven't known each other that long. You've never tried it with me. But that doesn't mean... I keep forgetting you can't remember."

He shrugged. "I can't imagine it's anything I'd find to be much of a thrill. Find a cave and snoop around inside. Stir up a few bats and step in stagnant water. Doesn't sound all that interesting to me."

She laughed a little, but she was getting the strangest feelings from him. Like unease. He didn't like talking about caves, much less, she imagined, exploring them. The idea of the small, dark spaces gave him an unreasonable amount of trepidation, or something. Something he was trying not to feel.

"There's a lot more to it than that, Ash. I've been miles into a cave, miles underground, in places where no one's ever set foot before. I've crawled through passages on my belly, only to emerge at a three-hundred-foot drop, then rappelled down it with nothing but my rope and carabiners." She shook her head, remembering that particular trip. She felt, just for an instant, the thrill she'd felt then race up her spine. An instant later, she sensed the small tremor that raced up his, only his wasn't caused by excitement. It was something darker. And then it was gone.

"Sounds dangerous."

"Risky is a better word. Of course, the more experienced you are, and the more care you take, the less the risk."

"And you're experienced?"

"Umm-hmm."

"And you take the utmost of care?"

She averted her eyes. "Pretty much."

"Interesting."

She glanced at him, saw his studious frown and wondered what he was thinking. Then his gaze dropped to the neckline of her blouse and narrowed.

"Ready for bed?"

She drew a sudden breath, then caught it, releasing it in a controlled manner. "I've been meaning to talk to you about that."

"I figured you had."

She licked her lips and swallowed. His eyes followed the motion. "For all practical purposes, Ash, we're strangers. I mean, for all you know about me, we could have just met today."

"Can't argue with you there."

She squared her shoulders and rushed on. "So I think it would be best if we used separate bedrooms."

He bit his inner cheek. "Because you don't believe in sleeping with strangers?"

She frowned hard. "What kind of a question is that?"

"A fair one, I think. I was wondering if it applied to all strangers or only the ones you happen to be married to."

For a second she gaped. She snapped her jaw shut with an effort and tried to control the surge of anger. "You're really a jerk, you know that?"

"I've been called worse." He was silent a moment. "Don't you think a good screw would jog my memory?"

"I don't give a damn what it would jog!" Even amnesia wasn't a good enough excuse for that kind of crudeness. She got to her feet, anger beginning to reach a full boil. "At the top of the stairs, turn left. That's your room."

He stood, as well. "You know, for a newly married woman you're not acting very wifely."

"I don't feel very 'wifely,'" she said.

He took a step forward, bringing him very close to her. He caught her shoulders in his hands. "I could fix that." With a tug, she was flattened to his body. She felt the hard planes of it through his shirt, and a tiny tongue of heat curled in some unexplored cave within her.

She drew back her hand and slapped him.

He released her, blinking in shock. "What the hell was that for?"

"For trying to push me into something I don't want."

His eyes hardened. "But you're my wife."

"And like most men, you assume that means I provide sex on demand, right? And if I refuse, you just go find it elsewhere. That's the way it works, isn't it?" She was angry, blurting things out as they entered her mind without thought to what he'd make of them.

He stepped away from her and gave a derisive snort. "You have one hell of a warped outlook, lady."

"I've seen enough to confirm it as fact. Good night, Mr. Coye." She turned on her heel and marched up the stairs.

"'Night... *Mrs.* Coye."

She stopped on the fifth step, her back stiffening. Then she forced herself to continue.

Chapter 3

His head throbbed, reminding him painfully of the very real injury behind his feigned memory loss. He had a hell of a concussion. He was lucky that was all he had, considering his brake line had been cut, and his car totaled from the impact with a city dump truck. He was still more tired than a man in the shape he was in had any business being.

Still, he wondered. Why hadn't Joey been willing to take him to bed to perpetuate her little lie? Was it just another cover? Did she know, somehow, what kind of woman he'd been looking for and intend to convince him that she was it? He didn't want a woman like his mother. He wanted one like . . .

The image that he'd held in his mind for so long floated before him now. A sweet, shy, sensible woman. One who would stay at home and raise his kids the way kids ought to be raised . . . not the way he'd grown up. One who would make pot roast for Sunday dinners. One who wouldn't hop into bed with him on the first date.

He didn't want a whore.

And he certainly didn't want a biker babe, or a thrill seeker. Joey Bradshaw didn't even come close to the model wife he was looking for. So it was a bitter irony that she was the first woman in a long time to say no to him.

Of course, just because she'd refused him didn't mean she made a practice of abstaining. She was just trying to keep him convinced she was on the up-and-up, fighting her natural tendency toward wildness. All that talk about stargazing and hiking in the woods. Right, next she'd want him to believe she was fond of daisy picking and orphaned puppies.

It was time to do a little serious investigating. He'd take out his frustration that way.

He knew perfectly well that this weekend he hadn't been getting married in Vegas. He'd been checking the details of a string of murders committed five years ago. Murders remarkably similar to the ones taking place in the Syracuse area now.

In the past, the victims had consisted of four men and one woman. All killed by a single, swift slash to the jugular. They had all been attacked between midnight and 3:00 a.m. No one had reported hearing anything, not a scream, not a scuffle, though the bodies had been found in busy areas. And none of the victims seemed to have had a thing in common, besides the manner in which they'd died.

So far, in Syracuse, three bodies had been found. All men. The MO was the same, from the nature of the wounds to the probable times of death. Only this time there was one more clue—cigarette butts found at all of the crime scenes, coral-frost lipstick stains ringing the filters. And for the first time, the police were entertaining the notion that the killer was female.

She'd have to be strong, but not unnaturally so. Just enough to grab a man from behind and draw a razor-sharp blade across his throat. It would only take an instant.

Ash thought again of the trim, firm shape of Joey Bradshaw's arms, and then of the weight bench downstairs. He shook his head, still finding it difficult to believe it could be her.

Then why's she lying, pretending to be my wife? And why did her sister make that remark about the murders getting Joey into trouble?

Again he shook his head. It just wasn't credible. But he found himself recalling her nasty remarks about men a few minutes ago, and wondering what made her so disdainful of his gender. Just how much of a man hater was she?

He began in the living room, and he went through everything. Every cabinet, every closet, every drawer. He found little of interest. Some high-topped, deep-treaded boots in the closet, along with a pair of helmets with lamps on top, and several neatly looped ropes with some sort of hardware attached. Looked as if she hadn't been kidding about the caving.

Then, on the top shelf of the living room closet, his hand closed around a cool metallic object. A chill raced through him as he pulled it down. A nine-millimeter Ruger. A full clip.

"Damn."

He glanced up the stairs. If there was anything to find, he'd more than likely find it in her bedroom. But how could he look with her sleeping right there?

Maybe the opportunity would arise later. He slipped into the kitchen and picked up the phone, quickly punching in Radley's number. A sleepy voice answered.

"Rad, it's Ash. What have you got on her?"

"Nothing yet, pal. I'll have a full report for you by tomorrow. I've got people on it. How's it going?"

"Damned if I know. She's not...she's not a run-of-the-mill-type woman, Radley."

"In what way?"

Ash sighed hard. "She packs a cannon and rides a Harley, for starters."

"She rides a... Holy crap. Listen, Ash, this might be something. I got a look at the police reports today. They put a woman on a motorcycle at the scene of two of the three murders. She showed up when the bodies were found. A gaper, you know. They only started taking notes the second time around."

"Description?" Ash wondered why he felt so disappointed.

"Small woman, large bike, dark helmet with a tinted visor over her face."

Ash swore fluently.

"Maybe you ought to pull out of there, Ash."

"I think I'll stick with her awhile."

"If you're sure..."

"I am. Let me know when you get the rest of the info, Rad."

Ash replaced the receiver. Before he mounted the stairs, he took the clip out and replaced the gun in the closet.

She knew she was asleep. It wasn't a normal dream, it was lucid. And she knew she didn't want to see it, but she also knew she had to. She might learn something, see something she hadn't seen before. So she didn't struggle against it. Struggling wouldn't make it go away. It would only distract her from paying attention.

There was Ash. He was falling in slow motion. Falling, his back hitting the carpeted floor hard, then his head. His eyes were closed. He wasn't getting up. A hand came then, blocking the view of Ash. The hand seemed to linger before the lens of her vision. It was gloved ... a black glove. Buttery-soft kid leather. She could smell it. And there were two small buttons at the wrist. The hand clutched a jeweled dagger ... and the end of the dagger was stained dark, and she knew the stain came from blood.

The vision clouded, faded and began to solidify again in her mind's eye. This time there was only a still form, face-down on the floor. The baggy T-shirt's back was covered in crimson stains. The long, multicolored hair reached into the blood, its ends soaked in it. Near her head, the bloody jeweled dagger rested.

"Caroline!"

Then she felt it, the insidious creeping sensations that were not her own, but echoes of someone else's feelings. Rage, so intense she felt her body shake with it. The shadow of a black soul eclipsed her own for just an instant, and terror held her in an unshakable grip.

Joey sat up in bed, eyes wide in the darkness. She couldn't go on like this! She wouldn't! Tears flooded her eyes, and her throat spasmed. She wished to God she could escape this thing people called a "gift." It was a curse, and she didn't want it anymore. Why should she be the only one to know what was going to happen? Why should she be the only person in the world who could prevent her sister's murder? God, she was so afraid she'd fail.

Her bedroom door swung open and Ash filled the door-way. "Joey?"

She reached out, flicked on the lamp. He stood there in nothing but a pair of white boxers, looking anxious. "I'm okay. Bad dream."

He came in, approached the bed and finally sat on its edge. He did it all slowly, as if waiting for her to object. She kept quiet.

"You don't look okay." He lifted one hand, brushed the tears from her face, then looked at his hand as if it had acted without his consent. "You're shaking all over."

It was then that she realized she couldn't keep him from being killed while she slept. She had to be close enough to prevent it, at all times. It meant her sister's life. She had to break the killer's chain—and she had to break it beginning with Ash.

"You screamed... your sister's name, I think. Was the dream about her?"

She bit her lip. It was so difficult, lying all the time, hiding the things that troubled her the most. "I don't remember." Her throat closed off. "It scared the hell out of me, whatever it was."

She tried to catch the sob before it escaped, but she failed. She heard him swear softly just before he slipped his arms around her and pulled her to his chest. "It's okay, Joey. It was just a dream. It's over now."

Her tears dampened the crisp hairs of his chest. Her cheek was pressed tightly there, and his scent completely invaded her senses, drowning out the memory of that alien presence in her mind. His arms around her were strong and hard and felt as if they could be barriers against the dark invader. She snuggled nearer without quite meaning to. That damned chemical attraction she'd felt before she'd even met him came to life inside her.

"You want me to stay?"

She sniffed. She was glad he'd offered, so she wouldn't have to ask. She did have to be near him at all times, attraction or no. It had been foolish of her to let her temper make her forget that earlier. What if the killer had struck tonight? Ash could be dead already, and the Slasher on his way to his next victim.

Caroline.

She lifted her head and met his gaze. "I'm not going to have sex with you, Ash."

"I didn't ask, did I? What do you think, that's all I ever think about?"

She felt something then, and it made her frown. Nightmares. God, he'd had nightmares all the time...a long time ago. That's why he was reacting this way to hers.

That was all. Just that tiny kernel of revelation. Then nothing.

She sighed, shook her head and settled back under the covers. Ash lifted them and slipped in beside her. They both lay on their backs, looking at the ceiling, saying nothing. She wondered if his body was as stiff with tension as hers was.

She had her answer a second later. He swore and rolled onto his side, facing her. "This is ridiculous. Neither one of us bites. Roll over."

She did, facing away from him. A second later she went rigid as his arms came around her from behind and his body snuggled close to hers. "Relax, Joey. I'm not up to anything. I promise."

She did relax after a moment. Actually, it was rather cozy lying this way. Incredibly warm and sort of... safe feeling. It was a real shame she had to lie awake and wait for him to fall asleep. It would have been so easy to simply curl into his strong embrace and drift off.

But an hour later, when his deep, rhythmic breathing told her he slept, she eased his arms from around her waist and slid carefully to the edge of the bed. Then she paused, listening. His breathing pattern didn't alter. She slid to the floor and tiptoed out of the room, going down the stairs.

She went to the closet in the living room and took down the gun. Without checking, she knew it was unloaded. She removed the clip. Empty. A little chill snaked up her spine. She could have sworn she'd left the gun loaded. She'd deliberately put it out of reach of her two nieces. So who had taken the bullets out?

A tremor worked its way from her toes as she dragged a footstool nearer, climbed onto it and reached farther into the closet, to the shoe box in the back. She removed the shoes and pulled out a box of cartridges, reaching for the extra clip. She didn't get down first. She filled the clip right there, while standing on the stool. She slipped it up into the hollow handle of the gun, then slammed it home with her palm. On unsteady legs, she stepped down. Checking the front door, she made sure the lock was engaged, glancing at the broom handle lying lengthwise in the sliding-glass door's track. Then she rushed downstairs, to assure herself the back door was locked, as well.

It was. So who had taken the bullets out of the gun? There was only one answer. Ash. And if he'd found the Ruger, then he must have been snooping. And if he was snooping, then he must not trust her. He must suspect something.

She had to be more convincing. She couldn't mess this up. Not when her sister's life—when Ash's life—depended on it.

Her nerves jangled. Her muscles twitched. She paced the floor for a while, until her pacing took her to the kitchen cabinet where she kept the cigarettes. She rarely smoked anymore. Only in times of extreme stress. She invariably finished by vowing never to light up again. And she invariably lit up again anyway when things started getting to her.

She lit one now and paced as she smoked it. Something was wrong. Something more than just the suspicious mind of the man upstairs, sleeping in her bed. Some darkness loomed too close, reaching out its gnarled, ugly claw. She shivered, took a final drag from the stump of the cigarette and ground it out in an empty tuna can she snatched from the recycle bin.

Only then did she slip silently up the stairs, the gun held at her side. She paused at her side of the bed, glanced once at Ash and frowned. He wasn't in precisely the same position as before. She watched him a moment. His dark lashes rested on his face. A shadow of beard darkened his jaw, giving him a fierce look and making her want to rub her hands over his bristles. His arm was on the outside of the covers, and she could tell easily that his disapproval of weight training applied only to women. She wanted to touch his arm, to feel the iron in those bands of muscle when he tensed beneath her fingers.

She shook her head quickly. This was stupid, this moon-eyed staring at him as he slept. She was a grown woman, not a love-struck teen. But even with the dread embedded in her soul, she felt the attraction. It was impossible to forget it, even for a minute.

She thought about slipping the gun under her pillow, but was afraid he'd touch it in his sleep. If it hadn't been Ash who had taken her bullets, then he still didn't know about the gun. What on earth would he think if he knew? She decided on the drawer in the nightstand beside the bed. She could reach it quickly and with a minimum of effort.

As she closed the drawer, Ash moved. She swung her head around quickly, but his eyes remained closed, his breathing steady. He'd only rolled onto his back, exposing the chest that so disturbed her, its crisp, springy curls that lured her lips. It also revealed the ripples of his abdomen. She could see the "six-pack" beneath his skin, even as he lay there, completely relaxed. She had the absurd image of running her hands over him, feeling the hard shape of his muscles, the warmth of his skin, the springy hairs tickling her palms. She almost groaned aloud.

Shaking her head, she gently eased herself into the bed. A second later she was imprisoned by his arm snagging her waist, and one hair-roughened leg covering hers. Rather than struggling free and waking him, she opted to relax and go to sleep. She told herself it was so she wouldn't wake him. In truth, his weight was more a comfort than a burden, even if such closeness was more likely to keep her awake than lull her to sleep.

He couldn't rest easy after she'd sneaked away to get the cannon and had returned, tucking it within easy reach. He told himself it was okay, that he'd removed the bullets already. But he couldn't be sure she hadn't reloaded it, and he couldn't be sure she wasn't a lunatic who was planning to use it on him. He figured at least with his arms around her, he'd know if she went for the gun.

Unfortunately this close he could smell the lingering aroma of cigarette smoke that clung to her hair. Radley's words floated into his mind like filmy ghosts. "She lights up a cigarette, my friend, you get the hell out... think about those butts with the coral-frost lipstick stains on them...."

He tried *not* to think about those butts, even as he wondered what shade of lipstick she used. Then he asked himself if he was the one who was stark, raving mad. Despite the fact that he had every reason to believe she might roll over at any minute and try to blow his head off, his body was beginning to respond in some very primitive ways to the feel of her.

Beyond the clean, crisp feel of the sheets, he felt the silky texture of the nightgown she wore. Beyond the musky smoke in her hair, he could smell the shampoo she used. Under the weight of his thigh, hers was like silk, and firm, and so shapely he wanted to trace the length of it with his lips.

The image jarred him, and he had to back off a little so she wouldn't feel his response to her tight, rounded backside pressing into his groin.

How could he lust this way after a woman who might be out to kill him? Maybe that head injury had done more damage than he knew.

Eventually, after hours of restlessness and several changes in position that did nothing to ease his discomfort, he must have slept. When he woke she was not in the bed. He couldn't believe it. The rising sun slanted through the window, spilling over the empty pillow where she'd been. He sat up quickly, glanced around the room and found it empty. He yanked the drawer open. The gun sat there, like a stern reminder. He did a quick check and found the damned thing had been reloaded ... to the hilt. He slammed the drawer, swearing, flung back the covers and leapt up just as she stepped in from a door that apparently linked bedroom directly to bathroom.

She wore a pair of narrow-legged, tight-fitting jeans, and a tank top that fit like a second skin. Her hair was a mass of long wet straggles. Water beaded on her neck. His gaze moved lower, to the round breasts beneath the clingy material, to the luscious rise of them visible at the scooping neckline and the droplets that clung there. A rush of blatant, animal lust seared him from the inside out, and he cursed himself for idiocy. Even then, he let his glance sweep down to her denim encased thighs, curving calves and adorable little bare feet.

He swore yet again, and didn't realize he'd spoken aloud until she said, "Sorry. I tried to be quiet."

"You were." He lifted his gaze, by sheer force, to her eyes, slanting and green and full of mystery. "Leave me any hot water?"

She smiled, and he felt an inexplicable hope that whatever she was doing she had a good reason. "I left you plenty. And while you're showering, I'll make us some breakfast."

"I thought you couldn't cook."

"I didn't say I couldn't. I said I didn't...much. I can scramble eggs and nuke sausage."

"Well, I can butter toast and mix up frozen orange juice, so we ought to survive." He glanced down at his body, clad only in skivvies. "I don't suppose I have a change of clothes here?"

"No. Sorry. Right after breakfast we'll go over to your place, if you want. Maybe being in your own apartment will sweep some of those cobwebs out of your rafters."

And that was when he noticed the running shoes dangling from one of her hands. "You going out?"

"Coming in, actually." She walked to the closet and tossed the shoes carelessly inside.

He frowned. Dammit, how could he have slept right through her leaving the house? He was lucky he hadn't woken up dead. Why hadn't he heard the car, or the bike? "Where did you—?"

"I run every morning. I hope I didn't bother you when I sneaked out."

Sneaked out.

"I never even knew you'd left. What time—?"

"A little after five." She smiled softly and her eyes traveled over his face. "You were sleeping like the dead, Ash. I think your body has a little recovering to do yet."

Right. He must have been out cold. And the last time he remembered glancing at the clock's luminous digits, it had been twelve twenty-something. She could have been gone half the night, for all he knew. He had nothing but her word for it.

The entire time he spent in the shower, he kept thinking about the famous scene in *Psycho*. But nothing happened. He emerged, groped for a towel and smelled the scent of scrambled eggs and sausage wafting up the stairs.

He pulled on his jeans, but didn't snap them closed. The sight of the clothes she'd left discarded on the bathroom floor distracted him. He bent to pick them up. Shiny black spandex leggings with hot pink racing stripes. Thickly woven white socks. Her damp towel was still there, too. She wouldn't win any housekeeping awards. He stuffed the clothes into the hamper, then opened the medicine cabinet, rubbing one hand over his scruffy face.

There was a tap on the door. He went to it and swung it open.

Joey didn't say a word. Her lips were parted, as if she'd started to speak, but nothing came out. Not even, he thought, a breath. Her wide green gaze moved down his bare chest, pausing for a moment at the slightly gaping fly of his jeans, then jerked upward to his face again. Her cheeks pinkened.

His ego spiraled upward. He leaned one shoulder against the doorjamb. "Did you want something?"

Her tongue darted out to moisten her lips. She shook her head. "No. I just—the razors. They're in the closet, top shelf. Shaving cream, too. I thought you'd be looking for them."

She wanted something, all right. Her eyes said it all. And why the hell did it give him such a thrill to know a murder suspect was lusting after him?

"Thanks. I was just looking for them." He turned and opened the closet, pulling down the cream. She still stood in the doorway. He glanced at the pink can. "Powder-fresh scent?'' He looked at her again, standing so flustered and flushed and sexy, her still-damp curls falling over her shoulders, cat's eyes fixed on his.

A mischievous smile played with her lips. "It's the best I can do for now."

"It won't be so bad. I like the way *you* smell."

She cleared her throat and lowered her gaze.

"So how's that breakfast coming? *It* doesn't smell half bad, either."

Her head flew up again. "Oh, God, my eggs!" She whirled and raced down the stairs. He chuckled and turned back to the sink to begin applying the lather to his face.

A few minutes later he heard the phone ring, and then her voice, cussing long and fluently. He stuck his head out the bathroom door. "Want me to get it?"

"Please!" she yelled back.

He wiped the last of the lather from his face and ducked into the bedroom to snatch up the receiver.

"Ash?"

Radley's voice was strained. The bottom fell out of Ash's stomach.

"We've got another one," he said when Ash didn't answer him.

"When?" Ash tried to keep the turmoil from his voice.

"He was found half an hour ago. Coroner's putting the time of death between two and three this morning with what he has so far. We'll know more later."

Ash swallowed hard. He couldn't be sure of Joey's whereabouts between two and three this morning. He only had her word that she'd left the house around five. He didn't want to ask the next question, but he knew he had to.

"Where?"

"Phoenix, Ash. A couple of miles from where you're sitting."

Ash shook his head as it began to throb again.

"Ash, did she leave the house? Was she away from you at all between two and three?"

"It's circumstantial."

"Dammit, Coye—"

"I don't know, okay? I fell asleep."

"You fell—"

"I know. I'm an idiot. Shoot me. Save her the trouble."

"You really think—?"

"It was a sick joke." He didn't think she was out to kill him. Or anyone else. Hell, the idea was ludicrous. "Look, we don't know anything yet. Keep this to yourself until we do." Why in God's name was he trying to protect her? He ought to call the cops himself.

"Too late for that, Ash. They have the plate number of that bike from the last time. Now, with this murder practically in her backyard, don't think they won't be over there to grill her."

Ash closed his eyes. His mind was spinning. He just couldn't make himself accept that the woman he'd held in his arms last night, the woman whose tears he'd wiped away after a nightmare had scared her half to death—could also be a cold-blooded murderer. "Thanks for the warning, Radley."

"You want me to be there when they show up?"

Ash chewed his lip. He looked up at the sound of her steps, light and quick. She stopped in the doorway, her eyes just as huge and innocent as an angel's. "I burned our eggs."

She looked so damned remorseful he couldn't help but smile at her. He covered the mouthpiece. "That's okay. I hate eggs."

Her face brightened immediately. "Raisin bran?"

"My favorite," he lied.

She grinned and trotted back down the stairs. Ash stared at the empty doorway until Radley's voice brought him out of his trance.

"You want me to come over or not?"

Ash stiffened. "Only if you're going to back me up. And I mean one hundred percent."

There was a long pause. Then, "What are you going to do?"

"Trust my instincts. They haven't been wrong yet, have they?"

Chapter 4

His facial muscles were too tight. There were a pair of brackets etched between his dark brows. He kept looking at her across the table. Not saying anything, just *looking* at her between bites. It gave her a squirmy kind of feeling. As if he was searching for something, as if he was trying to read her mind. He finished his raisin bran and rose, rinsing the bowl, then stacking it in the dishwasher.

"Are you going to tell me what's wrong, or just keep frowning all morning?" But she already knew, didn't she? She'd felt the eerie restlessness in the middle of the night. She'd paced and shivered and given in to her craving for a cigarette. She'd sensed the ugly blackness closing in.

He turned to face her, smiling a little. "I didn't realize I was frowning."

"It was that phone call. You've been messed up ever since." She rose, too, leaving her cereal bowl, spoon still inside, on the table. "Who was it?" She felt sick to her stomach. The dread she'd felt so strongly last night returned, and she braced herself for his answer.

"Rad Ketchum." He didn't elaborate.

"Your editor." The darkness gathered around the edges of her mind. Something bad had happened last night. Something she'd sensed . . . maybe even as it was happening. Something she should have been able to prevent. What good was the damned "gift" if she was too afraid to use it? God, when the coldness, the darkness, came to her, she did her utmost to push it away, to ignore it, when she should look closer, examine it and try to see what it meant. And it was coming again now, the cold, clammy hand clutching her heart and squeezing. It was getting harder to breathe. And then there was only the white heat searing her throat.

She gasped in pain and sat down hard when her knees buckled without warning. Tears choked her even as Ash shot forward, startled, grabbed her shoulders and asked if she was all right. She lifted her head and stared up at him, the most horrible, gut-wrenching fear she'd ever known throbbing all through her. "It isn't her," she whispered. "It isn't Caro. Tell me it isn't Caro . . ."

His puzzled frown—or was it a worried one?—deepened just before Joey closed her eyes against a flood of tears. "Why would you think . . . ? Joey, Caroline is fine. This has nothing to do with your sister." He shook her a little, hands tightening on her shoulders. "You hear me?"

She drew a deep, shuddering breath. Then another. She forced her eyes open as the tide of panic receded. "Then who?"

His dark eyes narrowed, and through the haze of dread she realized she was giving too much away. He'd wonder how she knew. If she told him, he'd think she was insane, or worse. She bit her lip and tried to think logically, coherently, even with that shimmering gloom hovering in her peripheral vision. It was getting closer. Getting harder to ignore.

"Something's happened to someone. I can see it in your eyes. Your editor called and told you something and..." She bit her lower lip and watched as some of the suspicion faded from his eyes. "Just tell me."

"Okay. There was another murder last night. Early this morning to be exact."

He watched her face, observing her every reaction, she thought. "The Slasher?"

He nodded. "The victim was found a little over an hour ago... in Phoenix."

She knew her eyes widened. She felt them expand until her head ached. Phoenix! She'd sensed the darkness was getting closer, but...

She shot to her feet, catching the front of his shirt in both fists. "Caro lives in Phoenix—"

"She's fine, I told you—"

"And the girls? Brit? Beth?"

"It was a *man*, Joey. The name hasn't been released yet."

She sighed as every muscle in her body went limp. The hands bunching the material of his shirt relaxed, and she sagged forward without even thinking about it. His arms came around her, maybe as automatically as hers encircled his waist, as instinctively as her buzzing head rested against his warm, hard chest.

It felt good. Like some kind of armor against that darkness, that chill. Like she was being infused with calmness and strength, and she'd be able to stand on her own again if he'd just hold her a little longer. She hadn't known being in a man's arms could feel like that.

When his tight hold on her eased, she stepped away and looked up, seeing the same surprised expression on his face that must have been on hers. And there was something else.

As if he'd come to some kind of conclusion, or made a decision.

"Joey, the police might come here this morning. They might want to ask you some questions."

She frowned. "Me?"

He opened his mouth to say more but the doorbell chimed. The *front* doorbell. Ash licked his lips. "If anyone asks, Joey, you don't smoke. Never have. Okay?"

She shook her head, bewildered, searching his face for an explanation.

"Just trust me."

She nodded, sensing that she *could* trust him. Too bad he was the one person she had to lie to in order to save her sister's life...and his own.

He gave her shoulders a final squeeze and let go. She walked through the living room, looked through the glass door to the officers standing there. The woman was tall, built like Lady Atlas, and blond. She exuded the kind of raw, rugged sex appeal most men find hard to resist, and her cold blue eyes on Joey seemed to be trying to intimidate her from the first glance.

Joey stared right back, not blinking, and pointed one finger at the decal that read, Please Use Other Door."

"Go around back." She said it loudly, and her voice didn't shake at all.

The cops show up to question her about a murder, and she tells them to use the back door. She had backbone, he had to give her that much. Not that she'd seemed all that solid a few minutes ago. But he'd known her fear for her sister was genuine, even if it didn't make much sense. And if it *was* genuine, then she couldn't have been the killer, right? She'd have to know who the victim was if she'd committed the crime herself.

He stood beside her at the door as Sgt. Beverly Issacs and two male officers filed in. Bev dwarfed them both by a good four inches. Her head was level with Ash's when she stopped in front of him. Joey, at his side, looked like a pixie in comparison.

"Hello, Bev."

"Well, Ash. Seems like every time I turn up a clue in this case, I find you there before me. You wanna tell me why that is?" Her voice was frosty, but her eyes glinted so he knew she wasn't really angry or suspicious of him. Just running out of patience.

"Oh, I'm not here for any clue. I got married. Hadn't you heard?"

Her smile was wide and instant. "Right. And I'm running for mayor."

He felt Joey's gaze on him and looked down to see her frowning. "You *remember* her?"

Whoops. "Bev and I go way back, Joey. But I only remember her because she questioned me at length right after my accident." He'd almost slipped. Even the police weren't aware his amnesia was anything but genuine. He had to be more careful; Bev was sharp. He glanced at her again. "Bev, meet my wife, Joey Bradshaw . . . Coye," he added quickly, hoping Bev hadn't noticed the slight hesitation.

Bev's ice blue gaze darted from him to Joey and back again. "You're serious."

Ash nodded.

Bev shrugged. "Well, married or not, Ash, I have some questions for your *little* wife here." She glanced down at Joey. "You don't mind, do you, Ms. Coye?"

Ash smiled inwardly as Joey stiffened her spine and rose to her full height. Her chin came up, and her gaze never wavered from Bev's for a second.

"I don't mind at all."

Bev nodded and nudged one of the officers, both of whom flanked her like the servants of some great, powerful queen. The officer yanked a pad and pencil from his pocket and stood ready. "Ms. Coye, you own a motorcycle. Is that right?"

Joey didn't blink. "Yes."

"A black Harley-Davidson, New York plates, 352H4?"

"It's a black Harley. I don't have my plate number memorized, but you're more than welcome to take a look."

"Not necessary. It's registered to you."

"If you already know, then why are you asking?"

Ash slipped his hand around Joey's and gave a warning squeeze. It wouldn't do to be hostile to the police. They would wonder why.

"That bike's been seen at a couple of crime scenes recently, Ms. Coye. You want to tell me why?"

"I was curious. Is there a law against that?"

Beverly's gaze turned angry. Ash had felt it coming. Damn, Bev was not a good person to tick off. "What kind of cigarettes do you smoke, Ms. Coye?"

"I don't smoke, Ms. Issacs."

"*Sergeant* Issacs," Bev said through gritted teeth.

"Whatever."

Bev looked at Ash, and he could see her temper simmering near a full boil. "You *married* this?"

"Easy, Bev. She's upset. You would be, too, if someone implied you were a serial killer, wouldn't you?"

Bev sighed and swung her head toward Joey again. "Where were you last night and early this morning?"

She opened her mouth, but Ash spoke first. "She was in bed, with me."

"All night?" Bev looked skeptical.

"All night," Ash replied.

"But she could have slipped out, while you were sleeping."

"We're newlyweds, Bev. We barely had two days together before the accident, and I've been in the hospital ever since. You really think I *slept* my first night back?" As he said it, he slipped an arm around Joey's shoulders and squeezed her to his side.

Bev's wary gaze kept shifting to Joey, and Ash hoped she wore a convincing expression on her face. He kept his own gaze level with Bev's, not looking away once.

Bev shook her head. "You lost your memory—"

"But not my mind."

"If I find out you're lying—"

"I'm not."

She nodded, casting a skeptical glance down at Joey. The sergeant shook her head, then turned on her heel and left the house. The two officers followed, and Ash closed the door.

For a long moment he didn't turn to face Joey, knowing the questions he'd see in her eyes.

"You lied to her."

"Yeah." He turned around slowly and looked at her. There was some sort of ache in her eyes that he hadn't expected. As if he'd hurt her somehow. Impossible.

"Why?"

"A husband wants to protect his wife. Human nature."

"Or maybe you thought I needed an alibi."

"If I thought you were a killer, I wouldn't be here."

She blinked three times, each downward swipe brushing more moisture from her eyes, only to have it quickly replaced. "You know this Beverly pretty well."

He nodded. Then added, "I used to, anyway. Or so I'm told."

She stared at him harder. "You've slept with her."

He had, but how the hell could she know that? Was his face that transparent? He squirmed for a second, then remembered he didn't have to give her a direct answer. "Maybe. I don't remember." For just a second she looked furious. Then she covered it. For crying out loud, was she actually jealous?

"*She* does." Joey looked at the floor. "And she'd like to do it again."

He gave his head a small shake. "Did I miss something? Did you and Bev have a heart-to-heart while my brain went out to lunch, or what? Where are you getting this? What the hell did she say or do to make you think—?"

"Nothing. She didn't have to. It was obvious."

She turned to walk away, but he caught her arm before she reached the stairs and turned her to face him. "Obvious, how?"

"I know what I know, okay?"

She knew, all right. And she didn't like it a bit. And for some reason, he *liked* the idea that she didn't like it.

He followed her up the stairs, trying not to grin in satisfaction. She was more worried about his one-nighter with Bev Issacs than she was about the police department's suspicions of her. Further indication she was not the Slasher, to his way of thinking.

She stalked into the living room and paced the floor. He sat down in the recliner and watched. He watched the sway of her hips as she walked away from him, the way her thighs moved as she walked back. She was no hooker. He didn't know why he felt so certain of that now, but he was. She was no killer, either. He didn't know what she was, but he knew he wanted to find out. And he knew something else, too. She was in trouble. It was fear he saw in her eyes at times, not cunning or cold-bloodedness. She was lying to him out of ice-cold fear.

He rose and took her shoulders, stopping her nervous pattern. "Hey." She looked at him, those eyes so wide and vulnerable he thought he'd probably believe anything she told him. "Whatever it is, Joey, I'm on your side. Okay?"

He saw the guilt that flashed over her face along with the surprise. "You don't even know me. How can you—?"

"I want to know you."

Her eyes widened. Her lips parted and she stared at him. "I might be able to help, if you'd just talk to me."

She licked her lips, then shook her head, but her gaze remained riveted to his. "I . . . can't."

He shrugged. "You will. I can wait." His eyes focused on her full lips, and he felt himself tightening up inside. He wanted to kiss her. He wanted it badly. He moved his head lower.

She stepped away, turning around quickly, averting her face. "If we're going to your apartment to pick up your things we ought to get at it, don't you think?" Her voice was strained, and too soft.

He steeled himself against the desire stirring in his groin. "Sure. Okay."

There was just too damned much to deal with!

She paced his living room while he rummaged around in the bedroom, tossing clothes into a suitcase. She couldn't shake the attraction. It was absolutely monstrous in proportion, and growing all the time. And he felt it, too, which complicated things still further.

To top it off, he was protecting her. Probably only because he thought it was his duty as her husband. But he'd lied to the police, likely jeopardized his career, for a woman who was no more than a stranger to him. How would he feel about her when he learned the truth, that she was nothing to him, that he'd put himself on the line for a woman he didn't even know? She hated the guilt she felt because of that.

And what about his relationship with Lady Atlas? Maybe they'd actually had some kind of affair, and he just didn't remember. Maybe Joey's lie was now going to ruin whatever they'd had together. That Beverly Issacs still wanted Ash practically appeared in boldface type across her forehead whenever she glanced at him, at least it did to someone as sensitive as Joey. But how did he feel? Was he attracted to the woman? He must have been once. It was hard to imagine any man who wouldn't be. And why did the thought make Joey feel like throwing up?

She paced faster. Another man had died last night. She'd felt it coming, and done nothing to prevent it. She'd have to do better if she were going to keep her sister and Ash alive.

He emerged, suitcase in one hand and something smaller in the other, something that looked like a miniature briefcase with a small, plastic handle attached to it. She frowned at it.

"My laptop," he said. "I'm still on leave from the *Chronicle,* but I'd like to work from the house."

She nodded. His face was pinched, and she realized his head was throbbing. She picked up a lot of his feelings, more than she usually did with anyone—except, perhaps, for the Slasher. She shook that thought away. "You need to lie down, Ash. Didn't the doctor prescribe anything for the pain?"

His eyes narrowed. "How'd you know my head was splitting?"

She forced a smile as she sought an explanation. If she kept slipping like this, he was going to catch on. She gave him what she hoped was a sly glance. "I'm your wife. I can read you like a book."

He nodded, but was still looking at her rather oddly when he followed her out the door.

He used the time she left him lying in her bed. *Her* bed, he noted with interest, not the one in the room she'd assigned him originally. She'd hustled him up here the second they had returned from his place and insisted he lie down. It was almost as if she could feel the way his head was pulsing every time she looked at him.

But pain or no, he had work to do. While he believed Joey was innocent of the Slasher killings, he was still all too aware of her dishonesty. He thought she might have a good reason for the lies, or at least what she must believe was a good reason. But he couldn't help her unless he found out what it was. And he had a feeling, a bad, creepy kind of feeling in the pit of his stomach, that it all revolved around the Slasher killings. She'd known something had gone down last night. She'd known it before he'd told her. There was no doubt about that.

He slipped out of bed after she'd been gone for a while. His gaze fell on his suitcase. She'd left it here, in this room. It was pretty obvious she intended for him to stay here. His ego would have liked to believe it was out of pure, overwhelming desire for him. His brain, however, knew there must be more to it.

He sat on the edge of the bed, picked up the phone and poked at the numbers. When he heard Radley's voice on the other end, he kept his own low. "What have you dug up on my wife?"

Rad snorted. "Wife, huh? You wouldn't be getting attached to that phrase, now would you, Ash?"

"Knock off the comedy and give me an answer."

Rad was quiet for a moment, and Ash could hear papers riffling. "It's weird, I can tell you that much."

"Weird, how?"

Rad cleared his throat. "She does free-lance work for some major corporations."

Ash frowned. "That's what she told me, but I didn't believe it."

"Yeah, well, I find it kind of hard to believe myself."

"Why?" A ripple of alarm went through him.

"She's a psychic, Ash."

Ash didn't say anything for a long time.

"You still there?"

"Yeah."

"Okay, here's the skinny. Say a company is considering a merger, or a major move, or maybe they have an officer embezzling funds but aren't sure who. They take it to J. B. Bradshaw. She comes into the firm as a secretary or some such, snoops around a little, talks to people, gets a feel for the place and then she gives them their answer."

"Right. You want to get serious now, Rad?"

"It's gospel. I've had it triple-checked."

Ash shook his head. He didn't believe in mind readers. "And she gets results?"

"Sometimes she does. Word is, she doesn't charge unless she can help. She hasn't always been able to. But she's never been wrong. She either comes up with the right answer, or no answer at all."

"Uh-huh." Ash wasn't buying a word of this. "And she lives off this?"

"Her fees are pretty hefty, Ash. And she's getting quite a reputation in corporate boardrooms. I've heard she works pro bono for small, struggling firms who can't afford—"

"Have you got anything legitimate for me, Rad, or just fairy tales?"

Radley made an aggravated noise into the phone. "Skeptic. Okay, she doesn't have a police record. Not so much as a traffic ticket. She holds a valid handgun permit, and the records list a nine-millimeter Ruger as her only weapon."

"Anything else?"

"What do you want, a biography? Nothing you don't already know. One sister, Caroline Dryer, married to Theodore 'Ted' Dryer, formerly of Clark County, Nevada. Two nieces, aged six and sev—"

"Clark County, Nevada?" Ash jumped to his feet. Vegas was in Clark County.

"I already checked, Ash. Dryer's lived in New York State since '84."

"That doesn't mean he hasn't gone back to visit...maybe in the summer of '89, the summer the Slasher did his hunting in Vegas."

"Maybe."

Ash swallowed. He hadn't wanted to believe Joey was involved in this ugliness. But maybe she was. Maybe she was protecting her brother-in-law. Or even her sister. Picturing Caroline as a murderess was harder than envisioning Joey in the role. He shook his head. Anything was possible.

"Thanks for the help, Rad."

"You lied to the police, didn't you?"

Ash frowned at the phone. "I thought you didn't want to know."

"You could get your ass tossed in jail. Especially if you're withholding evidence."

"I know that."

He could almost see his friend's frown over the phone. Rad said nothing more, just broke the connection. Ash sighed and put the receiver back in its cradle. He went to the door, opened it and listened for a minute. Not a sound.

He slipped down the stairs and glanced around. She was sitting on the couch, legs curled under her. Her face registered extreme agitation as her eyes scanned the pages of a fat book. A thick, wavy lock of silky hair fell down over one eye, and she shoved it back with a sweep of her small hand. Her brows bunched tighter; her green gaze was intense. He glanced at the title and almost swore out loud. *Inside the Mind of a Serial Killer.*

Dammit straight to hell. He shook his head in frustration and backed up the stairs. Psychic. Hell, she was no more a psychic than she was a killer. But it was becoming increasingly evident that she was obsessed with the Slasher. Why? Did she know anything, or was it just morbid curiosity? He wondered if he'd ever figure her out.

Well, at least she was occupied for a time. He went to her dresser, pulled open the bottom drawer and pawed through it, then opened another.

The phone rang, and he stiffened. Then he relaxed when it didn't sound again, and she didn't call to him. Must have been for her. Good, she was still distracted.

His headache eased slightly, probably due to the maximum-strength nonaspirin pain reliever she'd insisted he take, and the hot, herbal tea she'd made him drink afterward.

His hand dipped into the top drawer, and his gaze was drawn downward. He was wrist deep in sheer, silken underthings. He couldn't move for a minute. When he could, he found himself pulling a nearly transparent, lace-edged, ruby red teddy from the drawer. He held it up, eyeing the high cut of the leg openings, the sheer lace that bisected the bodice. He could picture her in it. Her little body would be perfect for such a creation—that tiny waist, curving hips. Those breasts. God, he wanted to touch them.

He blinked fast and shoved the garment back into the drawer. What was he, some kind of a pervert? Had it gotten so bad that he now had to resort to pawing her underwear? He looked again at the mounds of lace and silk and satin in the drawer, and an ugly, unfamiliar feeling crept into his mind as he wondered when she wore them, and for whom. From the wide selection under his hand, she must find need for these kinds of garments often. Too often.

Disappointment and irrational anger flooded him, along with burning, red-hazed memories.

She'd called herself Lila, and her brassy red hair came from a bottle. She'd look so beautiful those nights, just before she'd lock him in. But it was fake, like a Halloween costume. He would sit in the corner, in the tiny, pitch-black closet. He'd hear the sounds she made. Sounds that made him think someone was hurting her. And he'd wonder if they would kill her and she'd never come to let him out. Sometimes she didn't, not until very late the next day. Those were the times when she'd been too drunk to think of him sooner. Those were the times when he'd see the ugliness behind the mask.

Her name wasn't Lila, it was Liz. And she wasn't pretty. Not with her watercolor hair in matted straggles and black mascara smeared under her eyes and the stench of regurgitated liquor on her breath.

When the closet door opened on those mornings, he didn't want to look at her. And he couldn't, anyway, because he'd be in a hurry to run to the bathroom. And always, on the way, he'd pass the empty bottles and unwashed glasses, the overflowing ashtrays, the rumpled bed, and always, always, there would be a sheer, silky nightgown lying on the floor.

His first assumption had probably been right, after all.

Joey Bradshaw must be a pro. No woman would buy so many of these things unless...

He looked down at the tag dangling from one thin strap that hung out of the drawer.

Unable to resist, he picked it up again, frowning. Then his gaze moved over the other items in the drawer, spotting more tags, and still more.

"Ashville, what do you think you're doing!"

He spun fast, still clutching the teddy. Joey stood in the doorway, her face as red as the satin that caressed his fingertips. "I, uh, I was just...looking for a place to put my clothes." He stuffed the teddy into the drawer and slammed it. "Sorry."

Her expression didn't ease. Her cheeks were pink with embarrassment. Her eyes glittered with anger at his invasion of her privacy. "Did you ever think to ask?"

He just looked at her and shook his head. How could she look so innocent? Was he a complete idiot?

"I'll make some room for you. In the meantime, you really ought to be lying down." She still didn't meet his gaze. She lifted a hand that held a pair of tightly rolled dampened cloths. "I brought a hot pack for your head. Thought it might help."

He complied and went back to the bed. She perched on its edge, leaned forward and gently laid one of the moist, hot cloths on his forehead.

The swell of her full breasts, the crease between them, was so close to his face he could feel the heat rising from her skin to his. He could smell the scent of her. A rush of desire seared him from within, and he knew he still wanted her. Good or bad, chaste or promiscuous, he wanted her, and it was infuriating to admit that, even to himself. He puckered his lips and blew gently, warm breath bathing her breasts.

She straightened at once, eyes widening.

"When are you going to be willing to sleep with me, Joey?" He'd asked the question before he could tell himself not to.

She blinked fast, avoiding his eyes. "When you get your memory back."

"What if I told you I was getting it back already? What if I said I remembered every minute of our...wedding night?"

She swallowed hard. "I'd say you were lying."

He nodded. "Can't blame a guy for trying." He looked toward the dresser. The strap of the teddy still hung out of the drawer. A confused jumble of anger, disappointment and desire pummeled him. He tried to ignore it and licked his lips. "What if I never remember?"

She shook her head. "You will. I'm going to help you."

"I think seeing you in that red number would help me a whole lot, Joey."

"I really wish you wouldn't talk to me like that."

He smiled slowly. "Makes you hot?"

"Makes me angry. You're obnoxious as hell, you know that?" She glanced down at the second hot pack in her hand and slapped it onto his chest. "Here. This one's for the back of your neck. You can do it yourself."

She stood and turned to go. Driven by his own demons, Ash lunged from the bed. "You've never worn them, have you? None of them."

Her back stiffened. She said nothing.

He grabbed her arm, turned her slowly to face him. He forced himself not to hold her too tightly, or to jerk her around in his anger. It made no sense to feel this angry. "Answer me, Joey. You've never worn them, have you?"

"No. I've never worn them. Why is it so damned important, anyway? What do you think, that I put them on and parade through the streets? Jump out of cakes? What?"

Why this feeling of relief? She could be lying through her teeth for all he knew. God knew it wouldn't be the first time. And why the hell did he care what she wore, or for whom?

He released his breath and sat down on the bed. He lowered his head, and for the first time he really wondered why she would buy the things and not wear them.

"So you're stocking up on silk and satin, huh, Joey? Got some big plans in the making? Expecting a prince on a white horse to come along?"

She stood perfectly still, her eyes searching his, hurt, but more than that. Searching. Trying to see what drove him. "Princes turn into frogs, Ash. Happens every time. I almost forgot that for a little while today. Thanks for reminding me."

He heard the real confusion, the pain in her voice and wished he could take back his words. Dammit, the idea of her wearing those things for someone else had filled him with rage. The thought that she could be anything like Liz... He'd just wanted her to deny it.

"No danger of that with you, though, is there? You were a frog to begin with." She turned away, reached for the door handle. "By the way, we're having dinner with my sister and Ted tonight. I hope you'll try and fake a few princely qualities while we're there."

Chapter 5

Dinner.

Pot roast with baby potatoes and tiny carrots and whole onions cooked right with the meat. Thick, creamy gravy, mashed potatoes, sweet peas, homemade rolls, real butter.

Damn, it was too bad Caroline was already taken. She was the type of woman he'd been looking for. The kind who'd have babies and not go all to pieces because she'd put on a few pounds. The kind who would adore her life, not go looking for excitement elsewhere.

But there was something wrong with the picture. Because no matter how hard he tried to make Caroline's image fit the one in his mind, just to remind himself of what he wanted—what he'd always wanted—he found himself looking toward Joey, instead.

All right, he might as well cut to the heart of the matter. He wanted Joey...in a purely physical way. But lust wasn't everything. Just because it had hit him between the eyes like it had never hit him before didn't mean he had to rethink his priorities. And to be perfectly frank about it, he probably wouldn't want her so badly if she wasn't holding out on him so well.

"I had no idea you two even knew each other, and then you stand there and tell me you're married," Caroline was saying.

Ted's laugh was low and contained. "I wish I could have seen the look on your face."

Ash frowned. He couldn't remember the look on Caroline's face. Only the devastation and panic on Joey's. "I'd have married her sooner if I'd known your dinners were a fringe benefit, Caroline." He made an effort to keep up the conversation, to appear the polite, friendly new brother-in-law trying to get to know his wife's family.

"What blows me away," Ted went on, "is that you two were able to put it together at all, after the accident and everything." His brown hair was sprinkled with gray, and his face was too lean. Like a weasel's face.

"Ted, maybe Ash would rather not talk about that," Caro put in.

"No, it's okay." Ash reached out and grabbed the glass of milk Bethany had just set on the table's edge. He snatched it just before it tipped into her lap, sent her a wink and kept on talking. "Truth is, I don't remember a thing about Joey and me. It's like that day she showed up at the hospital was the first time I'd ever met her."

Ted's gaze narrowed, and he sent Joey a probing glance. She ignored it.

"Where *did* you meet, Joey?" Caro asked her sister.

Ash speared a succulent piece of meat and relaxed in his seat to listen to her answer. Ought to be entertaining.

"I'll bet it was something to do with that Slasher case, wasn't it?"

Ash frowned, brain instantly going on alert. He swallowed his food and sat straighter. "Why would you think that, Ted?"

Ted shrugged. "Well, you were investigating it. She's been obsessed with it since the first—"

"Ted, I haven't been obsessed. You're exaggerating."

"Interested is probably a better term," Caro put in quickly, as if she was jumping to her sister's defense. "But no more than most of the people who live around here."

Ted frowned hard at his wife, and she sent him a silent message, a powerful one. A puzzled expression settled over his face, but he shrugged and leaned back in his chair.

"I certainly understand her interest in the murders better now. She was seeing you, Ash, and you were investigating them. It's only natural she'd want to know all she could."

Ash nodded, but kept glancing at Joey's face. She looked about as uncomfortable as if she were sitting on a pile of thumbtacks.

"There was another one last night, you know," Ted put in, and when Ash glanced at him it was to see him watching Joey's face, as well.

"Another what, Daddy?"

"Another of the great ice-cream robberies," Ash said quickly, not missing a beat. "Three gallons of Heavenly Hash. Someone's going to have a whale of a belly ache this morning."

Brittany giggled, and Caroline shot Ash a grateful glance. Ash felt something warm press against his calf and looked down. A black-and-white cat the size of a small cow looked back, purring loudly. "Well, now. Who's this?" Ash stroked the cat's head and fed it a bit of his meat.

"Felix," the girls chimed in unison.

"He likes you, Uncle Ash."

"I think he likes everybody who feeds him."

The cat moved on to the next seat, panhandling for scraps, and Ted picked up the conversation. "Where *did* you two meet?"

Joey shifted in her seat. "At the theater...the one at the Carousel Mall. We were both there to see that Harrison Ford film, and we ended up sitting together."

It wasn't bad, as far as lies went. Wasn't good, either, but it wasn't bad.

"And the next thing she knew, I'd spirited her off to Vegas and married her. Right, Joey?"

She bit her lip, nodded and applied herself to her dinner.

"You ever been there?" His question was directed to Ted. He disliked the man, though he couldn't quite pinpoint the reason. Maybe it was the depth of scrutiny with which Ted kept watching Joey. As if he knew something...or suspected something.

"Used to live there," Ted said, glancing away from his sister-in-law for once.

"You miss it much?"

"Not really."

"Oh, yes, you do, Ted." Caro smiled in Ash's direction. "You ought to hear him in the winter."

"Well, who wouldn't miss the sun when there's three feet of snow outside the door?" Ted chuckled, but it had an uneasy sound to it. It seemed strained.

Ash nodded, smiling. "You get back there often?"

Ted stiffened, his fork pausing halfway to his mouth.

It was Caro who piped in with the answer to Ash's question. "We used to spend vacations there, but it's really not much fun for little girls. They were toddlers last time, remember, Joey? It took all three of us just to keep up with them."

Ash's stomach clenched. "Joey went with you on vacation?"

Caro nodded. "To help with the girls. These days, we opt for places with theme parks nearby."

Ash was itching to ask if that trip happened to occur during the summer of '89. But he couldn't just come right out with it. These people were not stupid. They'd know he suspected something, even if they might not know what.

"Time for dessert?" Bethany asked.

"It's Aunt Joey's favorite," Brittany sang.

"Caro, you didn't . . ."

Caroline smiled at her sister. "Of course I did. And don't start going on about calories and fat content or I'll be insulted." As she spoke, Caro rose and began clearing away dishes. Joey rose to help, and Ash automatically stood, as well.

Moments later, they sat with luscious cheesecake and wonderful coffee, groaning almost in unison that they couldn't hold another bite.

"You play pool, Ash?"

Ash almost answered yes, then caught himself. "Damned if I know." He tapped his head with a forefinger by way of explanation.

Ted laughed. "I have a new table downstairs. What do you say we find out?"

Ted Dryer was an electrician. TD Electric had its "headquarters" in the shoe box of a building he'd put up beside the house, complete with a professionally crafted sign and a "company" pickup truck with magnetized ads stuck to the doors. Ted walked Ash outside to show him around. The pickup was less than two years old, the building freshly painted. From all appearances, business was good. Ted unlocked the door to the shop and ushered Ash into the office portion. It was raw, consisting mostly of a desk and chair, a phone, a file cabinet and a little rack to hang keys on, tacked to the wall just inside the door. The pickup keys dangled there on a key ring that read, My Other Car's A Mercedes.

Later, they knocked the balls around the green plush table, and Ted seemed friendly, but perhaps a bit too curious.

"So tell me about Joey," he said at one point during the game. "I can't quite picture her settling down to be someone's little wife."

"Me, neither." Ash met Ted's glance and they both laughed. "Hell, Ted, you can probably tell me more about her than I could tell you." He shrugged. "I must have known her so well once, but now..." He let his voice trail off, hoping Ted would take the bait.

"She's pretty up-front," Ted said. "I mean, she's not the kind with hidden agendas and plots. She's just about what she seems. Calls 'em like she sees 'em, says what she means...most of the time."

"Most of the time?"

Ted shrugged and bent over the table, drawing the cue stick back slowly, aiming its tip at the white ball. "We all have our hang-ups." He struck the cue ball. It struck two others, one of which rolled neatly into the corner pocket. Ted straightened and walked around the table, reaching for the chalk.

"And what's Joey's?"

Ted's brows raised. "Ah, now that's the question of the hour, isn't it? I thought I had her figured out. Thought she hated anything male and always would." He laughed and shook his head. "Guess I was wrong, huh?" He grinned.

But Ash didn't feel like smiling. "Why'd you think that?"

Ted chalked the cue. "Always assumed it was because of her father." He looked up, frowning. "Hasn't she talked to you about this?"

Ash shook his head, sensing Ted's reluctance to say more.

"Well, she ought to. It isn't my place to say any—"

"Ted, telephone." Caroline's voice rang down the stairway.

Ted sighed, set the stick down and went up the stairs. Ash followed. He found his gaze drawn to Joey's face. Her eyes were round and concerned, fastened to Ted as he spoke quietly and hung up.

"Well, I'm afraid I have to go out."

"But, Ted—"

"It's an emergency, Caro. Mrs. Peterson's power is out, and she says the box smells hot. I really have to go." He gripped Caro's shoulders, drew her forward and kissed her quickly. Then he turned to pump Ash's hand. "Good meeting you, Ash."

"Same here," he replied.

Ted faced Joey. His jaw tightened as he looked at her. "Take care, Joey." The words were heavy with meaning. And then he was hurrying out the door.

Caro sank onto the sofa, her face obviously straining to hide her misery. Ash wasn't sure what to do, but he caught Joey's glance. She nodded her head toward the two girls stretched on the floor watching television. She looked worried about her sister and Ash knew what she wanted.

"Hey, you two angels. Isn't it getting close to bedtime?"

Two blond heads turned in his direction. "Not yet!"

"Can't we stay up? Mommy?"

Ash shook his head in mock disappointment. "Well, I was going to read you a story. I never had any little girls to read bedtime stories to before. But if you'd rather stay and watch TV—"

They were on their feet in a flash, and Ash felt himself being tugged, one girl holding each of his hands, down the hall toward the bedrooms. He glanced over his shoulder at

Joey, caught her grateful smile and sent her an encouraging wink.

She was worried. Right now, it was about her sister, but it went deeper, Ash thought. She hadn't relaxed all night. And while it was obvious she was still lying to him, and to her sister, as well, it was equally obvious that she hated every minute of it. And it did nothing to dampen the desire he felt for her every time he looked at her.

Joey slowly opened the bedroom door and peered inside. Ash sat in a rocker, a girl on each knee, a book open on his lap.

"And as the princess gently kissed the frog, something magical happened. The spell was broken, and he turned into the handsome prince he truly was. Falling down on his knees, he took the princess's hand in his and told her how much he loved her. They were married in a great celebration, and of course they lived happily ever after."

He closed the book. "Well, how was that?"

Joey smiled, an unfamiliar warmth curling in the pit of her stomach. She'd been furious with him earlier, but she'd reasoned with herself until she thought she understood him. He believed she was his wife. He probably felt frustrated and hurt that she'd rejected his physical advances. His rotten attitude was no more than another result of all he was going through right now. She had to forgive him. "They're asleep," she whispered.

Ash glanced at the blond heads lolling upon either of his shoulders. Joey stepped forward and scooped Bethany from his lap. She carried her to the white four-poster and tucked her in. When she turned, it was to see Ash installing Brittany in the bed's twin, on the other side of the room. Felix had already settled himself on the foot of her bed and looked dead to the world.

"You know, these two are just about the most precious things in my life."

"I'm not surprised," he said, his voice low. "They've charmed my socks off already."

She met his gaze across the room. "You're terrific with them."

"I love kids."

She went to the rocker and picked up the book. The process of forgiving him was suddenly complete. *"The Frog Prince?"*

Ash met her in the room's center. "Seemed appropriate," he said softly. "It's a fascinating theory, don't you think?" He took the book from her hands, set it aside. "I know I acted like a frog earlier. I didn't mean it."

"I know."

He slipped his arms around her waist, drawing her close. She stiffened, but he shook his head quickly. "One kiss, Joey. Not so much for a husband to ask from his wife, is it? Besides, how else will you know if there's a prince hidden under this frog skin?"

She moistened her lips. What she saw in his eyes made her blood warm, and she was assaulted once again by the attraction that wouldn't go away. She wanted to kiss him, not to convince him that they were truly man and wife, but to feel the touch of his mouth on hers, the pressure of his arms around her, the crush of his chest. She nodded. "All right. One kiss."

Ash smiled. Then his mouth covered hers. His arms around her waist tightened, drawing her body to his. She parted her lips, curious, eager, excited, all at once. His tongue swept into her mouth like a loving caress, touching her in a probing search as if he were an explorer, the first to enter there. She felt as if he were tasting her, and liking what he found as his tongue dipped and danced around her mouth. She felt herself begin to shake.

It shocked her. She tried to analyze it. She wasn't shivering with cold, or with fear. Her arms curled tighter around his neck. Her body pressed harder against his, and her fingers threaded into his hair. This was good. Whatever this was, it was incredibly good. When he withdrew his tongue, she thrust her own into his mouth. But hers was hungrier, more demanding, and she felt him shudder in response.

He tasted wonderful, and Joey didn't want to stop. Her body was responding to this closeness, this excitement, in primitive ways she couldn't deny. Her breaths came quick and shallow. Her skin heated and felt so sensitized that every movement of him against her sent her into another realm of awareness.

This was getting out of hand. It was more than a kiss, what they were doing. She ought to stop it, right now. Because he was losing himself in her as much as she was in him. She felt his heart hammering, heard his rapid breathing. All because of her. She was giddy as his mouth fed from hers. The feel of his hands at the base of her spine, their pressure holding her tight, was erotic, as was the gentle, exquisite way he sucked at her tongue.

She was so hot she thought she'd go up in flames. And then the sound of Caroline clearing her throat sent her to the opposite extreme. Ice coated her, extinguishing the heat. She stepped away guiltily, suppressing a shiver. The fire in Ash's eyes still burned bright.

"Caro... I—I'm sorry. I... we just—"

"It's okay. I remember when it was like that. Go on home, you two."

Ash blinked, then turned, slipping a possessive arm around Joey's shoulders. "You sure you don't want us to stick around, until Ted gets back?"

The pain that lanced her sister was visible, but Caro only nodded sharply. "No, he's liable to be...late. As long as the girls are asleep, I guess I'll turn in myself. It's been a long day. Good night."

Joey sighed as her sister turned and walked away. Ash kept his arm around her while they walked together to the front door. Joey turned the lock before closing the door.

Ash looked down at her and she met his gaze for a long moment before she had to look away. He wanted her. His eyes were telling her so in no uncertain terms. And dammit, she wanted him, too. But she couldn't let this thing with him develop into anything more than it was. She couldn't let herself begin to feel anything for him. God, she didn't ever want to suffer the way Caro was...the way their mother had.

He walked her to the car, opened the driver's door and stood aside. Joey shook her head and handed him the keys. "Go ahead, Ash. I'm too worried. I'd probably put us in a ditch."

He got in and she went around to the other side. "You want to talk about it?"

She frowned hard as he started the car. Strangely enough, she did. Why, for God's sake? What good would telling *him* do? "Caro thinks Ted's cheating on her." Joey shook her head and thumped her fist on the dash as the car backed out into the street. "Damn him. She has so little self-esteem left as it is. How can he do this to her?"

Ash shook his head. "Don't you think he deserves a trial before you string him up, Joey?"

"My sister wouldn't think it unless the evidence was pretty strong. She doesn't *want* to think it now, but it's getting harder not to."

"Why?"

She looked up at him, looked at the way the lights of other vehicles played over his face. His beard was coming in again, a darker shadow on his jaw. Her fingers itched to run over it. "There's money missing from their accounts, and he won't explain it. He has these murmured conversations on the phone and hangs up when she comes into the room. He's secretive. She knows he's keeping something from her. And that was the second emergency this week for Mrs. Peterson."

"So?"

"Mrs. Peterson's first name is Veronica. She's a thirty-five year-old widow who'll take on anything wearing pants."

"Mee-ow." He sent her a grin.

She scowled back at him.

"Well, have you ever met the woman?"

She lifted her chin. "No. But Caro has—"

"And you don't think she might be a little biased?"

"My sister isn't like that." She felt his gaze on her, but didn't look back. "Why do men do it, Ash?"

"What? Cheat?"

She nodded, still not facing him.

"All men don't do it."

She released a clipped, forceful sigh and shook her head. "Right."

"Your father did, didn't he?"

She looked up quickly, startled. "How do you know—?"

"Ted mentioned you had a problem with your dad. The rest was just deductive reasoning. You've talked about your mother several times, but never your dad. You and she must be very close."

"We were." She swallowed the lump in her throat.

"Damn," he muttered. "I'm sorry, Joey. I didn't know... Was it...recent?"

"Last year. Stroke." She drew a breath and willed herself to go on. "He was with his mistress the night she died. He moved her into my mother's house two months later."

"And you can't forgive him?"

"I hate him."

He nodded. "Hating people takes a lot of energy, Joey."

"I'm used to hating him. I've had a lot of practice."

"Been doing it a while, hmm?"

"Since the first time I saw him with someone else. I was twelve. The thing I never understood was why my mother put up with it. She had to know. God, if I could see it, I know she could. Why did she stay with him?"

"That's probably something only she could answer."

She nodded, but remained quiet.

"You know, growing up like that might make a lot of women wary. Maybe even a little quick to jump to conclusions."

She faced him as he turned her car into the long, graveled driveway and drove slowly over it. "You think that's what Caro is doing?"

He shrugged. "Could be. I got the feeling Ted was hiding something, but it didn't seem like it was an affair."

She frowned. "What else could it be?"

"I don't know. Whatever it is, he'd be better off being honest with Caroline about it. The truth probably isn't as bad as what she's thinking."

Joey blinked, for the first time wondering if there could be another explanation for Ted's behavior.

"It's important, I think. Being honest," he went on. He steered the car onto the blacktop portion of the driveway and killed the headlights, then the motor.

She had to turn her head away. Even though he couldn't see her in the darkness of the car, she could feel his eyes on her. She could feel that he knew she'd been less than honest with him, and she couldn't deny it.

"You're right." Her voice was almost a croak. "But sometimes there are things that are more important." She thought of her beautiful nieces, growing up without their mother, of the beautiful man beside her lying still and cold in a grave.

"Okay, I'll concede that point." He was silent a moment. "Will you answer me one question?"

"If I can." She lifted her head.

She heard him move, and then the interior light came on. He looked at her, rubbed his stubble-coated chin. "You see any signs of a prince emerging here?"

"Not a one." He looked crestfallen, and she laughed softly. "But you know, I'm beginning to think the frog isn't as bad as he pretends to be."

He slept in her bed again that night. It was an unspoken conclusion that he would. He still wasn't sure why she wanted him there, if she didn't want *him*. Of course, she did want him, she just wouldn't let it happen. So why share a bed?

Not that he'd turn her down. There was always a chance she would change her mind, right?

He showered, toweled off and stepped into the bedroom, only to find her already asleep, her back to him. He sighed in frustration, but he crawled in beside her.

Sometime that night he had the dream. He tried to wake up, but as always, he couldn't. He could only lie there, heart racing, skin beading with sweat, and live the damned thing over again. He should have been used to it by now.

But then it left him, all at once. Suddenly there was warmth in the cold little room. There was light. Someone was there with him, and it was all right.

In the morning, he almost choked. Joey was curled into his arms, her head nestled in the crook of his neck where her breaths bathed his skin. Her hair tickled his chin. Her legs twined with his, one lying over his, bringing the center of her tight to his own hardness.

Yes, hardness. That was what woke him. And how was he *not* supposed to get hard, with her pressed up against him this way?

She'd worn an oversize football jersey to sleep in. It was hiked up to her waist. Her panties were brief, and they were too small a barrier. His shorts weren't much better. He could feel her warmth, and without his own permission he arched harder into her.

She responded by sighing softly, wet lips brushing his collarbone, and wriggling against his arousal.

He was in hell. He'd died during the night, and this was to be his eternal torment. He couldn't move without waking her. And if he woke her, and she felt the undeniable proof of where his mind had wandered, she'd probably be furious with him for the rest of the day. As if he had a choice in the matter. *He* wasn't the one twined around *her* like a jungle vine!

She moved slightly, and the friction made him bite his lip. Then he bit it harder. Maybe pain would dampen his responses. He tried to back away a little, but her leg tightened around his.

He groaned out loud.

Her eyes fluttered open, unfocused. He closed his fast. Maybe he could pretend he was still asleep.

Joey couldn't believe the way she'd wrapped herself around Ash as she'd slept. Then she remembered the dream, and she knew why.

It had been vivid, the nightmare. And it hadn't been her own. It had been his. She'd experienced every part of it right along with him. There was no imagery in the dream. No sights. Only darkness, and the sensation of smothering in it.

There had been a deep-seated fear that made his heart race, the gasping for breath that went on and on. The certainty that he'd be abandoned, alone in the dark, in a crushingly small place for a long, long time, had jumped out at her. And then there had been the sudden awareness that he wasn't alone.

She wasn't really there, in the small, black prison. *He* was. It was Ash's nightmare. But in the midst of sleep, she'd gone to him. She'd wrapped herself around him, wanting to shelter him from the darkness, the cruelty, the fear.

He'd clung to her, and the dream had lost its power.

She shook her head and gently loosened her grip on him. Easing her head from his chest, she drew her leg away from his. Then she looked at him, lying there in the golden light of early morning. So big. His long, powerful legs stretched to the very edge of the mattress. And so strong. His bare chest bulged, rippled. His biceps were as big around as her neck.

Yet he hadn't always been this way. He'd been young, and small. He'd been afraid, and so very alone. He'd had nightmares.

And somewhere, right now, today, beneath all the sinewed strength of the man, that little boy lived still, as vulnerable as he'd ever been. Ash kept that child in tight control. But he couldn't control the boy in his dreams.

Why, God, why did that one small glimpse inside him make her want him even more?

She lifted her trembling hand to touch his face. She ran her fingertips very lightly over his cheek and felt tears well up in her eyes for the boy he'd been. She slipped her arm around his waist and lay close to him again, wanting him to feel that closeness, wanting to keep his nightmarish memories at bay.

Tears spilled over, dampening the crisp hairs of his chest. Then his hand came to her face and very gently brushed them away.

"You're crying." He moved away from her, looking down with a deep frown. "Joey, what's the matter?"

She shook her head, staring into his eyes and seeing more than she ever had before. There was so much more to him than she'd known. So much she still had to learn.

"Bad dreams," she whispered.

Ash's frown only deepened.

Chapter 6

She was a puzzle.

No matter how he tried he couldn't figure her out. And he was beginning to feel more desperate to understand the workings of Joey Bradshaw's mind than he was to identify the Syracuse Slasher. Because he wanted her...more than he'd wanted any of the "party girls" he'd taken to bed in search of the elusive Miss Right.

Across the table, he watched her delve into the omelet he'd made this morning. She closed her almond-shaped, emerald eyes—those rare precious gems that seemed to hold the secrets of the universe when she was serious, and seemed brighter than the sun when she smiled. She licked her full, cover-model lips, and Ash felt his gut twist into a hard little knot.

"God, this is good. Where did you learn to cook like this?"

"Trial and error, mostly," he admitted. It wasn't his best effort. It definitely needed more salt.

"No, it's perfect," she said. But as she said it, she reached for the saltshaker and handed it to him.

He took it, shook a little onto his eggs, then stopped. He looked at her and blinked. "I didn't ask for the salt."

"Didn't you?" She pretended his remark meant nothing, but she seemed to have trouble swallowing the last bite. "I must have seen you looking for it, and guessed."

"I wasn't looking for it." He shook his head and studied her face. His conversation with Radley came back to him. *He* thought she was some kind of psychic. "You do that a lot, you know."

"Do what?"

"Answer a question before it's asked. Hand me something I want, but haven't mentioned." He recalled that she'd appeared in the bathroom, just as he'd been searching for a razor, to tell him where they were.

"Maybe it's just that I know you so well, Ash."

But he knew she barely knew him at all, so again she was lying. She just had a keen instinct, he supposed. It was no more than that. There *was* no more than that.

"You know what I was thinking?"

He swallowed his coffee. "Nope. I'm not the mind reader." He said it just to gauge her reaction. She tensed and shot him a look of alarm. So maybe she'd rather he didn't know about her hocus-pocus leanings. He grinned to ease her mind and was rewarded with a smile that nearly knocked him off his chair.

"I was thinking we ought to stay a night at your place."

"Why's that?"

She bit her lip. "Your memory doesn't seem to be improving at all. It worries me. Maybe if you were around familiar things."

Even the aromas of the ham and cheese and onion he'd added to the eggs hadn't drowned out the freshly showered scent of her skin, or the whiffs of strawberry her hair was emitting. He thought there just might be another reason behind her suggestion, but he didn't say so. He would only find out by going along with it, and keeping an eye on her. "If you want to. We can go over tonight. I ought to be working, anyway."

"How much time off are they giving you?"

He detected a hint of worry in her voice, and he wondered about that. "Only what I'll take sitting down. I'm itching to get back to that story, especially since there's been another—" He stopped when he saw her go a shade paler and replace her forkful of food on the plate. "What is it, Joey? You don't want me to go back to work?"

She licked her lips and met his gaze. "What did the police tell you about your car accident?"

He frowned, trying to keep up with the way she hopped from subject to subject. "Not much. Wasn't much to tell. Brakes failed—"

"I thought it was a new car?"

He sipped his coffee, giving himself time to collect his thoughts. Nothing had been mentioned about his car having been tampered with. The cops were playing this one close to the vest. "New cars break down, Joey. Accidents happen."

"What if it wasn't an accident?"

He set his cup down and stared at her. Did she know something? And if she did, was it because of her alleged ESP, or because she had an inside track with the Slasher? "What do you mean?"

She lowered her gaze, shook her head. "You were trying to expose a serial killer. What if... what if you were making the Slasher nervous?"

He drew a deep breath and released it with utter control. That was exactly what had happened. So how did Joey

know about it? He pasted a false smile on his face and
chucked her under the chin. "Hey, I'll go along with any
theory that makes you worry about me. I kinda like it."

She faced him, brows raised in apparent anxiety. "This
isn't a joke, Ash. I really don't want you going back there.
Especially to work on the Slasher story. Not until..." Her
voice trailed off.

"Not until the Slasher's caught?"

He reached across the table, closed his hand over hers.
"You really are worried, aren't you?"

She nodded, and Ash found himself believing her. It felt
kind of warm and fuzzy having someone worry about him.
It was a feeling he thought he could get used to. "Let's not
worry about it at the moment, okay? I have a full week to
go before I get the doctor's okay to go back to work. '

She sighed long and low, but nodded.

"You haven't been working yourself lately."

"I'm self-employed. There's nothing pressing right now."

"Have you been turning down jobs, Joey?"

She met his gaze and he thought she was going to lie to
him again. He was relieved when she didn't. "A few. But I
can afford it."

"Why?"

"Why?" she repeated.

"Why haven't you been working?"

She shrugged, hesitating, and picked up her fork, pushing her omelet around her plate. Finally she met his gaze.
"What I do takes a certain amount of...concentration. And
instinct." She shook her head slowly. "Lately I just haven't
had it."

So her supposed *powers* were failing her.

"What's distracting you? Me?"

She looked up fast and shook her head. "No. I don't
know what it is. It doesn't matter, anyway. It'll pass." Now

she was lying. He had no doubt. The way her eyes couldn't quite hold his, the quick tightening of her jaw. It was surprising how quickly he'd learned the signs.

She shoved her plate away, obviously ready to change the subject. And again it was clear to him how much she disliked lying to him. "You know, I'm getting a little bored with this sitting around the house all the time. Are you up for a little recreation?"

"What did you have in mind?"

"Something that requires physical exertion."

He cocked one brow. "You're not thinking of dragging me into a cave somewhere are you?"

She laughed aloud. "Not until your head is a little better. And we won't bother with the exercise room because I don't want to hang around the house." Her gaze traveled down to his chest and a speculative gleam lit her eyes. "You're in great shape. What do you do to keep from going to pot?"

"You mean you'd be willing to try a little one-on-one?"

She leaned forward, hands propping her chin, elbows on the table. "Only if you're talking basketball."

"You wouldn't stand a chance. Too short."

"Sounds like a challenge to me."

An hour later she was standing on a concrete outdoor court, wearing a loose-fitting tank over a pale gray sports bra, a pair of black spandex shorts, white slouch socks and Nike high tops. The court was behind a school, but school was out, so they had it to themselves. The grass had been mowed this morning, and it smelled so potently fresh that the air was almost tinted green. The sun blazed down onto the blacktop, heating it. The ball wasn't old. It still had that new-ball scent.

She dribbled close to the ground, which was an advantage of being short. The rough texture of the ball felt good on her palm. The sun on her back felt even better. Ash towered over her, arms spread, trying to keep her from making any progress. She faked right, then drove left, ducking under his arm and charging to the basket for a lay-up worthy of the NBA, she thought.

The ball hit the blacktop, bounced twice and rolled to a stop at Ash's feet. He didn't look at it. He was looking at her with something that might best be labeled amused wonder.

"I never would have guessed."

"Don't just stand there, big guy. We're here to sweat, remember?"

He picked up the ball and began a lazy dribble away from the net as she came nearer to guard him. Then in a burst of speed he spun backward, pivoted to face the basket and executed a perfect jump shot from a foot beyond the line.

In no time at all they were both damp with sweat beneath the July sun. Joey's neat, high ponytail dripped straggles that stuck to her face, no matter how often she swept them away. Ash swiped a hand across his forehead. His dark hair curled wildly and his face was alive with color. The sleeveless, collarless sweatshirt he wore had dark spots under both arms and in the center of his chest and back.

"What do you say we take a break?" Joey tossed the ball into Ash's chest. He caught it with a quick, reflexive move.

"Admitting defeat, are you?" He smiled as he said it.

"Not on your life. I just don't want to have to carry you back to the car."

"Fat chance. You're just afraid *I'll* end up carrying *you* to the car."

"Ha!" She put her hands on her hips in a taunting gesture. "You're so wiped out you couldn't if you had to!"

"Lady, you just made a tactical error." He dropped the ball and lunged forward, scooping her up so fast she didn't have time to dodge him. She struggled, but she was laughing so hard it weakened her. He held her tight to his chest, one strong arm under her knees, the other just beneath her shoulders.

"What about the ball?"

"Oh." He bent over it, letting her pick it up, then straightened and strode off toward the car. He picked up speed, nearly running over the sidewalk.

"We'll see who's wiped out."

"Watch out for that cat!"

He skidded to a halt, frowning at the sidewalk just ahead. "What cat?" No sooner had he spoken, however, than a calico cat scrambled across the sidewalk just ahead of him. He looked down at Joey and shook his head. "How the hell do you *do* that?"

"Don't be silly. I saw it coming."

"Then you must have eyes in the back of your head."

She waggled her brows up and down. "Well hidden by my hair, aren't they?"

His gaze changed just a little. He looked down into her face, into her eyes, and something stirred in his. Her arms around his neck held on tighter as he lowered his head. His lips found hers, nuzzled, then parted and possessed. She let her head fall backward as his tongue delved into her mouth, into her throat. She clung to him for dear life as her pulse rate skyrocketed.

This wasn't fair. She wasn't supposed to feel this way toward him. It was an act... an act that was necessary to save his life, and Caroline's. And yet she had no defenses. As his wife, how could she refuse even to kiss him? She was lucky he hadn't yet insisted on a lot more. She didn't need ESP to know he wanted her. And if she kept refusing, he was going to guess the truth, or at least wonder about it. Kissing him was another part of her cover.

Right. Get honest, she told herself. She was kissing him because she *wanted* to kiss him. The feel of his mouth covering hers, his demanding tongue, the warm, sticky sweat at the back of his neck where she clung, all combined in an ardent assault on her senses. He was storming the gates she'd erected, and she had the insane urge to help him tear them down. Deep down inside, she knew she wanted more than his kiss. Much, much more.

They stopped at a convenience store for deli meat and sub rolls on the way back. When they arrived at Joey's place, clothes still damp and hair in tangles, Caroline's car was in the driveway. Ash was craving a shower, and he figured he'd probably get first crack at one. Joey would want to speak in private with her sister.

He sent her a reassuring glance as she shut off the motor and then they both got out and walked around the house. Brittany and Bethany were chasing each other around the back lawn, near the house. It looked like a spirited game of tag. Caroline sat in a lawn chair, watching them. Her hair, as always, was up in a ponytail. She wore sweats again. Ash took a moment to note how alike the two women were. If Caro would get some spunk, go to a gym and hold her head up a little higher, she'd be a knockout.

What was that? Was he just thinking she ought to be more like Joey? That the dedicated house mother should be more like her hellcat sister?

Then he recalled the way Joey had let him kiss her on the sidewalk, the way she'd kissed him back, and he knew he hadn't yet succeeded in convincing himself she was all wrong for him. His mind knew it. But, God, he was having trouble proving that to the rest of him.

Caroline rose and met Joey halfway. Her eyes were red and her cheeks showed tear tracks. She hugged her sister and a sob ripped through her. "I'm...l-leaving him."

Joey met Ash's eyes over Caroline's shaking shoulder. "It's all right. It's going to be all right, I promise you. You're tough. You can get through this." She sent him an apologetic glance. "You and the girls can stay right here with Ash and me."

He made a grimace, then remembered that they were planning to spend some time at his apartment anyway to help restore his memory. For someone who would be "found out" as a result, Joey certainly seemed eager for him to regain his memory.

Joey released her sister and turned to unlock the back door as Bethany and Brittany came running toward her. Caroline averted her tearstained face while her daughters crowded inside.

"You should have gone inside, Caro. You didn't need to wait for me."

"I didn't want to intrude."

"If I minded, I wouldn't have given you a key, silly."

Ash stopped in the doorway, sensing the turmoil in Caro, the pain seeing it caused Joey. "I'll get the groceries," he said. "Leave you two alone."

"No need." Caroline sniffed and seemed to stiffen her spine. "You're family now, Ashville. And please don't worry that we're going to move in on you. I'm taking the girls to Miami to visit Dad and Rhonda for a couple of weeks."

Joey frowned as she and her sister stepped outside. "I'd rather have you here."

"You're newlyweds—"

"So are they." Joey's voice was tinged with bitterness. She shook herself, though, and put an arm around her sis-

ter as they followed Ash along the path around the house.
"We'll talk. Look, stay for lunch. Ash is making subs."

"I don't want to impose..."

Ash turned, letting them catch up. "Hey, you haven't
lived until you've had an Ash Coye special. Make you into
a new woman." He sent Caroline a smile and felt Joey's
gratitude bathing him as he walked with them out front to
get the groceries from the car.

Ash took the key from the switch and moved around to
open the trunk. He reached in for a bag, vaguely aware of
the slamming of the screen door coming from the back.
Joey bent to grab the second, her worried eyes scanning her
sister's face. Caroline bit her lip as tears filled her eyes once
more.

"I don't think I can stand this. God, Joey, what am I going to do?"

Joey shifted the bag she held to her hip, freeing one arm.
Her big green eyes moistened as she reached for her sister.
Then she went rigid, her arm stilling in midair. Her eyes di-
lated and her face went white. "Brittany," she choked. The
bag slid from her grasp, splitting and spilling its contents on
the blacktop. "Brittany!" It was a scream the second time,
delivered as Joey whirled and began running full tilt around
the house.

Ash didn't take time to wonder what the hell her problem was. He followed her, dropping the brown paper bag
back into the trunk. Caroline ran after her, too.

Joey flew over the back lawn, heading for the river. Ash's
stomach wrenched when he caught sight of one golden
blond head, only one, dangerously close to the sloping
bank. Bethany stood near the red wooden dock, her small
body convulsing with sobs. Ash ran faster. His feet hit the
dock just as Joey sprang into the air over the side, knifing
into the murky, fast-running water.

In the space of a heartbeat, he glanced out over the water. He saw nothing. Then he was following Joey's path, into the cold. If she thought Brittany was in the river, then he wouldn't waste time questioning it.

He submerged, but was unable to see in the greenish water. When he broke the surface again, he caught sight of Joey. She was out farther, in the force of the current, moving away from him rapidly. As he watched, she bounced up and dived under. He stroked toward her, his heart hammering forcefully enough to break his ribs, his eyes straining, his arms putting forth superhuman effort.

He almost jumped when Joey broke surface a few feet ahead of him. Her face was pale, haggard, her eyes a dull green, a color that seemed to scream with pain. Her arms tugged a limp, blond-headed form from beneath the water, and she struggled to hold the child's face above the waves. She saw him.

"Ash..."

Then he had her. But there was no way in hell he could fight the current and hold on to both of them.

She pushed Brittany into his arms. Joey looked horrible, and he had a sickening feeling there was a lot more wrong with her than the cold, dirty water or exhaustion. He held the little girl firmly with one arm as she began to whine and struggle and choke. He reached for Joey with the other.

"You'll sink. I'm okay, just get Brit out of the water."

He shook his head. "You're hurt. Joey, what is it?"

"She needs to get out of the water. Go now. I'll be right behind you, but don't wait for me. I'm a slow swimmer."

Her pupils told another story. With one arm he pulled her arms back around the child, speaking softly to calm Brittany as he did. Then he hooked his own arms around them both. "Hold her tight, Joey. Don't let her go." He side-stroked toward shore. They would end up yards from the dock, since the current was pulling them downstream. His head was under more than it was above, but he managed to keep both Brittany's and Joey's faces out of the water.

Then he was in the shallows and Caroline was there, up to her waist, reaching for her daughter, sobbing hysterically. Bethany came running along the shore, eyes wide.

As soon as Caroline had Brittany in her arms and was carrying her onto the bank, Ash wrapped his arms around Joey and picked her up. Her head fell backward. Her eyes were glazed. He swore and trudged onto the shore.

A jagged tear through both black spandex and tanned thigh gushed blood at a rate that made him dizzy. He laid her on her back on the ground, tugged the baggy tank top over her head and wrapped it around the wound, tying a knot and tugging it fiercely tight. Her eyes fell closed.

"Joey?" He caught her face in his hands.

"Dizzy," she whispered. "Brit?"

He looked up to see Brittany sobbing and choking, white-faced, in her mother's arms. "Caroline, you have to call an ambulance."

"I did." The small voice came from behind Caroline, and it shook with fear. "I r-ran to the house and called 911. The lady said they would be here soon." Her lower lip trembled. "Is my sister gonna die?"

Caroline opened her arm to encircle Bethany's shoulders. "No, honey. She'll be fine." Caroline looked toward Ash for the first time. "Joey... Oh, God, Joey..."

"Easy, Caro. She cut her leg on something, lost some blood, I think, but the bleeding's stopped now. She'll be okay." Ash's hold on Joey tightened and he searched her pale face. "You'll be okay." It was almost a prayer. Something inside him moved, twisted, ached. How had she come to matter so much to him in such a short time? What the hell would he do if she *wasn't* okay?

Chapter 7

"Mommy, I'm scared!"

Joey tried to whisper a reassurance as Brittany was settled onto the stretcher next to hers, which sat beside the river on the green mat of lawn. Mom would have had a fit at them driving over her grass. The thought flitted in and out of Joey's mind like an errant breeze.

She was dizzy and having trouble keeping her eyes open. Her voice, when she spoke, was slurred and the words came slowly. She felt drunk and weak. All she could smell was the odor of river water. She was soaked with it.

Caroline looked helplessly from frightened, still-pale Brittany to sobbing, terrified Bethany, clinging to her waist. "I thought they were inside. I should have been watching." She'd whispered the same two phrases over and over until Joey worried she was more shaken than Brittany was.

"I don't want to go in the ab'lance," Brit whined. "I'm *scared.*"

"How about if I ride with you?" The deep voice was Ash's. He was right there, beside her, close to Brit, one hand smoothing Bethany's hair. He was calm and strong and solid, and Joey couldn't imagine anyone she'd rather have here with her now. "Your mom and Bethany can follow right behind us in the car. If you want, I'll hold you up so you can see them out the window."

"Mister, there isn't going to be much room. You'd be better off changing into dry clothes and following us yourself."

Joey focused on Ash, saw the stern look he sent in the paramedic's direction. "I'm riding in the ambulance."

"I want Uncle Ash," Brittany said softly. Her voice trembled as she was installed in the ambulance. Then Joey's litter was lifted and snapped into place. Ash climbed in, settling himself between the two. She was ridiculously glad he was here.

Caroline stuck her head in the back. "I'll grab some dry clothes from the house and be right behind you." She leaned in farther, snagged Ash by the neck and hugged him hard. "Thank you," she said on a broken sob.

A moment later they were bounding over the lawn and then the driveway. Brittany twisted until her head was off the litter, resting it on Ash's knee. Joey saw his crooked half smile. She watched his big, tanned hand as it stroked Brittany's dripping wet hair away from her face, then moved to tug a blanket over her shoulders.

When the driver gave a siren blast to clear traffic, Brittany jerked and began to cry.

"Hey now, you're not afraid of a little noise, are you?"

She nodded, choking on a sob.

"Would a story help?"

A short sniffle, wide blue eyes gazing upward, another nod.

"Well, let me think. I'm not real up on fairy tales... except for the *Frog Prince*." Joey felt his warm gaze on her and she forced a weak smile for him. "Do you have a favorite, Brittany?"

"Red Riding Hood."

"Oh. Well, let me think a minute." He pretended great concentration, a furrow forming between his brows. "Okay. There was this little girl, see. And they called her Red Riding Hood because..." He looked at Brittany with mock seriousness. "Because she was a redhead and she liked to go riding dressed up like a hood."

Brittany released a peal of laughter. "Noo, Uncle Ash."

"Hmm. Oh, I have it. Because she had a red car and she was always riding on the hood."

"No." Brit giggled, relaxing back onto the pillow. "Because she wore a red *hood*."

"Right. That would have been my next guess. Anyway, she was walking through the woods one day... I think she missed the bus. And along comes this big bad raccoon." Brit squealed. "Squirrel?" Ash attempted. "No, wait, it was a possum. I'm sure it was a possum... or a deer."

Joey closed her eyes to the sound of chuckles coming from the front of the ambulance, as well as the lilting laughter from her niece. And then...

"I love you, Uncle Ash."

"I love you, too, kiddo. No more swimming in the river, okay?"

"I didn't mean to. I fell."

"I figured that."

"I caught a frog, but he got away, and when I tried to get him, I slipped."

"Well, no more frog catching near the river, then. At least, not without me. I'm a world-class frog catcher, you know."

A miserable feeling settled like a shroud on Joey's shoulders. What had she done? How devastated would Brittany and Bethany be when they found out the uncle they were fast growing to adore was no uncle at all? And Ash? How much pain would the truth cause him?

He left the treatment room when Caroline arrived. Brittany was fine, and glad to see her mother and sister. Ash hurried through the corridor and started toward the room where they'd taken Joey, only to be stopped outside the door by a stern-faced nurse.

"You can't go in there."

Ash shook his head, frustration pulling at his nerves. "The hell I can't—"

"Sir, the patient is—"

He started to push past her. "The *patient* is my *wife*." Then he stopped and stood still, blinking. For just an instant, he'd believed it was true. For the briefest moment in time, he had stopped playing a role. He wasn't pretending. He actually felt like a man desperately worried about his wife. He drew a calming breath.

"At least tell me what's going on."

The nurse smiled gently. "She's fine. The doctor's suturing her leg. Why don't you sit down? I'll let you know as soon as you can go in."

He grated his teeth, and stuffed his hands in his pockets to keep himself from bodily moving the slight woman and charging into the room. He couldn't sit. He paced, keeping that closed door always in his sight. The nurse went in and it took all his will to keep from following. What seemed like hours, but in truth was only minutes later, a doctor emerged. The nurse came out behind him and sent Ash a nod.

He rushed into the room, then stood inside the door as relief sapped his nervous energy. Joey sat on the edge of a bed, wearing a thin white hospital gown that covered her thighs. Her bare legs dangled over the side.

She met his eyes and smiled. "You look like a drowned rat."

He glanced down at his wet shorts and the sweatshirt that still stuck to his skin. Then he glanced back up at her. He crossed the space between them and pushed the cloth up, away from her injured leg. Thick, white bandages padded the length of her outer thigh. The memory of the way it had looked before, torn, bleeding, made him close his eyes for just a second.

He felt her palm on his cheek. "Hey, it's all right. I'm fine."

Reaction must be setting in. And it was a powerful reaction. He felt sick. He stared hard at her face, the green eyes that were already regaining their sparkle, the slightly puzzled smile. He studied it, just to prove to himself that she was really okay, even as he wondered just when she had dug her way under his skin.

"Brittany is fine, too," he told her. Mainly just for something to say to cover his jumbled emotions.

"I know. Dr. Fritz told me."

"Dr. Fritz?"

She bent her head and tugged the rubber band from her wet, tangled hair. "His last name is unpronounceable. Ouch." She scowled at the hairy rubber band before tossing it toward the wastebasket.

She was okay. It was finally sinking in, and as it did, the questions that had been overshadowed by his worry came to the surface. Questions that made him uneasy.

"So what happened?"

She ran her fingers through her hair, trying to comb out the snarls. "I think it was a rusted-out barrel. I felt it slice into me when I dived in. I didn't see it, so I can't be sure."

He bit his lip and watched her intently. "That's not what I meant." He caught her hands, stopping their movements. She faced him again, frowning. "How did you know, Joey?"

"How'd I know what?" She knew what he was asking. It was clear in her eyes.

"That Brittany fell in. We were all there together. You just went white all of a sudden, yelled her name and took off for the river. So the question I'm asking is, *how did you know?*"

Her tongue darted out to moisten her lips, and she hesitated before answering. "I . . . heard a splash."

"From that distance?" He shook his head. "No one else heard a thing, Joey."

"Well, I did."

"So how'd you know it was Brit, and not Bethany?"

She bit her lip, her gaze lowering. "Bethany is afraid of water. Brittany is a little fish. Or, at least, she used to be. Maybe that will change now."

Ash stood close to her, his thighs touching her legs where they dangled from the edge of the bed. He studied her face, wanting to be angry with her for holding things back, which he knew she was doing, without doubt. But he couldn't. He was just so damn glad she was alive. He replaced her hands in her hair with his own and shook the still-damp tangles out. For the first time he questioned his own skepticism. Maybe there was actually something to this psychic thing.

"You saved my life, Ash. Brit's, too. You could have drowned trying to pull us both out."

She was grateful. She meant it. Her eyes were like billboards announcing her true feelings. He knew when she was lying, when she was hurting, when she was scared. He knew when she was wanting him, and fighting it. "No chance of that, princess. Frogs are great swimmers."

He stiffened then, because she slid her arms around him, beneath his, and lowered her head to his chest. "I'll never be able to repay you for this. There aren't any words. If I'd lost that little angel..." She shook her head. "How am I ever going to thank you?"

"You could try trusting me, Joey."

She lifted her head, meeting his eyes.

"All frogs aren't the same, you know. Some of them are pretty decent characters, given half a chance."

She blinked as moisture gathered in her eyes. "I'm afraid..."

"Of what?"

She shook her head quickly. "That you'll go away...that you'll stay. That I'll become a gullible fool like so many others before me." A tear spilled onto her cheek.

"You're a lot of things, Joey. But gullible isn't one of them. Maybe you ought to try trusting your instincts."

She shook her head. "That's what my mother did, and then my sister. Look where it got them."

"It doesn't have to be that way."

She looked at him then, her eyes so intense he felt them penetrating his mind. He leaned forward. He'd kiss her senseless. He'd show her, make her believe... He was brought up short when the door opened and the same petite nurse stuck her head in.

"Your sister asked me to bring you these." She set a paper bag on the floor. "Dry clothes." She left them alone again, and the door swung closed.

He cursed the woman's timing. The mood was broken. Joey lowered her arms and averted her eyes. Sighing, Ash picked up the bag and pulled a pair of shorts and a T-shirt out of it. Joey slid from the bed to the floor and winced when she put weight on the leg.

"Easy now." Ash set the clothes on the bed and gripped her around the waist, lifting her right back up to the bed again. He grabbed the shorts and crouched in front of her to slip them over her feet, pull them to her knees.

She grabbed the waistband. "I can take it from here." She slid down, landing only on her good leg this time, and tugged the shorts up under the gown. She tried balancing on one leg while reaching behind her to undo the ties in the back, but wobbled and would have fallen if he hadn't caught her.

"Enough with the modesty, Joey. Turn around."

She looked at him, and he knew she was about to object. Then she sighed and presented her back to him.

Ash untied the bows. He couldn't keep his eyes from traveling over the gentle curve of her spine. And he knew it wasn't really necessary for his palms to slide slowly over her skin as he pushed the gown down over her shoulders, but they did it, anyway.

It landed on the floor. He stood utterly still for a moment, fighting the demon that drove him to turn her around, to look at her, to touch her. It was a hard battle, harder because it was one he didn't want to win. But he stiffened his resolve and reached past her for the T-shirt. As she gripped the bed for support, he pulled it over her head, holding it in place while she inserted one arm, then the other. And it really was accidental that the backs of his fingers brushed over her breasts as he pulled the shirt down over her body.

He felt her shudder, though. He lifted her hair out of the shirt's collar, and then he held it aside and lowered his lips to the back of her neck. He didn't think about doing it, wasn't even aware he was going to until his lips brushed over her nape. He heard the breath escape from her in a rush, and he felt something akin to pain squeeze his chest.

Then he straightened and stepped away from her. He had to, or God only knew what the little nurse would see the next time she popped through the door.

There was too much tension, too much confusion. He cleared his throat as she turned to face him, her eyes searching his. "You, uh, want to hobble, or ride on my back and let me hop you out of here?"

She smiled, but it was shaky, uncertain. "I can walk." As if to prove it she took a step, but then gasped audibly.

He got in front of her, bent his knees and crouched down. "Climb on."

"Ash—"

"Don't argue with your husband, lady." He looked over his shoulder at her with mock severity. "Climb on."

She gripped his neck and slid her legs around his waist. Ash held her soft-skinned legs to his sides. She started to droop, so he reached behind him, palms to her firm backside, and shoved her up higher. "Rrribbit."

She laughed aloud. "You're crazy, you know that?" He walked with her on his back into the corridor and down it. "No wonder you were so great with Brit in the ambulance. You're just a kid yourself."

He frowned, remembering the fear in the little girl's huge blue eyes. "I can't stand to see a kid scared witless, and she was ready to climb the walls in there."

"You were afraid a lot when you were growing up, weren't you?" she asked softly, her words pinpointing the most vulnerable target possible.

Without hesitation he nodded. "Yeah. I was." It wasn't until after he'd confirmed it that he wondered how she'd known.

Her head dipped down, and he felt the brush of her lips across his cheek. "Whatever it was didn't stop you from becoming a hell of a man, Ashville Coye. A hero, in my book. My hero.''

He shook his head. ''Poor princess, waiting for a knight on a charger to show up, and instead you got a frog on a lily pad.''

She started to say something, but they emerged into the waiting room then, and Caroline came to meet them. Brittany looked a good deal better, and Bethany's face glowed with joy.

Both girls lunged for Ash's legs, hugging him violently.

''Can I ride next?'' Bethany shouted.

''No, me,'' Brittany said. ''I'm the one that almost got drowneded.''

''Well, your Aunt Joey is the one who hurt her leg, so I guess she has you both beat. How about when we get back to the house I give you both a turn?''

Squeals of assent preceded the girls being hustled into an elevator, and then out to Caroline's station wagon. Ash lowered Joey in through the open hatch door, so she could keep her leg stretched out. And when they reached the house, he scooped her up again and carried her into the house. He saw the suitcases near the door and glanced at Caro.

''They're ours. I took them out of the car before I left for the hospital.''

Joey's face was tight when Ash lowered her to the sofa. ''You should have locked the door, Caroline.''

''Sorry, little sister. I was too busy wondering if you'd survive the trip. Sheesh, at least I thought to toss the groceries into the fridge. Bags and all, but what the heck?''

Joey's frown deepened. Ash leaned closer to her. ''What is it?''

''I don't know.'' She shook her head slightly. ''Something...''

"Rides now, Uncle Ash!"

He turned Joey on the couch, lifting her injured leg onto a pair of throw pillows. "But I was going to make you my superdeluxe combo subs for lunch."

"Go change your clothes, Ash. I can start the subs," Caroline offered.

"I'll help—"

"*You* will sit there and rest," Ash told Joey. "Doctor's orders." He turned to Caro. "Five minutes." Then he ran upstairs to put on clean clothes. He returned and approached the girls. "Bethany, for courage above and beyond the call of duty, for remembering what you learned in school and calling 911 for your sister, I award you the first ride." He hunkered down and a giggling Bethany clambered onto his back, wrapping her small arms around his neck. "Careful not to choke the old guy now." Ash straightened and began a mock gallop around the living room, into the kitchen and out the other side. All the time, though, as he gave each child a turn, he watched the worry on Joey's face increase. It scared him.

The subs were made and devoured in record time. When they finished, Caroline stood. "We have to go."

"Go where?" Joey sat straighter on the couch.

"Airport. I told you, Joey, the girls and I are going to Miami."

"You didn't say today!"

"Well, I was going to, but..." Caro didn't finish the sentence. A car pulled in, and seconds later the back door thudded open, footsteps pounding up the stairs.

Ted stopped in the doorway, his gaze jumping from Caro to the two girls who were still munching potato chips in the kitchen. His eyes fell closed in apparent relief, and he moved toward Brittany, dropping to his knees and gathering her into his arms.

"You okay, Brittany? Hmm?"

She nodded hard. "I fell in the river, but Aunt Joey and Uncle Ash swimmed out and got me."

Ted's arms tightened. He kissed Brit's cheek and put her back in the chair.

"And I called 911," Bethany put in proudly.

Ted ruffled her hair. "You're a good girl, Beth." He looked up, met Caro's gaze. "Were you even going to tell me?"

"I was going to call—"

"I should have been there, Caroline. I'm her father."

"Did you bring your suitcase, Daddy?"

"'Course he did," Bethany told her sister. "See, Mommy, I told you Daddy would come to Grandpa's house with us."

Caro bit her lip as Ted's gaze widened. He opened his mouth to speak, but Joey was quicker. "Look, you two obviously need to talk." She slanted a meaningful glance toward the girls. "Alone."

Ted didn't seem to hear her. He stepped into the living room toward Caroline, shaking his head. "You're *leaving?*"

She only nodded, her eyes filling.

"Caro, this is crazy. I know what you've been thinking, but you're wrong—"

"Am I?"

He looked as if he'd been punched. Then his face hardened. He turned on his heel and rushed back down the stairs. Ash wasn't sure why, but he followed. Something about the sudden pain on the guy's face hit him, and wouldn't stop.

He stopped Ted at the door. "You're just letting her go?"

Ted's hand tightened on the doorknob. "For now, yes." His voice was choked, and his eyes narrowed in apparent pain when they fell on the suitcases on the floor. "Doesn't look like she's giving me much of a choice, does it?"

Ash sighed hard, pushing a hand through his hair. "You could talk to her. Tell her—"

"Look, Coye, this really isn't any of your damn business. And with you and Joey up to your elbows in this Slasher thing, I'm beginning to think it isn't a bad idea for Caro to get the hell out of Dodge for a while. At least she'll be safe." He thumped a fist on the door.

"I wasn't trying to butt in." Ash opened his mouth to say more, then threw his hands in the air. "You're right, it's none of my damn business."

Ted gripped the door, jerking it open. He started to step through it, then stopped, his back to Ash. "There is no other woman, but Caro isn't going to believe that. It's her father... Sometimes I'd like to slit that bastard's throat for messing those two up the way he did."

Then he left, slamming the door behind him. And Ash couldn't help but ponder his parting words. Slit the bastard's throat. Not break his neck, or blow his head off, but slit his throat. Did it mean anything?

He went back upstairs to see Caro gathering the girls, apparently ready to leave. "Caroline, are you sure this is what you want to do?" Why did he want so badly to fix this mess? He was letting himself get carried away with his role as a member of this family. Caroline only nodded. "Because you *can* stay here, you know. I'd hate to think you were going south because of me—"

"It's better if she goes," Joey announced loudly. Ash frowned. She'd done a complete turnaround since he'd been downstairs with Ted. A few minutes ago, she'd hated the idea of Caro and the girls leaving.

Joey glanced at the clock on the wall. "You'd better hurry, or you'll miss your flight."

"She's right, Ash. But thanks for the offer." Caro hugged her sister, and the girls flung themselves at Ash's legs.

He picked them up, one in either arm. "All right, then, how about one last ride out to the car?" He spun in a circle as the girls giggled. "You'd better send me a postcard, you hear?"

The Slasher had been here.

The sickening sensation had settled in the pit of her stomach from the second they'd entered the house, but she hadn't been able to pinpoint the source. Then it had hit her all at once. What she was feeling was a presence. Someone was in the house, or had been very recently. Someone with a soul of pure evil.

And somewhere in the darkest dungeons of her soul she knew who. And she'd had to get Caro and the girls away from here.

As soon as Ash went outside with the girls, she retrieved her gun from its new hiding place atop the kitchen cabinet, checked to be sure it was loaded and started up the stairs, wincing with every excruciating step. The feeling grew stronger with each second that passed. Before she reached the top she was breathless. Moisture stood on her brow. She held the gun in a two-fisted grip, muzzle up, and glanced around at four closed doors.

Directly ahead was the room she'd designated as the girls' when they visited, filled with toys and coloring books and dolls. To her left was the guest room she'd offered to Ash that first night. To her right, side by side, were the doors to her bedroom and the bath.

She stood frozen at the top of the stairs, concentrating on those doors, sending out invisible feelers. If she chose poorly, and the killer were still here, she might get caught from behind.

"Joey?"

She whirled, gun first. Ashville stood on the bottom step. Why did he have to be so quick? She pressed a finger to her lips to silence him and held a palm outward to tell him to stay where he was.

He came up the stairs, anyway, but he kept his voice low.

"What the hell is going on?"

"Someone...has been here. May be still here. I don't know."

He frowned. "Where?"

"It's strongest near our room." It came out that way without her giving it conscious thought. She lifted the gun again, taking a step nearer.

Ash's hand on her shoulder stopped her. He took the gun from her hands and pushed her back to the wall. "Wait here."

"Ash, no. You shouldn't even be here. You could get killed." Panic gripped her. She didn't want him anywhere near this dark menace.

Ash ignored her, stepped forward and shoved the bedroom door open. As he stepped in and looked around, Joey threw the bathroom door wide, afraid the Slasher had slipped through the adjoining door from the bedroom. No one.

"Joey."

She hurried to the bedroom at Ash's call and froze in the doorway, half expecting to come face-to-face with evil incarnate. But there was no one there. She stood, trembling, while Ash checked the other rooms. When he came back to her, he didn't speak. He just looked at her, waiting.

"You think I'm crazy."

He shook his head. "No. I think you're nervous, jumping at shadows, terrified for your sister and, for some reason, for me, too. What I don't know is why." She said nothing. "Joey, talk to me, tell me what made you think someone was—"

"I don't think it, I *know* it. Someone was in this house while we were gone."

His voice became placating. He stroked her hair. "Honey, you've been through a rough day. There's no one here. There's nothing missing. Look around, everything is just as we—"

He stopped there, his muscles slowly tensing under the skin where her hands rested. She turned, followed his gaze and saw the laptop opened on the dresser. The little pouch that he kept his diskettes in was unzipped and empty. She drew a sharp breath, feeling, for just an instant, the distinct sensation of an ice-cold blade tearing across her back.

What was *that?*

Then Ash was touching her, his hands on her shoulders. "We won't touch anything. There might be prints."

"No." She leaned back against him, letting his warmth chase the cold, tearing feeling from her shoulder blades. "There were gloves. Black, kid-leather gloves, with two little buttons..." She held up a hand and touched the back of her wrist. "Right here." She could feel the gloves, too tight on her large hands. Only they were *not* her hands at all.

"Who?"

Her eyes flew wide. "Where is Caro—?"

"On her way to the airport. Safe and sound. Now dammit, Joey, tell me what the hell is going on. Who wears gloves? Who is it you think was in here?"

She sniffed, trying frantically to control the fit of violent shaking that began at her fingertips and raced its way up her arms to her shoulders, down her spine to her legs. She couldn't say it. She couldn't tell him that his murderer was getting closer. God, she didn't want to lose him. It was so much more important now. More than just a means to stop the Slasher before Caro became a victim.

She turned into Ash's arms, clung to him. "We have to get out of this house."

Chapter 8

Radley Ketchum's office at the *Chronicle* was little more than four stark walls surrounding a paper explosion. He paced toward the closed door, then back again, and handed the coral-frost lipstick to Ash. Ash took it and shoved an overflowing ashtray aside before sitting on the edge of the desk.

"You could get your ass tossed behind bars for evidence tampering, Coye." It was little more than a harsh whisper, delivered as Radley glanced over his shoulder. "You know better than this crap."

Ash dropped the small cylinder into his pocket, trying not to think about what the lipstick's presence in Joey's makeup bag might mean. He was guilty of more than evidence tampering. He was obstructing justice, and he knew it. He glanced beyond Radley, through the glass in the office door, and saw Joey on the other side. She clutched a ceramic mug with steam rolling off the top and sat on the edge of the little chair in front of Ash's desk. One foot tapped rapidly on the floor. One hand, the one that wasn't holding the mug, kept flexing and relaxing on her wounded thigh. She'd have been pacing if she could have managed it.

"Look at her, Rad."

Radley turned his head slowly and stared for a moment. "Yeah. She sure doesn't look like a killer, but—"

"Not that. Look at her face. Her eyes. Radley, that's one scared woman sitting out there." Ash shook his head. "She won't go back to her house, wouldn't even stick around and wait for the police to show up."

Rad shook his head slowly, facing Ash once more. "Yeah, but scared of *what?*"

"Of the Slasher, I think."

"Or maybe scared of getting caught. Maybe she's scared you're close to finding out *she's* the Slasher." Rad shook his head, crossed the room slowly and straightened the photo of his sister, the ugliest woman Ash had ever seen. She was built like a tank.

"That's bull," he said quietly, glancing again where Joey sat.

"Use your brain, Ash. Why would *she* be afraid of the Slasher? All five victims have been men."

"Four, Rad."

"What?"

"Four victims. You said five, but there's only been—"

"Four, five—what difference does it make? There'll be more. The police haven't got much to go on, and you're hiding anything they might *get* to go on. They're getting desperate."

"That's what I'm afraid of." Ash jumped down from the desk and walked closer to the door. "They need a suspect, even if it's just to take the heat off for a while, and I'll be damned if it's going to be Joey. They could ruin her life, Rad, all on the basis of one tube of lipstick."

"That happens to be the same brand, even the same shade, that was found ringing those cigarette butts found at the crime scenes."

"Coincidence. Look, I can't stand by and let her get railroaded."

"Why the hell not?" That Rad's patience was reaching its limit was evidenced by the deep color rising in his face and the tightening of his jaw. "It's due process. If she's innocent she'll be cleared, and if not she'll pay. That's the way the system works, isn't it? She's nothing to you, right? Just a lead you wanted to follow up, isn't that what you said? Or has gettin' in her tight little pants changed your mind—?"

Ash had him by the collar before Rad could finish the sentence. Two fists bunched Rad's dingy white shirt at the front and drew him forward.

"See what I mean, Ash?" Rad ground the words out between clenched teeth as Ash glared down at him, wanting to knock out a few of his teeth. "You're not objective anymore. You're messing around with evidence, protecting a suspect, risking your job...." He glanced pointedly down at the fists that held his shirt, and Ash sighed hard, releasing him.

"You're wrong." He turned and paced away slowly. "Not that it's any of your business, Rad, but I haven't slept with her. And I'm on top of this story. Objectivity intact."

Rad was silent a long moment. Then, "I don't think so, Ash. I'm going to put Harris on the Slasher case."

Ash whirled. "The hell you are!"

"You aren't yourself. You're—"

"Quitting."

Rad's mouth fell open, the rest of his sentence left hanging unfinished in the air, silenced by a single word.

"That's it. Your choice. Give the story to Harris, and I walk. And if I walk, you'll probably be behind me in the unemployment line, because the paper will fire you for losing their star reporter. Now what's it going to be, Rad?''

Rad's eyes conveyed his anger. He didn't like being backed up to the wall, but Ash was saying no more than the truth, and Rad knew it. "What are you planning, Ash, besides trailing along after the bimbo like a hungry pup and hoping she drops you a crumb?"

Ash glared right back at him. "Go to hell, Rad."

"Damn you, Coye—"

"All right." Ash held up one hand. "Truce, okay?"

Rad stuffed both hands deep into his pockets and nodded. "What are you planning?"

"To talk to a psychiatrist, an expert on serial killers. Try and get a profile of our suspect. And I want to see some of these executive types Joey's worked for, find out what they have to say about her... abilities."

It was Rad's turn to stare through the window at Joey. "You still think she's a fake, right?"

Ash hesitated before answering. "I'm beginning to wonder."

"Why?" Rad turned, frowning. "You're a dyed-in-the-wool skeptic about that kind of crap, Ash. What's she done, read your mind or something?"

"Or something."

Rad's face seemed to relax all of a sudden, all the tension going out of it. He turned again toward the door and looked through it, eyes blank. "Well, now. Isn't that interesting?"

Ash shook his head slowly, reaching for the doorknob. "Don't go asking her about it. She thinks I don't know. And treat her right, Rad. She's my wife, don't forget."

"As long as *you* don't forget that she *isn't*."

She stiffened when she saw them coming toward her. She'd tried to concentrate on their conversation in Mr. Ketchum's office, but as usual, the harder she tried to focus, the less she picked up. In a newsroom that was bursting with wall-to-wall desks, rushing people and the constant clicking of keyboards, it was tough to hear herself think, let alone pick up what someone else might be thinking. She sensed, though, that a lot of the time they'd been talking about her. Not knowing what was said made her uncomfortable and self-conscious.

"Mrs. Coye." Radley Ketchum nodded toward her. "Feeling better now?"

She nodded politely. "Yes. Thanks for the coffee."

Ash stood in front of her, putting both hands on her shoulders. "Bev called while I was in Rad's office."

Bev. Detective Lady Atlas, he meant.

"They've finished at the house."

"Did they find anything?"

Ash squeezed her shoulders. "A few prints, they're being analyzed but—"

"They're ours. I told you, the person wore gloves..." She stopped, blinking. Ash would have her committed if she didn't stop going on about the gloves. She glanced up to see if his boss found her as nutty as Ash must, but he only stared at her, his gaze dark, probing.

"Anyway, we can go back now—"

"No."

He shook her so slightly it was barely palpable. "Joey, we can still stay at my apartment. But don't you think you ought to pick up a few clothes? Your toothbrush?"

"I'm not going back there."

Ash shook his head, and she knew he thought she must still be distraught over the intruder, stressed out from all that had happened today. The truth was, she was calm, and thinking as clearly as she ever had in her life. She simply did not want Ash in that house. A sense of danger loomed at the very thought of it.

"Okay. All right, if that's what you want." He turned to Rad, who still stared hard at her. "I'll be in touch."

"Good." He smiled at Joey. "Hope to see you again soon, Mrs. Coye." Then he turned and walked away.

Ash drove to his apartment, a few short minutes from the offices of the *Chronicle*. He unlocked the door, and Joey preceded him in, limping slowly, senses on alert. She was more wary than she could ever remember being. She stepped into the short, dark hallway and felt the wall for a light switch.

Ash beat her to it, and as soon as he flicked it on Joey stepped farther inside. Still, she was careful. She poked her head through the archway on her right, into the kitchenette, leaning heavily on the doorframe and fumbling for that light switch. When she saw nothing there, aside from the gleaming white cupboards and checkerboard tiles, she returned to the hall and hobbled through the door on its other side, into the small bathroom. She turned that light on, as well.

She knew Ash stood in the hallway, leaning against the wall, just watching her peculiar behavior. Stubbornly she glanced around the little bathroom, even going so far as to open the frosted-glass doors on the three-sided shower stall in the corner and to peek inside.

Sighing her relief, she stepped back into the short hall. Ash put an arm around her. "You'd better relax, Joey. You're jumping at shadows. No one's here but us."

"Better safe than sorry," she quipped. "And I'm not jumping. Just checking." The hall opened into the large living room of Ash's corner apartment. At the far end, glass doors led out to a balcony. Darkness gathered beyond, dotted by Syracuse's lights, only visible in the slits between the vertical blinds. The bedroom was on her right. She checked both before she sank onto the modular sofa's forest green plush.

"Feel safe now?" There was worry, as well as a hint of amusement, glinting in his eyes.

She smiled at him. "It isn't *me* I'm—" She stopped herself. "Yes. Perfectly safe."

"You're sure?"

She squinted at him. "Why so interested?"

"Just checking. Thought I'd go out for some supplies."

"Like what?" She was no longer relaxed on the sofa, but leaning forward, tense.

Ash shook his head and sat down beside her. "Like food. I haven't been here in a while. The place isn't exactly well stocked."

She turned to face him, wanting to beg him not to leave her side—not for an instant—but knowing how insane that might sound to him. "I'm not all that hungry, anyway."

"Well, I am. Look, I know you're still shaken. Just stay here, okay? Take a hot shower, watch some TV, drink a glass of wine. Loosen up. I'll be back in thirty minutes, I promise."

She shook her head slowly. "We can order in."

"Joey—"

"Don't go, Ash." He frowned, searching her eyes for a long moment. "Just...don't go."

He sighed, and his chin dropped to his chest. When he lifted it again she saw the impatience in his face, the frustration. "You want me to stay, then you're going to have to tell me why. What is it you're so afraid of, Joey?"

She blinked, turning her face away. "I—I'm not afraid, just—"

"Bull." He caught her face in his hands and brought it around, then stared deep into her eyes. "Stop keeping things from me. Joey, I want to help you, but I can't if you won't tell me what's wrong. Can't you trust me even that much?''

She said nothing, and after a second he dropped his hands, sighed in anger and rose from the sofa. "Dammit, Joey, I'm not your father, and I'm not Ted. I'm not going to betray you. But I guess it's too much to ask you to believe that, hmm?"

He started toward the hall, then down it, and Joey lunged off the sofa after him. The pain in her thigh screamed, but she forced herself to run, and she gripped his arm just as he reached for the doorknob. She jerked him back.

"Don't! Don't leave, Ash, you can't..."

He stood motionless, not even turning to face her. "Give me one good reason, Joey. And if it's another lie—"

"The Slasher is going to kill you."

There was utter silence after she said it. He was going to laugh at her, call her crazy. But it would be better than letting him go out and end up dead.

He turned slowly and looked down at her. "How do you know that?"

He was watching her face so damned closely she knew he'd see through any lie she concocted. She caught her lower lip between her teeth and took a single step backward. "I just do."

"How?" he demanded, advancing. "Do you know the Slasher, Joey? Is that it?"

She shook her head from side to side, and when he reached for her she took another hasty step backward. But she'd forgotten her injury, and she put too much weight on it, too suddenly. She cried out. Her knee buckled as white-hot pain shot through her leg, and she stumbled.

Ash swore as he reached for her, caught her around the waist and kept her from falling. He hauled her up and forward, hesitated for an immeasurable instant, then pulled her closer, tight to his chest. His arms closed around her, and Joey pressed her face against the cool fabric of his shirt, inhaling his scent.

"It's not firsthand information." He murmured the words into her hair and slowly began to rock just slightly back and forth. "It's not that you're a part of this insanity. I know that, Joey. But for God's sake, you have to tell me what it is."

She nodded, moving her head against his chest even as her arms crept up around his neck and tightened there.

He turned her slightly and then scooped her up. He carried her down the hall, but didn't stop in the living room this time. He turned left and carried her into his bedroom instead.

As he lowered her onto his oversize bed, Ash studied her face in the too-bright lights of the bedroom. *Tell me the truth this time, Joey. I'm trying to believe in you, but, God, you're making it tough.*

He propped pillows behind her and eased her onto them. He pulled the extra blanket from the foot of the bed, shook it out and covered her, tucking it around her shoulders. The apartment was chilly. He hadn't thought to adjust the thermostat when they'd come in. He hadn't been thinking about much at all lately, except the mystery that was Joey Bradshaw and how he might solve it.

He looked at her huddled on his bed like a frightened child, at the way her hair tumbled over her shoulders, and the way her lips were slightly parted and moist and full. He'd been thinking about those lips, too, and how they tasted. And those thoughts led to others, until he was surprised he could remember how to breathe, let alone investigate a string of murders. Maybe Radley had been right about that.

He pushed a hand through his hair and turned away. He went to the living room and heard the anxiety, the raw fear, in her voice as she called his name.

"I'm not going anywhere," he called back. "Just stay put." He stalked to the kitchenette and found a bottle of white zinfandel in the fridge. For a minute he just looked at it, sitting there, unopened, waiting for the notorious Ashville Coye to introduce it to his latest conquest. There was an instant when he was disgusted with himself and his endless search for the perfect woman. Who did he think he was, anyway, that the perfect woman would be interested in him? And where did he get off, listing the standards she had to meet? What did he know?

Nothing. Not one damn thing. Joey Bradshaw was proof of that. He'd written her off the day he'd met her, and as it turned out, she was probably the closest thing to perfect he'd ever seen.

He slammed the fridge closed and fumbled in a drawer for a corkscrew. He felt things for Joey. Things he didn't want to feel. Hell, in all his big plans involving the wife of his dreams and the perfect nuclear family, he'd never given much thought to actual *emotions* being involved. He guessed he'd just assumed some deep, abiding fondness would come with the package.

What an idiot!

So he meets a woman who's as far from what he'd thought he wanted as was humanly possible, and starts wishing he could have her—wishing he could *always* have her. And it has to be a woman who's lying to him every time she opens her mouth. A woman who can't trust him. A woman who gives every indication of being mixed up in murder.

The cork popped and Ash threw it, corkscrew and all, onto the shiny white counter. "And she thinks she can read

minds, to boot. It's crazy." He reached into the cupboard
above for two wineglasses, and filled them both. Then he set
the bottle aside and just stared into the pinkish liquid, remembering the way she'd known little Brittany had fallen
into the river, the way she'd known a lot of things she
shouldn't have. The thoughts made him uneasy. He gripped
one glass and tipped it to his lips, draining it. He set it down
and filled it again.

"Maybe I'm the one who's crazy."

"Ash?"

God, she was so afraid to let him out of her sight! Why?

"Right here. I'm right here." Maybe now she'd come
clean with him, tell him why she'd started this game. Why
she was pretending to be his wife, and what she knew about
the Slasher.

He carried the two glasses back to the bedroom, sat on the
edge of the bed and handed her one.

She gave him a wary look and took a sip. Then another.
"This is good."

"Talk to me, Joey."

She licked her lips and nodded, taking a bigger gulp of
wine. "You won't believe me. You'll think I'm a flake." He
only watched her, waiting. She cleared her throat. "Sometimes I *know* things."

"What kinds of things?" He wasn't going to help her. He
needed to know if she would be honest on her own.

She averted her eyes. "Like when Brit fell in the river."

"You said you heard the splash."

"I wasn't...being honest. I didn't hear anything. I
just...*felt* it. In my mind, I saw Brit fall in, and I knew."
She licked her lips and rushed on. "That's how I help the
companies that hire me as a consultant. If I'm around people, I sometimes sense their dishonesty and I..." Her voice
trailed off.

IT'S FUN! IT'S FREE!
AND IT COULD MAKE YOU A

MILLIONAIRE

If you've ever played scratch-off lottery tickets, you should be familiar with how our games work. On each of the first four tickets (numbered 1 to 4 in the upper right) there are Pink Strips to scratch off.

Using a coin, do just that—carefully scratch the PINK strips to reveal how much each ticket could be worth if it is a winning ticket. Tickets could be worth from $100.00 to $1,000,000.00 in lifetime money ($33,333.33 each year for 30 years).

Note, also, that each of your 4 tickets has a unique sweepstakes Lucky Number... and that's 4 chances for a **BIG WIN!**

FREE BOOKS!

At the same time you play your tickets to qualify for big prizes, you are invited to play ticket #5 to get brand-new Silhouette Intimate Moments® novels. These books have a cover price of $3.99 each, but they are yours to keep absolutely free.

There's no catch. You're under no obligation to buy anything. You don't have to make any minimum number of purchases — not even one!

The fact is thousands of readers enjoy receiving books by mail from the Silhouette Reader Service™. They like the convenience of home delivery... they like getting the best new novels months before they're available in bookstores... and they love our discount prices!

We hope that after receiving your free books you'll want to remain a subscriber. But the choice is yours—to continue or cancel, anytime at all! So why not take us up on our invitation, with no risk of any kind. You'll be glad you did!

PLUS A FREE GIFT!

One more thing, when you accept the free books on ticket #5, you are also entitled to play ticket #6, which is GOOD FOR A GREAT GIFT! Like the books, this gift is totally free and yours to keep as thanks for giving our Reader Service a try!

So scratch off the PINK STRIPS on all your BIG WIN tickets and send for everything today! You've got nothing to lose and everything to gain!

Here are your BIG WIN Game Tickets potentially worth from $100.00 to $1,000,000.00 each. Scratch off the PINK STRIP on each of your Sweepstakes tickets to see what you could win and mail your entry right away. (SEE BACK OF BOOK FOR DETAILS!)

This could be your lucky day—GOOD LUCK!

FOLD AND DETACH ALONG THIS DOTTED LINE—RETURN ALL GAME TICKETS INTACT.

TICKET 1

Scratch PINK STRIP to reveal potential value of cash prize if the sweepstakes number on this ticket is a winning number. Return all game tickets intact.

LUCKY NUMBER

4I 771546

TICKET 2

Scratch PINK STRIP to reveal potential value of cash prize if the sweepstakes number on this ticket is a winning number. Return all game tickets intact.

LUCKY NUMBER

2S 662864

TICKET 3

Scratch PINK STRIP to reveal potential value of cash prize if the sweepstakes number on this ticket is a winning number. Return all game tickets intact.

LUCKY NUMBER

9R 786920

TICKET 4

Scratch PINK STRIP to reveal potential value of cash prize if the sweepstakes number on this ticket is a winning number. Return all game tickets intact.

LUCKY NUMBER

7L 646869

TICKET 5

Scratch PINK STRIP to reveal number of books you will receive. These books, part of a sampling program to introduce romance readers to the benefits of the Reader Service, are free.

AUTHORIZATION CODE

130107-742

TICKET 6

All gifts are free. No purchase required. Scratch PINK STRIP to reveal free gift, our thanks to readers for trying our books.

AUTHORIZATION CODE

130107-742

YES! Enter my Lucky Numbers in The Million Dollar Sweepstakes (III) and when winners are selected, tell me if I've won any prize. If the PINK STRIP is scratched off on ticket #5, I will also receive four FREE Silhouette Intimate Moments® novels along with the FREE GIFT on ticket #6, as explained on the back and on the opposite page. 345 CIS AQYL (C-SIL-IM-10/94)

NAME _____

ADDRESS _____ APT. _____

CITY _____ PROVINCE _____ POSTAL CODE _____

Book offer limited to one per household and not valid to current Silhouette Moments® subscribers. All orders subject to approval.

© 1991 HARLEQUIN ENTERPRISES LIMITED.   PRINTED IN U.S.A.

019561919-L2A5X3-BR01

SILHOUETTE READER SERVICE
PO BOX 609
FORT ERIE, ONT.
L2A 9Z9

MAIL ⟹ POSTE

Canada Post Corporation / Société canadienne des postes

Postage paid
If mailed in Canada

Port payé
si posté au Canada

Business
Reply

Réponse
d'affaires

01956l9199   01

"So you're a psychic."

She closed her eyes. "Don't laugh at me, Ash."

He took the wineglass from her hand and set it on the bedside stand, placing his beside it. "I wouldn't do that."

"I can't control it. I'm not sure I want to."

He wasn't sure he believed it, even now. "Is that how you knew someone had been in the house? You just *felt* it?"

She lifted her head and nodded.

"And what you said about the gloves—"

"I saw the hands...the gloves."

He sighed, licked his lips. "What else have you...seen?"

Her eyes widened and took on an intensity he hadn't witnessed before. "Ash, you're in danger. You have to believe that. The Slasher wants you dead, and I can't let it happen."

"Because I'm your husband?"

Tears gathered until her emerald eyes glittered. "Because...I care about you. I don't want to lose you, and that's nothing but the truth."

It was some kind of pain that twisted inside him when she said that. Some kind of excruciating, wonderful pain. She was telling part of the truth, at least. Or what she believed to be the truth. But it was difficult to swallow. He'd never put much stock in farfetched claims of extraterrestrials, or Elvis sightings, or ESP.

"You don't believe any of it, do you?"

He reached toward her, brushing a single tear from her cheek with his thumb. "I believe you care." He shook his head. "Can't imagine why, but you do. And I think you're convinced of this...this mind-reading thing. I just..." His hand fell away from her face. He got up and reached for his wine, then paced the room, carrying it. "It's damned hard to buy into, Joey." He took a huge gulp and went on. "Maybe if you could *show* me—"

"I'm not a magician, Ash, and this isn't some parlor trick."

He turned to face her, seeing the anger rising in red blotches on her cheeks. "I didn't mean—"

"Yes, you did. You were going to ask me to read your mind, tell you what you were thinking while you evoked some unlikely image. It doesn't work that way. I told you, I can't control it. I can't just look inside your head and read your thoughts as if I was reading a book. God knows I've tried."

He felt his brows shoot up as her anger ran its course. "You have?"

She nodded, looking miserable.

"And you couldn't read me, huh?"

She shook her head, then paused. "Well, except..." She bit her lip and didn't finish the thought.

"Except what?" Why did his voice sound so eager? Was he actually hoping she could prove her claims?

She sighed, reaching for her wine and finishing it. "You had a nightmare one night. A bad one. One you have a lot."

He stiffened, suddenly feeling as if someone was invading his most private hell. But it was silly. He'd probably tossed and turned, broken into a sweat, maybe muttered in his sleep. Anyone would know he'd been dreaming.

"I did, huh? I don't remember."

She looked at him, her anger vanishing like mist. "You were alone, in a very small, very dark place. You felt like you were suffocating, you couldn't breathe, and you—"

"All right." He didn't mean to snap, but she was picking at an old wound. More gently he said, "All right, I believe you."

"I'm sorry." She got out of the bed and limped toward him. "I know it still hurts—"

"Well, your ESP is flawed, because it doesn't."

She stopped two feet from him. "You can tell me about it, talk it out—"

"It's not something I talk about." He finished his wine and looked down into the empty glass.

"Maybe that's the problem."

"My only *problem* is that my *wife* won't let me out of the apartment to buy food, and my stomach is empty."

She lowered her head, and he knew that she would let the topic slide.

"Help yourself to the bathroom, Joey, and something to wear to bed. I'm gonna call a deli that delivers." He turned to go, then turned back. "Hey, you wouldn't happen to be *sensing* any great hoagie joints that are still open, would you?"

His attempt at humor worked, he thought. She smiled, reaching back to the bed for the pillow and throwing it at him. "I suppose I'll be pummeled with ESP jokes for the rest of the night now?"

"You read my mind."

Chapter 9

She couldn't eat. But he didn't seem to have any trouble. Nor was his sleep disturbed in any visible way. He'd been snoring loudly when she'd slipped out of his bed. He had to know she was lying, keeping things from him. It was in his eyes whenever he looked at her. But she'd told him as much as she could. If he knew she wasn't his wife, he'd probably send her packing...and she couldn't protect him if she wasn't with him.

She stood on the balcony and stared down into the twinkling lights below. The warm summer breeze played with the shirt she wore. His shirt. It held his scent, wrapped it all around her, and she found she liked that sensation. Maybe too much.

She drank the wine she'd helped herself to, and told herself she was stupid to get so attached to him. It wouldn't last. It couldn't, because his memory was coming back.

It hadn't hit her at first. Only as she lay in the bed beside him, watching him as he slept, wishing she had the nerve to reach for him, to kiss him, had the suspicion taken root. He remembered his nightmare, remembered its source. And he hadn't seemed at all unfamiliar with his apartment. His memory was returning, and when it did he would know she was lying about their marriage.

And then she would lose him. Even if she managed to keep up the charade long enough to save him from the Slasher, in the end she would lose him to her own lies.

Why did it hurt so much to know that? Why was she standing on a balcony, in the dark, sipping wine and crying like a little girl?

"Couldn't sleep, huh?"

She stiffened, but didn't turn around. She didn't want him to see her foolish tears. "No."

"Neither could I." He moved up to the rail beside her, slipping an arm around her shoulders. He wore a short terry robe, untied, over the briefs he'd slept in.

"Liar. You were sawing timbers when I left."

"*Until* you left." He turned to face her, looking down at her. "Hey, what's this?" He wiped the moisture from her cheeks with his fingertips.

"Stress, I suppose." She reached for the wineglass. He did, too, bumping her hand with his and sloshing the wine onto her wrist. She drew her hand away, but he caught and lifted it. He brought it close to his face, his lips. Then he kissed it, drinking the wine from her skin, his mouth moving slowly over her wrist and forearm.

She trembled, and he straightened.

"Cold?"

She shook her head, unable to speak. She wanted him so much, wanted this make-believe marriage to be real . . . just for tonight. And she knew he wanted it, too. His eyes glimmered in the darkness, with desire . . . for her.

She averted her gaze. This was insane. "The shirt will stain," she said to break the tension.

Then his fingertips were at her neck, and she realized he was releasing the buttons. And she stood there, not moving, with neither the will nor the desire to stop him.

He reached the lowest button and stopped. He looked into her eyes, not touching her, waiting for her to say no. She didn't. Instead she caught the front of the shirt in her trembling hands, parted it and let it slide down her shoulders to fall in soft folds at her feet.

And there, in the moonlight, he looked at her . . . the way a mother must look at her own newborn child the first time it's placed in her arms. Awe, sheer adoration, glowing from his face, he looked at her from head to toe. He blinked, and met her gaze again, lifting a hand to caress her cheek.

"Ah, God, Joey." It was a whisper, hoarse, as if he were in some kind of pain. His hand drifted downward, over her chin, her throat. His fingertips skimmed her breast, then his palm closed over it.

She closed her eyes and let her head fall back in reaction to his touch. His hand slid over the curve of her waist, around to the small of her back, and he drew her to him. Free hand driving into her hair, he brought her face level again, and then he kissed her.

It was slow, almost reverent in its tenderness, that kiss. As if it were the first one, as if he wanted to learn the shape and taste of her mouth, memorize it, savor it. She felt the roughness of a day's growth of whiskers razing her skin. She tasted the wine on his tongue as he lazily licked at the inside of her mouth. And his fingers, flexing in her hair in time with those spread at the base of her spine, were hypnotic and wonderful.

She brought her hands up between them and pushed his robe open, wanting more, needing the brush of his chest hair over her breasts and the feel of his taut skin under her hands. He released her with only one hand at a time to shrug the robe off, never breaking the sweet, erotic rhythm of his kiss.

His head angled. His lips slid over her face, and he nibbled at her jaw, then moved lower, the damp warmth of his mouth bathing her neck and the hollow below her ear. Her heart raced, drowning out the sounds of traffic below. Her senses filled with him, with wanting him, needing him.

He bent her backward and took one breast into his mouth. Her hands on his shoulders tightened, and she felt the shudder that ran through him. He suckled her, making her gasp for breaths that wouldn't seem to come.

"Ash...we should go...inside," she managed, her voice sounding weak and shaky.

He kissed a trail back to her mouth, pausing in between as he spoke, not lifting his mouth from her skin, so that his words were warm caresses against it. "No, Joey. There have...been others...in there." His fingers tangled in her hair and he lifted his face slightly from hers, staring into her eyes. "This is different. *You're* different. I want you here, where there's never been anyone else."

Tears burned her eyes, but she nodded, and twined her arms around his neck to bring his lips to hers. He lowered her to the floor, on a rumpled bed made by the shirt she'd worn and his robe. And he came down with her, his arm pillowing her head as his lips moved over her body. His mouth moistened her throat and chest, her breasts and her belly. His free hand roamed downward, and he gently parted her thighs to explore the valley between them. He caressed her, then probed, and her hips rose of their own will. She was damp, trembling, and her desire encompassed her mind and soul.

When he paused and turned away, she cried out his name, but he came back to her in a moment, smoothing her hair, kissing her mouth. "I'm right here...not going anywhere." He touched her again, his thumb finding and then fondling the center of her need. And then he nudged her thighs wider with his knee and settled between them.

When she felt his hardness touch her softness, she closed her eyes and gripped his buttocks, pulling him into her. Her eyes widened at the sensation as her body stretched around him. Then his hands slid beneath her to hold her to him, and he pushed still deeper.

"Tight," he said between kisses. "So tight...so good." He withdrew and moved in again, slowly, so slowly she wanted to scream. And then again, and again, keeping to that torturous pace, no matter how she arched against him or twisted beneath him in desire.

Over and over his steely strength caressed her from within, and all the while he kissed her and whispered softly against her skin. Words that had no meaning for her then, in her frenzied state. Words like "You're safe, Joey...always safe with me."

He pushed her, and he pulled her. Played with her as if she were a puppet on a string, driving her to the edge of madness only to let her hang there, begging for fulfillment in the language of her body. She writhed beneath him, longing for it, mindless in her need.

Then he gave her what she craved, quickening his pace, deepening his invasion into her body, driving into her as she felt his need grow to equal her own.

And then she exploded. Her arms and legs clamped around him and she screamed his name, clinging to him as spasms racked her entire being. It was only as her coiled muscles began to unfurl that she realized he'd stiffened, too. Moaning long and low into her mouth, he thrust himself into her desperately, and held her tight to him as he throbbed inside her.

He held her as she relaxed, then eased off her. Lying close to her, he curled her into his strong arms and held her head nestled against his chest.

He kept her there, trapped against him. Not that she tried to move away. Her arm wrapped around his waist and she pressed even closer. Which was good, because he hadn't yet managed to blink all the moisture away from his eyes, and he sure as hell didn't want her to see it there. He hoped her mind-reading talents were as undependable as she'd said they were. His thoughts, his feelings, right now were something he had no desire to share with her. He wasn't even sure he understood them himself. He'd never been moved near to tears by making love to a woman before.

Hell, he'd never thought of it as *making love* before. But damned if there was anything else to describe what had just happened with Joey. Until tonight, he hadn't been aware of the difference, hadn't thought there could be more than physical pleasure, mutual satisfaction, two adults sharing a few minutes of passion with the connection broken as soon as it was over. He'd never *expected* there to be anything more.

He almost laughed at his naiveté. Then he justified his ignorance. How could he have known it could be like this? He'd never seen it firsthand, never known a man and a woman to share anything deeper. His mother certainly hadn't been an example of it. At least his own experiences had been for pleasure rather than for cash.

He looked down at Joey, cuddled against him, and wished he were the one with the ESP. He'd kill to know if she felt anything like what he was feeling. As if she belonged to him now, and he to her. As if there was no one else in the world he could feel this way with. As if he'd never let her go...not now, not if it meant he had to battle an army to keep her.

The power of his feelings scared the hell out of him. Especially knowing she'd been lying to him from the start, and still not knowing why. But he would find out. He would dig until he knew everything about Joey, and he would find a way to make her trust him with the truth.

He rose to his feet, only smiling when she looked up at him with her delicate brows arched. He bent and scooped her into his arms, carried her inside and lowered her onto the bed. Then he got in beside her and held her close. And somehow he knew that as long as he did, the nightmares of his childhood would be powerless to haunt his sleep.

She was in the shower when the phone bleated the next morning and Ash snatched it up, growling a greeting. He hated the interruption, since he'd been about to slip into the bathroom to join her.

"Okay, Coye, you owe me big time for this one."

Radley sounded smug, and his opening line caught Ash's attention. "What have you got?"

"I saved you some legwork, pal. A lot of it. You were planning to sift all the information from the Vegas murders, but I did it for you, and two tidbits came up that I think you'll find pretty juicy."

"What're you, bucking to get back into reporting? I thought this was my story."

"It is, Ash. But your life's on the line here, right?"

"And you don't trust me to check the facts with an unbiased eye."

"Hell, what're friends for?"

Ash sighed into the mouthpiece, shaking his head. "All right, Rad. What've you got?"

Rad chuckled. "I knew you'd come around." Then he cleared his throat. "This first one might go down hard, Ash. Your little woman was in Vegas during the summer of '89 when those killings went down."

Ash felt his spine pull tight, as if it might snap in two at the base of his neck. "How do you know?"

"Hotel records. I still have a few connections from my reporting days, you know."

Ash released his breath in a rush, not bothering to ask how Rad had known which hotels to check. He'd either checked them all, or he'd had a tip. Either way, it had to be true. It would be too easy for Ash to verify and Rad knew that. "What else?"

"Your Christmas present. Like I said, you owe me one. I know you don't want to see the mind reader do time for this. I've found you another suspect."

His senses pricked to full alertness. "Who?"

"A cop. A cop who was fully involved in the Vegas investigation. The same cop who's heading up the local one."

Ash frowned. "Bev Issacs?"

"The same. She worked on the Vegas PD when the murders were committed. And she smokes the right kind of cigarettes."

Ash swore softly, his mind working full speed. "I can't believe she's a killer."

"No one believed Ted Bundy could be one either, pal. I'm just giving you the facts."

"Are the police aware of this?"

"I don't know. If they are, they aren't talking."

Ash licked his lips. "We need to get our hands on a sample of Bev's DNA. Compare it to what the cops got from the saliva on those butts at the crime scenes. That's the only way we'll know for sure."

Rad was silent for a long moment, and Ash heard the flick of a lighter, and then the sound of Rad blowing smoke. "Look, Ash, if we're checking DNA, don't you think we ought to have a sample of Joey Bradshaw's, as well?"

"Hell, no." He answered too fast, and automatically.

"Afraid it's gonna clinch the case against her?"

"It would clear her."

"Then get it. I'll get an independent lab to do the testing, and work on getting SPD to give me a copy of the workup they have on the killer."

Ash hesitated, chewing his lip.

"Look, Coye, we won't tell the cops a thing until we have the results."

He let his chin fall to his chest. "Yeah. All right. How long will it take?"

"Two weeks, minimum."

"That's too long."

"Nothing to be done about that, Ash. Can you get me a sample from Joey?"

Ash looked around the room, his gaze settling on the wad of bandages she'd taken from her thigh before going to the shower. There were traces of blood marring the white gauze. "Yeah. I can get it. What about Bev?"

"I'll handle it."

He didn't elaborate and Ash didn't ask.

"I think you ought to sit tight on this until we have some answers."

"No, Rad. I already have an appointment to talk with a psychiatrist. I want to see it through."

"It's a waste of time."

"It's my time to waste. I'm still on leave, remember?"

"Pigheaded son of a—"

"It can't hurt, Rad. The more we know about who we're dealing with, the better."

"No shrink's gonna tell you anything you don't already know. They're quacks, all of 'em." Rad sighed hard.

"Ben Kramer's been studying serial killers for years. I've only been at it for a few weeks. Come on, Rad, ease up."

"Kramer, eh? Never heard of him."

"He's from Ithaca. I'm heading down there this afternoon."

"Your *wife* going along?"

"Well, I'm sure as hell not leaving her alone here until I get to the bottom of this. Not that she'd let me." Ash glanced toward the bathroom and smiled slightly.

"Why *wouldn't* she let you?"

"This psychic thing she has—"

"She's got you *believing* it?"

"Yeah. And she thinks the Slasher's added my name to the hit list. And now that you mention it, while you're checking on Bev, keep your eyes open for a pair of black gloves, kid leather, two small buttons at the wrist. Joey says that's what the killer wears."

Rad was silent for a long moment. Then, "Gee, Ash, why don't you just ask her who the killer is? If she's that good, she ought to be able to figure it out. Save us some time and effort."

"She doesn't know, but maybe she will in time. She can't control what she, you know, what she *sees*. But when she does get something, it's so damned accurate it's scary."

"Never thought I'd hear you talking like that about an alleged psychic."

"No less than I did." Ash heard the shower stop running. "Later, Rad."

"Right."

Ash hung up just as Joey stepped out of the bathroom, wrapped in a towel. He got up, stark naked, and met her halfway across the room, pulling her towel away. She squeaked in surprise, but he silenced her with a kiss. God, she tasted good. He picked her up, carried her into the bathroom and turned the shower back on.

Dr. Benjamin Kramer's office seemed more like a living room, and Joey was glad of the comfort after the two-and-a-half-hour drive down from Syracuse. They'd stopped at the house and Ash had made coffee and filled a thermos jug while Joey had packed a few things. He didn't see her stuff her two helmets into a duffel bag, and she was glad. She wasn't sure her attempts to get him into a cave would be successful and she was sure they wouldn't if he had time to think about it.

Shivers of dread had rippled up her spine when she'd entered her bedroom, but the sense of a menacing presence had faded a bit overnight. Still, she packed quickly, wanting to get out of the house as soon as possible.

Now she reclined in an armchair, extending her aching leg in front of her. Kramer frowned at her, his bushy gray brows bunching behind round tortoiseshell glasses. Then he pushed a footstool in front of her. She smiled gratefully and propped her leg on it.

"Recent injury?" He settled himself into a rocker, his paunch protruding slightly over the waistband of his cream-colored trousers.

"Very recent," she replied.

"Can I get you anything? Aspirin?"

"No, thank you, I'm fine."

He nodded, and turned his attention to Ash. "Now then, the reason for this visit. You're interested in serial killers. No doubt due to the string of murders you're investigating."

Ash nodded. "I'm hoping you can give me an idea of the kind of person we're looking for."

He shrugged. "Perhaps. The papers haven't been very forthcoming with details. It's difficult to judge without knowing more. Have the murders been particularly grisly?"

Ash glanced at Joey. "A single slash to the throat, Doctor. The victims bled to death. And there were..." He frowned a little. "Of course, I'm counting on your discretion. None of this is public knowledge."

"You have my word, Mr. Coye. Believe me, I'd do nothing to jeopardize the investigation. Please, go on."

Ash bit his lip. "There were cigarette butts found at three of the four scenes."

Joey stiffened. He hadn't told her that.

"Any blood on them?"

"No. Is that significant?"

Kramer shifted, leaning forward in his chair. "Could be. If the killer smoked while killing, there's likely to be blood spattered on the cigarette. Likewise, if he smoked beforehand, say, while waiting for the victim, and tossed the butt aside, it would still be spattered in blood. A bleeding jugular would be quite forceful." He cupped his chin, tilting his head. "I see a man who slashes, then steps out of the way and calmly smokes while the victim lies bleeding." He shook his head. "He's a predator."

Ash shook his head. "*She,* Doctor."

"Ben, please," he admonished with a wave of his hand. "Do go on. What makes you think the killer is a woman?"

"The butts were ringed with lipstick."

Kramer smiled slowly and shook his head. "Well, now I see why the police are stumped. They're taking too much for granted."

Joey blinked. "Are you saying it *isn't* a woman, Dr. Kramer?"

He tilted his head to one side. "Highly unlikely, Mrs. Coye. *Highly* unlikely. Female serial murderers are as rare as snow in July."

"But not nonexistent?" Ash stood, obviously agitated.

"No, not nonexistent. Although, those few I've studied have been violent in their methods, violent to the extreme. Multiple stabbings, dismemberment..." The doctor's gaze slid toward Joey. "I'm sorry. It disturbs you to hear all of this. You're pale."

"I'm fine."

Ash sent her a worried glance. She nodded to assure him she could handle whatever was said, and he returned his attention to Dr. Kramer. "What about the victims being men? Does that mean anything?"

"Perhaps. Have they *all* been males, Mr. Coye?"

Ash had been pacing, but he stopped. "No. I don't think so." Joey frowned at him. He watched her face as he went on. "I think this killer may be the same one who committed a series of murders in Las Vegas. One of those victims was a woman."

"Ah, yes...June and July 1989. I'm familiar with the case."

"My God..." Joey said no more, but her eyes widened as she searched Ash's steady gaze.

Dr. Kramer rose from his chair and went to the window, pushing aside the curtains to look outside. "We're dealing with a predator, Mr. Coye. One who doesn't wish to be caught. He kills not in a fit of rage, but calmly...like an executioner. He's hunting for a man he believes deserves to die, which is why he stays around to be sure the deed is done. He might be acting in vengeance against a real man in his past, perhaps a man who is no longer around for him to kill. And I don't believe he'll stop until he feels that man has died at his hand." He turned to face them. "If that man is already dead, then the killer might never stop. I'm not sure of the significance of the single female victim. There are hundreds of possibilities there. I wouldn't presume to hazard a guess."

"You really believe the killer is a man? Some kind of cross-dresser or something?" Ash asked, his voice incredulous.

"The odds are that it is a man, though it is not impossible that it's a woman. The cross-dressing is arguable. Perhaps the lipstick on the cigarettes is a deliberate attempt to mislead police. Perhaps he dresses as a woman only when he kills. Perhaps not."

Ash pushed a hand through his hair. "You're not giving me much to go on."

Ben Kramer chuckled. "I'm not a psychic, Mr. Coye. I can give you a bit more, though. This kind of anger probably began in early childhood. I believe you're looking for someone who was horribly hurt by an adult male."

"Physically hurt?"

"Not necessarily, but that's likely. The killer believes this man deserves to die for whatever he did."

Ash looked at Joey, and she cringed, knowing he must be thinking about her feelings for her father. God, did he suspect *she* was the Slasher?

He didn't give her a clue as they left the office, and remained silent when he slid behind the wheel of her car.

She got in, fastened her seat belt and turned to face him. "You think it was me, don't you?"

Chapter 10

He looked at her. Just looked at her, his eyes probing so deeply she felt their touch. "No, Joey. I don't think it's you." He started the car and pulled into traffic.

"I despise my father. I blame him for my mother's death. You know that."

He nodded. "I know that."

She closed her eyes, wishing she could tell him everything, wishing she could believe he trusted her, even knowing about her lies. "Ash, I was *in* Vegas when those killings happened. I was there with Caro and Ted. I was—"

"I know that, too."

She felt her eyes widen. "And you told me not to tell the police I smoke. The cigarette butts they found—"

"Same brand as yours. And before you ask, so was the lipstick. Same brand. Same shade. Coral frost."

She pressed her fingertips to her temples. "Oh, God." She felt her stomach heave. "Oh, God," she repeated.

Ash pulled the car onto the shoulder, gripped her shoulders and turned her toward him. "How long you been smoking that brand, Joey?" She didn't answer and he gave her a little shake. "How long? Tell me."

She bit her lip and tears filled her eyes. "A month, I guess. I never liked menthols before. Then I quit for a while, and when I got the craving again I bought those. I... God, I don't know why." She was crying openly, sure he believed she was a killer, feeling sicker by the minute. "I didn't kill those people, Ash. I swear to you—"

"I believe you."

She blinked and looked up at him.

"I believe you, Joey."

She shook her head, confused, bewildered. "Why?"

He pulled her across the space that separated them and kissed her hard and long and deep. And when he finally lifted his mouth from hers she saw the passion and the caring in his eyes.

"That's why."

He let her go, pulled back onto the highway and drove a short distance in silence. "The lipstick is new, isn't it?"

She nodded.

"I thought so. Never bought that color before, did you, Joey?"

She frowned. "How did you know?" He said nothing, so she went on. "No. I haven't even used it more than once or twice. The shade's all wrong for me. And I never liked frosts, anyway. I bought it on impulse."

"You bought it because the killer bought it."

She frowned hard. "What do you mean?"

"I have a theory. And I want you to hear me out before you shoot it down. I think you're more connected to this person than you realize. You're picking things up from him... or her, and you're not even aware of it."

She thought about that. "Ash, do you hear yourself? You don't even believe in psychics." She shook her head, looking at her hands folded in her lap. "I'm not even sure I do. At least, I didn't. Before all this."

Ash frowned at her, then shifted his gaze quickly back to the highway. It was smooth, and the blacktop smelled new. The yellow lines were still glow-in-the-dark brilliant.

"How could you *not* believe in it? You've made a business out of it."

"But I never saw it as being... *psychic*. Just intuitive. Maybe as being more sensitive than other people. I never... never had visions or dreams or anything like that. Not until... these murders started."

Ash's head tilted to one side and he took a gentle curve too slowly, deep in thought, she presumed. "Maybe there's a reason for that," he said at last. "Maybe...maybe there's a connection between you and the killer that you just aren't aware of. Maybe it's someone you know."

She sighed hard, shaking her head at the ridiculous idea. "Like who?"

"Like Ted." He sent her a quick, curious glance. "You said it yourself, Joey—he was in Vegas with you when those murders went down. And he's been acting odd lately. Oddly enough that your sister thinks he has another woman."

Joey closed her eyes and tried to picture Ted as a killer. Ted dressing as a woman, or putting on coral-frost lipstick and... Her eyes flew wide. "Caro has the same lipstick, Ash. We were together when I bought mine, and she decided to try it, too."

"So we know Ted has access to it. Does he smoke, Joey?"

She shook her head, almost going limp with relief. "Not in years. He quit right after Brit was born, because the smoke used to make her wheeze."

"You remember his brand?"

Joey shook her head. "I don't think I ever knew it." She concentrated hard, trying to find the answers in her mind, but they simply weren't there. And she knew too well there were other reasons for her to feel connected to this killer, to feel like the bastard had invaded her mind. Compelling reasons. Her own sister was on the hit list. And so was Ash. Those two things alone might have some bearing on her uncanny abilities in this. It didn't have to mean the killer was someone she knew.

But she couldn't tell Ash about her sister, because he was going to get his memory back soon. And if he knew the truth—that she'd only come to him in order to save her sister, that she'd played cruel, wicked games with his already-fragile mind—he would hate her. And she couldn't bear that.

"What kind of background does Ted have? Was he close to his family?"

She jerked herself out of her misery and tried to focus on Ash's questions. "His mother and stepfather still live in Nevada. He doesn't see them much anymore, but it's not because of any discord. Just the distance. They all seemed to get along fine whenever I saw them together."

"And where's his natural father?"

Joey frowned and shrugged. "I don't know. I've never heard Ted mention him." Images danced at the fringes of her consciousness. Images she'd seen before, in the nightmare. Her sister, Caro, lying facedown on the floor, her regulation sweats and baggy shirt stained with blood, her long, calico blond hair tipped in red. And the hands, those leather-gloved hands, reaching for her.

Joey pressed her fingers to her temples and sucked air through her teeth. God, she just wanted it to stop!

"Joey?"

She glanced at Ash and bit her lip. "You're right. There's some kind of connection, but I don't think it's Ted. Whatever it is, it's getting stronger. I can hardly close my eyes anymore without feeling . . . that blackness . . . closing in."

Ash reached out and his warm hand pushed into her hair, stroking it. "We won't talk about it anymore today, hmm? We'll just . . ."

She looked at him, smiled softly. He really seemed concerned. "Just what?"

"Whatever you want. Dinner in the most elegant restaurant in town. Syracuse Stage for the latest play. Ballroom dancing. You name it, lady."

She felt a warmth creeping through her, and she nodded.

Ash couldn't get over it. And he couldn't quit looking at her, lying back with her head pillowed on a backpack. She wore faded jeans that were a little too big, their legs rolled up, and a pair of black army boots that laced up over her ankles. The flannel shirt she'd pulled on over her tank top was worn-blanket soft, and its plaid pattern was fading. Her hair was long and loose, falling over her shoulders from under the most ridiculous-looking hat he'd ever seen in his life. Her fishing hat, she called it, and it dangled with hooks and lures of every imaginable description. The white light from a Coleman lantern bathed her face, shimmered in her hair, and her green eyes darted every few seconds to the fishing pole propped in the crotch of a forked branch she'd stuck in the ground.

Still, baggy clothes, ridiculous hat and all, she was the most irresistible woman he'd ever seen. It made no sense, but she looked better to him than any glamorous cover model or starlet or swimsuit calendar girl ever could.

And she was relaxing. The tightness wasn't in her jaw, and the worry that had clouded her eyes earlier was all but gone.

He would sit out here with the mosquitos all night if it would ease her mind.

She tensed up all of a sudden, eyes on the water. "Ash!"

"Hmm?"

"You have a bite."

He dragged his eyes from her to the fishing pole and saw its end twitching sporadically. He'd much rather continue watching Joey, but he leaned forward, carefully picked up his pole and waited. When it jerked in his hands, he yanked it once, felt his success in the frenzied tugging and began to reel it in.

Joey stood, balancing precariously on her good leg, and reached for the line when it was in the shallows. "Oooh, it's a nice one, too." She grabbed the slick black bullhead and worked the hook free. Ash shook his head slowly. Squeamish, she wasn't. She dropped the fish into the waiting pail, grinning from ear to ear.

"You really like this, don't you?"

She handed him a can of worms and settled back down in her spot beside him. "What's not to like?" She extended her wounded leg carefully and drew the other knee up to her chest, wrapping her arms around it and gazing out over the calm, muddy water. Crickets chirped madly, and once in a while the deep croak of a bullfrog floated like a foghorn on the breeze. The night wind stirred her hair.

Ash baited his hook and, with a less-than-expert cast, sent his line sailing out over the miniature lake. "So how did you know about this place?"

He balanced his pole in his own forked branch and sat down, closer to her than before. But when he glanced at her face, it was troubled. "Joey?"

She swallowed, sighed softly. "My dad used to bring us here when I was a kid."

"Did you like it this much then?"

She didn't look at him, just kept staring out at the water. "Mom would pack more food than an army could eat. We'd build a fire, toast marshmallows." She laughed, just a little. "Caro would never bait her own hook. She hated touching worms, and she never caught a thing because she'd insist on holding her pole and she wiggled it around so much a fish would have to be nuts to try and bite. But Dad would hook one on his, and he'd let Caro reel it in."

Ash felt a twinge inside. Jealousy, maybe, for the childhood he'd never had. And then he felt something else, something sad, when her smile slowly died. "That was before I knew what he was really like. I thought he was superman back then."

"Tough image to live up to."

She said nothing, just looked away, up toward the starry sky. Her eyes shone a little too much, and she blinked quickly.

"Joey, have you ever sat down and talked to your father, heard his side of things?"

"There's no excuse for what he put my mother through, so why bother asking him to explain?" She shook her head. "No, Ash, I don't want to talk to my father."

"But maybe if you—"

"Or *about* him." She shook her head. "It hurts too much."

"If you didn't still care, it wouldn't hurt at all."

She looked him square in the eye. "Sounds like the voice of experience."

He clamped his jaw shut. He was certain what he'd said was true, in her case. But not in his. He didn't care at all. Never had. It was different.

"Were you close to your father, Ash?"

"I never knew my father." He got to his feet. "You know, that camp-fire idea isn't bad." He looked around, spotted some twigs and dried leaves and began gathering them.

"What about your mother?"

Ash deposited the kindling atop the charred remains of other fires, old ones. "You didn't happen to bring any marshmallows, did you?"

He felt her gaze on him for a long moment. Then she released her breath all at once. "Afraid not."

He looked at her and saw the knowledge in her eyes. He knew she was feeling his emotions just then, experiencing his private hell right along with him. And for some reason, it didn't feel like an invasion. More like a mental hug. When their eyes met, those fingers of horror from his past released their brief grip on his mind. Warmth and light took their place.

She got up and walked toward him, stopping right in front of him, and he straightened from his task of arranging sticks for a fire. Her hands slid up his chest, around his neck, and she stood on tiptoe to press her lips to his. His arms encircled her waist and pulled her closer, and then he opened his mouth over hers, kissing her deeply, slowly, savoring her taste and her scent and her sweetness.

God, what was this thing that filled him when he was with her? Not lust, though he wanted her more every time he looked at her. No, it was more than that, deeper, fuller, bigger than that. It seemed to ooze from his every pore and press in around him from without at the same time. It enveloped them both, he thought, trying to fuse them into one being.

He felt her fingers threading into his hair, and her body pressing to his. He felt the cool, damp breeze bathing them both with its marshy scent. He lifted his head, staring down at those glittering green gems.

She blinked at him, her eyes wide and wonder filled. "I'm so afraid of this," she whispered.

"Of wanting me?" He slipped his hands beneath her shirt and ran his palms over the warm, smooth curve of her back.

"Of... of *needing* you."

He closed his eyes at the impact of her words. "I know."

"It's overpowering. It's getting worse all the time, and I—"

"And I can't do anything to stop it," he finished for her. "I'm not sure I *want* to stop it." He took her hat off and tossed it aside. Then he kissed her cheek, her jaw.

She let her head fall back and he trailed his mouth over her neck. "It's out of my hands," she said softly, her voice wavering like the breeze skipping over the water's surface.

"Then just let it go." His lips moved over her throat as he spoke. "Let it go, Joey."

He brought his hands around between them and pushed the soft flannel from her shoulders. As it fell to the ground, he pushed the tank top up, wrestled it over her head and tossed it aside. She wore nothing underneath, and he feasted on her perfect breasts, first with his eyes and then his mouth. He loved the way her nipples hardened on his tongue, the way they pulsed when he nipped at them, the way she arched toward him in silent supplication. His fingers fumbled with the button and zipper of her jeans, and he shoved them down over her hips, letting his hands caress and squeeze her buttocks as he did.

She trembled beneath his hands, sinking slowly to her knees. Her fingers freed his erection, and then her lips touched him, parted, took him into their warm wetness. He tangled his fingers in her hair, shuddering. Her hands pressed against his backside, pulling him deeper into her mouth. He felt her tongue working him, the soft scrape of her teeth, the pressure of her lips, and he groaned long and low.

He gripped her shoulders, pulling her to her feet, conscious of how fragile she was, both physically and emotionally. He supported her, so she wouldn't step down on that leg. Then he kissed her again while she frantically unbuttoned his shirt, shoved it off him and pushed his pants down.

He clumsily shook free of his clothes, gathering her to him again, feeling the thrill of her silken flesh against his skin. He couldn't get enough of running his hands up and down over the curve of her waist, or of thrusting into her with his fingers to feel the immediate rush of her juices coating them.

He picked her up, hands on the backs of her parted thighs, carefully avoiding the bandaged wound. He lowered her over his arousal. Her tightness was like a hand, gripping, squeezing. He held her hips and moved her up and down over him. She clung to him, feeding on his mouth as if she were starved for it. Her breasts, their nipples pebble hard, brushed over his chest, driving him insane.

He sank to his knees, still inside her, and slowly lowered her to the ground, going down on top of her. Her legs wrapped around him, her ankles hooked at the small of his back. Her hips writhed beneath him as he drove into her, again and again. And he felt her body tightening, tensing, trembling as her breathing came in quick little gasps and her heart hammered beneath his.

His own muscles bunched and twisted, the tension within him building with every stroke, every soft moan she uttered into his mouth, every warm breath that he swallowed. His tongue thrust into her mouth in rhythm with his body into hers, and then she was clinging, shaking all over, sobbing his name. The convulsing of her around him was what pushed him over the edge, and he plunged deep inside her, pulsing with the force of his release.

He closed his eyes and relaxed on top of her, supporting a lot of his weight on his knees so he wouldn't crush her. Her hands stroked his back, and her lips moved over his face and neck. He smiled, smoothing her hair and lifting his head enough to look into her eyes. They sparkled, searching his.

"No one's ever made me feel the way you do, Ash."

His ego launched skyward. She had that effect on him a lot. "I was thinking the same thing about you."

"Faint praise from a man with no memory." She laughed softly, but her smile died seconds later. "But that won't be the case much longer, will it?"

Ash frowned, immediately alert. Was she on to him? "What does that mean?"

"Your memory. It's starting to come back." She averted her eyes.

"What makes you think so?"

"The nightmare. You must remember something about... about your childhood."

He licked his lips. She was too perceptive. He hadn't even considered the possibility that she would...read him so well. "As little as possible."

She ran one hand over his hair. "It was pretty terrible, wasn't it?"

He nodded, not wanting to talk about the hell of his past. She must have read that, too, because she went on. "And then there's the apartment. You seemed to know where everything was. Didn't seem disoriented or anything."

"Oh, that." He said nothing for a moment, kicking himself mentally for slipping. "It felt sort of automatic."

She smiled, but her eyes seemed so sad it tugged at him. "You're getting better and you don't even realize it. Soon you'll remember everything."

"You don't sound happy about that."

"I *want* you to get better, Ash. Don't doubt that."

"But?"

She closed her eyes, shook her head. "It doesn't matter."

"I think it does."

"Let's not talk about it, Ash."

He sighed hard, rolling off her and reaching for his clothes. For just a second there, he'd thought she might come clean, tell him everything, explain her lies. She had disappointed him.

Beverly Issacs paced the hall in front of the apartment door, looking fit to bite nails in half, when Ash and Joey emerged from the elevator. She looked at Joey as if she was looking at day-old garbage, then focused her attention on Ash.

"I've been trying to get ahold of you for hours." It had the ring of an accusation.

Ash's arm fell slowly from Joey's shoulders, and she wished he'd left it there. She disliked this woman instinctively, felt the hairs on her nape stand upright in warning.

"Why?" Ash stepped forward, frowning hard.

Bev's pale face hardened. "We found another one."

Chapter 11

Joey's blood ran cold. Her fingertips felt like ice and tingled. Another one. Another of the Slasher's victims. She slowly closed her eyes. God, when would it end?

"When?" Ash hurried past Bev to unlock his door. He shoved it wide and stood aside while the tall woman strode through.

"Three hours ago, in a run-down house up in Central Square." She spoke as she walked.

Joey saw Ash glance back at her. She stiffened her spine and made herself move forward. She didn't want to hear this, but she supposed she had to. At least this time no one could suspect her. She'd been with Ash all day, all night. Never once out of his sight.

"Victim number five," Ash quoted as Joey passed him. He closed the door, and the three walked into the living room.

"Two," Beverly Issacs corrected. Ash only frowned at her. "Number two. This one had been dead awhile. Older man, lived alone, no close neighbors. Probably still wouldn't have been found if some kid hawking magazine subscriptions hadn't noticed the smell.''

Joey spun away from them, her hand going over her mouth.

"Dammit, Bev, can you get any more graphic?" Ash stood behind Joey, his hands closing on her shoulders, squeezing.

"Sorry. Didn't know she was squeamish."

Joey stiffened, and slowly she turned to face the woman. She was *not* squeamish. She'd just cleaned and skinned a half-dozen bullhead. Her hand tightened on the paper-wrapped fish. She'd forgotten she still held them. She didn't say a word to the woman, just walked into the kitchen, dumped the package into the sink and turned on the water. As she washed them, she could still hear Ash and Beverly talking.

"So why were you so frantic to get ahold of me?"

"I wasn't until I couldn't find you. Then I got to thinking our friend might've decided to make you his evening's entertainment."

"That's a leap of logic, even for you, Bev."

"Yeah, well it's damn near 2:00 a.m. Who's out at this time of night? And then there's your new wife, who hangs out at murder scenes for fun. Add in all the information you have about the case—you know, the stuff you aren't telling me—and it isn't so farfetched."

"You know everything I do," he said, but even Joey could tell by the slight smugness in his tone that he was lying. Joey sprinkled the fish with salt, wrapped them in clean white paper and set them in the fridge. Then she scrubbed her hands.

"Oh, yeah? Well I don't know why a guy named Harris, from the paper, would come to see me about a routine burglary investigation, only to snatch a few butts from my ash-tray and not-so-surreptitiously slip 'em into his pocket. Can you explain that to me?''

Joey could picture the way Ash would shrug, his face all innocence. "Beats me. Nicotine fit, maybe?"

"So you're not talking?"

"Bev, will you relax? If I find anything solid, you'll be the first to know. You think I want this creep to go on kill-ing?"

"If I find out you're withholding evidence—"

"Now, Bev, you know me better than that."

"Stubborn son of a—" Beverly broke off, eyeing Joey suspiciously as she reentered the living room, then shook her head hard and started for the door. "God, I hate men!" The door slammed behind her when she left.

Joey licked her lips as Ash looked her over. "You okay?"

She nodded. "Is Bev Issacs a suspect, too?"

Ash shrugged and slipped an arm around her. "What, just because she hates men?"

He was being evasive. "What are you going to do with the cigarette butt?"

He sighed hard. "Rad's having it DNA tested at an in-dependent lab... just to be on the safe side. Turns out Bev was working in Vegas when those other murders went down. I don't really believe she was involved, but—"

"Did you give him something of mine to have tested, as well?" He didn't answer. Joey stared up at his face, and he didn't have to. She closed her eyes. "God, you really do think it was me."

"Joey, that's not true and you know it. I'm hoping the test will clear you."

"Hoping. But you're not sure, are you?" She looked away, speaking before he could answer. "No, don't say anything. There are already too many lies between us, Ash."

"Maybe if there weren't, I could give you the answer you want to hear." He held her shoulders, staring down at her, searching her eyes. "Talk to me, Joey."

She felt tears burning her eyes and blinked to clear them away. Telling him would mean losing him, and maybe getting him killed. "I can't."

She pulled free of him, shaking her head sadly, and went into the bathroom. He didn't try to stop her.

She woke from her makeshift bed on the sofa to the smell of hot oil, and the sound of the shrilling telephone. She sat up, still groggy, feeling a dull ache of emptiness she knew was due to sleeping alone. She hadn't realized how comforting she found being wrapped in Ash's arms all night until she'd spent a night without it. But she'd been unable to sleep with him, knowing he could suspect her of something so heinous. It only brought home to her how little they really knew each other, and made her feel cheap and easy. So she'd told him she would be more comfortable on the sofa, where there'd be no chance of his rolling over and jarring her leg. And he had gone along with it, knowing full well it was just an excuse.

He poked his head out of the kitchen, breaking into her thoughts. "Oh, you're awake." She heard sizzling, snapping sounds and then the phone jingled again. "You want to get that? My hands are kinda full."

She nodded as he ducked back into the kitchen. She reached for the phone. There was a lengthy silence after her hello, and she repeated it twice before she got a response.

"Sorry, Mrs. Coye. I'm . . . not used to calling Ash and having a woman answer. How are you?"

She recognized Radley's voice. "Fine." She was distinctly uncomfortable, knowing this man shared Ash's uncertainty about her, perhaps was even convinced of her guilt by now. "And you?"

"All right, I suppose."

"I'll get Ash. Just a—"

"Not just yet. I'd like to talk to you for a minute if you don't mind."

She swallowed hard, tensing, wondering if he'd come right out and accuse her.

"I don't mind."

"It's... well, it's a strange question on the surface. But I'm aware of your... your gift."

She felt the blood drain from her face. "Ash told you?"

"No, I found out on my own. The point is, I need you to tell me if you... if you begin to, you know, *sense* anything about this case."

She cleared her throat. "I see."

"I don't think you do. I know you'll confide in Ash if anything... comes to you, so to speak. But you've probably guessed by now that Ash could be a target. He doesn't always know what's best for him, Mrs. Coye, and even when he does, he doesn't always *do* it. It would be just like him to ignore a serious personal risk to get a story. Especially *this* story. So if you come up with anything, it might be best if you tell me first."

She kept her voice low, so Ash wouldn't overhear. "You really think he's in danger?"

"I'm afraid so. I've worked with Ash for three years now, and to tell you the truth, I like the guy. I just don't want to see anything happen to him."

She closed her eyes. "Neither do I."

"Then I can count on you to keep me posted?"

She hesitated, then sighed. The more people working to protect Ash, the better. "Yes."

His relief was evident in his tone. "Thank you. Now can I talk to him?"

"Just a sec." She put the receiver on the end table, threw off her covers and walked barefoot to the kitchen, limping a little less than yesterday. Ash was just piling aromatic, golden brown fish onto a platter. She saw another dish, heaped with home fries on the table, beside a stack of pancakes and a bottle of blueberry syrup. She shook her head in awe.

"Peace offering," he said softly. "Forgive me?"

Forgive him? She was the one keeping the secrets, telling the lies. But she smiled at him. She hated the tension between them, wanted it to end, even though she knew it couldn't. Not entirely. Not until she told him everything. "Your boss is on the phone."

"I missed you last night, Joey." He came closer, ran one hand through her hair.

She lowered her head. "Radley's waiting, Ash." When she looked up he was still staring at her, waiting. She knew what he wanted. "I missed you, too."

He nodded, as if satisfied with her answer, and left the room, calling behind him, "Don't start without me."

"Where the hell were you all night?"

Ash shook his head, scowling at the mouthpiece before bringing it back to his ear. "Some greeting. What're you, my parole officer?"

"I won't go into the five calls I had from your lady cop friend, or the number of messages I left on your worthless machine, or the gray hairs I got wondering if the Slasher finally caught up with you."

"I think you just did."

"Hear this, Coye. From now on, you let me know where you are, when you're coming back and what the hell you're up to."

"Or what?"

"Or you're off the story."

Ash swore fluently into the receiver.

"Dammit, Ash, I want this scoop as badly as you do, but it isn't worth losing my best reporter. Keep me posted. That's an order. Understood?"

"Fine." Ash agreed, but he didn't like it.

"Good, so the next time I can't reach you, I assume the worst and send in the police."

As threats went, it wasn't half bad. "Right."

"Okay. So what'd you find out from the shrink?"

"He's of the opinion that our killer is a man. Says it's rare to find a female serial killer."

"That's nuts."

"That's what I said, but he was adamant."

"What else?"

"Probably abused in childhood, maybe by a trusted adult male. Might be a cross-dresser, but just as likely might not be."

Rad cussed softly. "Sounds to me like you're more apt to learn who it is from your little wife than from this quack."

Ash glanced toward the kitchen. He could hear plates clacking together, silverware jangling. She must be setting the table. "Maybe."

"What's that mean? Has she said anything?"

"I just have a feeling she's close." Ash frowned. "And it scares the hell out of her."

Rad was quiet for a moment. "You think there's a chance she already knows and just isn't saying?"

"Why the hell would she keep it from me?"

"Why do women do anything?" Rad sighed. "Ah, hell, it was just a thought."

"It was a stupid thought. She'd tell me if she knew."

"Like she's been so honest up to now, right?"

"Dammit, Rad—"

"Okay. Don't call me out for insulting the lady's honor. I'm no good with pistols at twenty paces. I'm just trying to cover all the bases."

"Well, you're not even in the ballpark. And by the way, don't send Harris to do any more snooping. The guy's about as subtle as a sledgehammer."

"Bev saw him take the butt?"

"You got it. Maybe you'd better come up with some plausible explanation before you run into her again. Look, is there anything else? My breakfast is getting cold."

"Go eat. But don't forget—"

"Yeah, Rad. I'll fax you a written itinerary before I leave the apartment again, okay? You want it notarized?" He hung up while Rad was still swearing at him.

When he walked into the kitchen, Joey was pouring coffee. He stopped in the doorway, because the sight of her there slammed him in the chest. For a second, he just looked at her. She wore one of her own nightgowns. Not one of the slinky ones, just a plain white one with short, puffy sleeves and a hemline that hovered around her ankles. Her hair was loose, fluffing around her shoulders like a calico cloud.

He liked looking at her, fresh from sleep with her eyes still puffy and her hair unbrushed, standing barefoot in his kitchen, pouring his coffee. He'd like to look at her this way a lot.

She carried two cups to the table and sat down. "So how's the boss?"

"Like a mother hen. He was worried about me." Ash took a seat across from her and helped himself to a piece of fish and a scoop of potatoes.

"So was Beverly Issacs."

He met her gaze across the table. "She's only worried I'm keeping evidence to myself."

"No, she was worried about you. I think...I think she cares."

She was jealous. It was in those transparent eyes of hers. He would have been idiotically glad to know it, if he wasn't aware of her mistrust of men in general, thanks to her father. "Joey, I am not interested in having a fling with Bev."

She nodded, averting her eyes, filling her plate. "You told me once you don't believe in cheating."

"It was the truth. I don't." That should end her worry, he thought, and stabbed three pancakes with his fork, dropping them onto his plate.

"But what if...we weren't married? Would you be interested then?"

He sighed in exasperation. "If we weren't married, all I'd be interested in would be getting us that way!"

He blinked, and only shook himself to clear his head when he heard his fork clatter onto his plate. What in God's name had made him blurt *that* hunk of baloney? Frowning, he picked up the fork and stuffed a piece of fish into his mouth to prevent anymore absurdities from slipping out of it.

The doorbell buzzed. "Damn. Seems the whole world is conspiring to keep me from having breakfast." He chanced a look at her, but she was just staring at him with those big green eyes, looking as if he'd just told her martians had landed on the roof.

He pushed away from the table and went to get the door.

Ted Dryer stood there looking like a wrung-out rag. His shoulders slumped, his shirt was rumpled and his eyes had dark circles ringing them.

"I need to talk to Joey." There was no preamble, no greeting.

Ash swung the door wider and stepped aside, waving one arm with a flourish. "In the kitchen. Join us for breakfast?"

Ted didn't answer, he just walked in, hands stuffed into his pockets. Ash followed, in time to see him pull out a chair, turn it backward and straddle it. Ash took his own seat and resumed eating, though he was quickly losing his appetite.

"You talked to Caro?"

For someone who needed to see her so badly, he was awfully casual.

"Of course I have. Haven't you?" Joey finished the meager amount of food she'd taken and got up to carry her plate to the sink. She took out another cup, filled it with coffee and set it down in front of Ted.

"No." His voice was dead.

"Well, you could try calling *her.*"

He closed both hands around the mug. "I have. She won't talk to me."

Joey shook her head, and Ash could see she felt sorry for him, even though she probably believed the same thing her sister did. "She's upset, Ted. Give her some time."

He nodded and lifted the mug, closing his eyes as he sipped from it. "How is she?"

"Fine. And so are the girls." Joey reached out to touch his shoulder. "They don't know anything's wrong. She hasn't told them. They think it's one big vacation, and they're having a ball."

Ted looked at Joey and smiled just a little. It was the saddest thing Ash thought he'd ever seen. "Thanks for that." He glanced across at Ash, then looked pointedly at his plate. "You almost through?"

Ash shook his head and shoved the half-finished breakfast away, thinking it just wasn't meant to be eaten. "Tactless, but to the point. I take it this is going to be a private conversation."

Ted nodded.

"Well, hell, I *always* shower right after not eating. Knock yourselves out."

He left to go into the bathroom, and he did turn the shower on. But then he slipped back out to the living room, where he could listen in. It wasn't that he didn't trust Joey. He did, in spite of everything. It was Ted that worried him.

"You guys were out late last night."

"We went to the lake."

"Ah...the fish."

"Bit like crazy. I'd like to go back today, but—"

"Tell me the truth, Joey."

God, he'd heard that one before. Ash tensed, waiting for her reply.

"I don't know what you're talking—"

"Don't give me that. This marriage to Coye is a sham, isn't it? There's no record of it in Vegas, or here or anywhere else."

Silence. Then, "How did you know?"

"I checked, is how I know. This whole thing has smelled like bad meat from the start. Does Coye even know, or have you got this poor guy completely buffaloed?"

He heard her sigh, long and hard. "He doesn't know. And you can't tell him."

A chair scraped the floor. Heavy steps seemed to pace. "It's this Slasher thing, isn't it? It's all wrapped up in these murders. Dammit, Joey, you've been obsessed with this thing from the first day it hit the papers. What in hell's going on with you?"

Another chair moved, more gently. "Ted, I'll explain it all to you. I promise. But not now. Not yet."

Silence again. A longer one this time, and Ash could feel the tension in the air.

"You know who it is, don't you?"

"Not yet. But...I think I will. Soon. And then this nightmare will be over."

"Or maybe it'll just begin. Joey, if you keep sticking your nose into places it doesn't belong, you're going to get yourself killed."

Ash stiffened. Was that menace in Ted's voice? A threat? Or just genuine worry? Either way, enough was enough. Ash stripped off his shirt, dropped it on the floor and sauntered back into the kitchen. Both sets of eyes turned toward him, startled, guilty. Joey looked like a frightened doe.

"Sorry to interrupt. I forgot my coffee."

Ted's gaze turned skeptical. "You always take coffee into the shower with you?"

"Old habits die hard."

"So do cockroaches." Ted sent Joey a warning look, then shook his head and left them alone.

Ash watched him go, then faced Joey. "He seemed upset."

"Just like your editor. He's worried."

"About you?"

She nodded. "He's sees himself as some sort of father figure—has ever since he and Caro got married. It drives me nuts, but it's kind of endearing." She sighed and started clearing the table. "At least it was, before he hurt my sister the way he has."

"Fell off his pedestal, did he? Just like your old man?"

She picked up the platter of leftover fish. "You ought to have a cat."

But her face had tightened at his words, and anger had flashed in her eyes. Just for a second it occurred to him that Ted could just as likely be in danger from Joey, as the other way around.

She felt it all day, crushing in on her. *Danger.* No longer a subtle tingling sensation up her spine, but a big, suffocating hand slowly closing around her. Its grip steadily tightened, until she felt as if her brain was in a vise and someone was turning the screws. She knew the threat to Ash was drawing nearer all the time.

The Slasher was somewhere close, watching, waiting.

Ash spent the morning on the phone, talking to everyone involved with the old crimes in Vegas. Not witnesses—no one had ever seen the Slasher strike—but people who had known the victims, or who had been unfortunate enough to discover one of their bodies. He was milking them for every crumb of information, hoping something would click into place, giving him a clue to the killer's identity. But it was apparent from the increasing tension in his face and in his voice that he was getting nowhere.

He hung up the phone and stared hard at the filled pages of notes in his hand as if waiting for a line to jump out and grab him.

"We have to get out of here."

He looked up fast and frowned at her. "What's wrong?"

"We just have to get out of here. Ash, something's going to happen. I feel it. Let's just leave."

He crossed the room to where she stood, pulled her into his arms and hugged her hard. "Relax, Joey. We're going to be fine, I promise."

"I should have brought the gun. God, why did I leave it locked up at home? I must be insane." She wrapped her arms around his neck and squeezed. "Please, let's go somewhere."

She knew he could feel her trembling, but there was nothing she could do to stop it. "Where, Joey?"

"Anywhere. The lake. There wasn't this tension there. It felt safe."

He pulled slightly away from her, looked down at her face, then glanced once toward the phone. "This isn't getting me much, anyway. Okay. A picnic lunch at the lake, but you owe me."

She sighed her relief and grabbed his hand, starting for the door.

"Aren't we packing sandwiches?"

"We'll pick some up on the way." She tugged again, but he stayed where he was.

"I'd better call Rad first, or I'm liable to be out of a job."

She closed her eyes and released his hand. "Hurry."

He made the call short and sweet, but the whole time he kept looking at her as if he was afraid she might be cracking up. And even though he hurried, it seemed to Joey that it took forever to get to the car. She let him drive, wanting to be free to watch all around them. All the way out of the city her gaze was darting to the cars around them, the pedestrians, even the traffic cops.

It was only when they'd left the city far behind, and exited the highway to take winding, narrow roads, that she began to relax. Ash smiled at her and squeezed her hand. "Better?"

"Yeah." She let her head rest against the back of the seat, closing her eyes. "I wish we never had to go back."

The car passed over sun-dappled pavement, beneath leafy green bows and needled limbs. It bounded through dips and potholes, and Ash slowed down.

"This road, wasn't it?"

She nodded as he approached the narrow dirt track and turned the car onto it. He drove a little farther. The track simply ended at a copse of maple saplings. Coming to a stop, he twisted the key, and they both got out. He came around the car to meet her, put his arm around her shoulders and walked toward the barely discernable footpath through the trees. A short distance later, they emerged onto a mat of green rolling gently down to the shore of Lake Oshiaki.

Ash held her closer. "We forgot the fishing poles this time. Whatever will we do to pass the time?"

Joey tipped her head back, inhaling to experience the full impact of the place—the pines, the lake water, the wildflowers. "We could swim," she suggested.

"That wasn't exactly what I was thinking."

"I know." She smiled up at him, the relief she felt in being away from that sense of menace making her feel playful. "But we could still swim."

"We didn't bring—" he slanted her a mischievous glance "—swimsuits. But I don't see that as a problem."

She lifted her eyebrows and looked at the lake. "Could be snapping turtles."

"Trying to back out, are you?"

He lunged for her, catching her up in his arms and striding toward the water as if to throw her in, clothes and all. She laughed, and struggled with him, and they wound up on the ground in a tangle of limbs and laughter. She was on top of him, and he caught her face between his palms and kissed her thoroughly. Then he rolled her off him and rose to his feet. He reached one hand down to help her stand. She took it and let him pull her upright.

"Let's do something," he said. "Before I lose my head."

She lowered her gaze. "I like it when you lose your head, Ash."

He growled deep in his throat and drew her to him for one more searching kiss. "It's broad daylight, honey, and I'd never forgive myself if some hunter or someone else came along." He looked at her with mock severity. "No one sees my wife naked but me. Got that?"

Her brows shot up. "Well, I guess I'll have to start wearing clothes to the supermarket, then." When he stopped laughing she slipped an arm around his waist. "Let's walk a little."

"You sure you're up to it?"

She nodded. "A short walk won't kill me. It only aches a little today. Besides, if it gets too painful you'll have to be chivalrous and carry me."

He chuckled, put an arm around her and began moving along the lake's curved shore. "So what are you going to wear to the market? Leather pants and a biker jacket?"

"Of course not. I'm saving those for the PTA meetings I'll attend with our kids."

He stopped walking and turned to look into her eyes, his own filled with some unrecognizable emotion. She saw his throat move as he swallowed hard, but then he began walking again.

She licked her lips, realizing what she'd just said. "Our kids." God, was she going to keep letting herself forget that this marriage wasn't real? Why was that so easy to do?

"Come on," she said, changing the subject. "I'll show you some of the most private spots you'll ever find anywhere."

His brows lifted. "Oh, yeah? And just who showed them to you?"

She elbowed him in the side playfully. "You've heard of Lewis and Clark? Well, these woods were explored and mapped by the great team of Bradshaw and Bradshaw. Caro and I left no stone unturned, even though at twelve and fourteen our map-making skills left room for improvement."

He let her lead the way, enjoying just being with her, watching her hair move as she walked, her limp very slight, her pace slow, relaxed. He liked watching her eyes dart around, taking in everything.

When she'd mentioned having kids with him, something very fragile had taken root in him. Something that made his stomach feel queasy and threw his equilibrium out of whack. He tried to ignore it and pay attention to the things she pointed out as they picked their way silently through the dense woods—a deer track, a pair of chipmunks chasing each other and chattering madly, a hawk circling above, a bare, green spot on a sapling where a buck had rubbed his antlers, scraping away the bark. But he found himself more interested in looking at her. More intrigued by her scent, than that of the pines. More impressed by her grace as she practically danced through the trees, than by that of the hawk gliding above them in perfect circles. He felt good about himself today, filled with satisfaction. And all because she'd relaxed. He'd eased her mind by bringing her here. Taken away some of her turmoil. He couldn't think of a higher cause to strive for.

Until she stiffened and stopped walking. Her eyes went wide, her jaw tight. Her lips trembled slightly. She spun around, staring back the way they'd come. "No..." It was a bare whisper.

"Joey?" He gripped her shoulders, brought her around to face him. The fear in her green eyes made his heart flip over. "What is it?"

"The Slasher...is here!" She pulled free of his grasp, gripped one of his hands in hers and veered off the path, pulling him. "Come on. Run!"

Chapter 12

She was frantic. Her palm against his hand was too warm and damp. She pulled him off the marked trail into the dense trees, running like a scared rabbit with one lame leg. He knew that every step sent pain screaming through her thigh. She grunted softly with the impacts, and her face twisted into a tormented grimace. He had little choice but to go along with her, though he had to wonder if she had finally succumbed to all the pressure she'd been under. He hadn't heard a thing, and he was damned sure no one had followed them down here.

Still, she limped up a steep incline, dragged him behind a cluster of brush and pulled him down until he squatted on his haunches beside her.

He scanned her panic-stricken face, his worry increasing with her every hoarse breath, every shift of her wide eyes. One palm rubbed up and down over her injury. Damn, she could have ripped the stitches out with that little performance. "Joey, take it easy. It's probably nothing. You've been under a lot of—'' Her hand shot out to press over his mouth. Her other one rose, pointing down the wooded bank they'd just climbed.

He frowned as she moved her hand away and looked where she was pointing. And then he heard it. Brush crackling loudly beneath hurried steps. He squinted, trying to see through the dense growth. A shadow took shape beyond the branches, moving a few steps, then stopping, waiting, then moving some more.

The form finally stepped into a clear spot and Ash felt Joey go ice-cold. The Slasher was a tall, big woman. Not fat, just big. Powerfully built. Her long legs were encased in black nylons. He couldn't see her feet, but there was a tight black skirt and a loose-fitting knit sweater. Red. He waited for her to step farther forward, so he could see her head, her face, but she didn't. She just stood there, silent, as if listening. And then her hand lifted, and he saw that it was encased in a black glove, and holding a blade that glinted in the sun as she turned it slowly.

He felt Joey's death grip on his forearm and looked at her. She was pulling him, but her wide eyes remained riveted on the form lurking below. Ash followed, moving with softly placed steps. Joey carefully pushed a tangle of berry briars to one side, tearing her eyes from the Slasher to look at him, and then nod toward whatever she'd revealed. Ash looked and saw the black hole the briars had concealed. His gaze met Joey's, and he shook his head once.

''We have to,'' she whispered. ''Ash...''

He heard the rustle of brush below them and glanced down once more. The killer had turned toward them and was climbing upward. Personally he'd rather stay right here and face the bitch, blade or not, than go into that well of darkness Joey had exposed. But he couldn't risk Joey's life that way. She could be hurt. Killed, even.

He looked again at the cave, licked his lips.

"Trust me." She mouthed the words with trembling lips. He braced his spine against the tremors that were trying to shake it apart and nodded. Joey bent double and crawled under the briars, disappearing into the darkness. Ash got down on all fours and backed in, so he could check the ground to be sure they'd left no telltale signs. As soon as he was completely surrounded in inky blackness, Joey reached past him, gently tugging the briars back into place to conceal the entrance. Then she reached out, felt for his hand, found it and gripped it.

"You can stand," she whispered.

He straightened slowly. She drew him forward, deeper into the darkness, and he went, telling himself over and over that it was necessary. That the danger was outside in the sunshine, not here in this dank, black well. He didn't need to reach out to feel the narrow walls of stone on either side of him, or reach up to know the cold ceiling was inches above his head. He hated the closeness, hated the sensation of there being no air in here, hated that his breaths came short and quick as she pulled him behind her, at her slow, uneven pace.

He steadied himself, clenching his hand around hers, trying to concentrate on her pain instead of his own. She was in agony. She must be, after that uphill run. He fought to think of ways to alleviate her suffering so she wouldn't become aware of his. He wouldn't let her see what this place did to him. He prayed she wouldn't feel his hand shake or sweat. It was the damned darkness! If only there was a light, even a faint glimmer, to break the pitch. But there was no light, and the memory began swirling in the pit of his mind.

There had been darkness then, too. And the feeling of four close walls looming around him, closing in as he crouched on the floor with his knees pulled tight to his chest.

No silence, though. His little cell's walls had been thin, and he could hear the sounds that came through them. His mother's sounds. Animal sounds. As if she was hurting, dying. And if she died, he would remain in the closet forever, behind the locked door, a prisoner of the darkness.

He stopped walking. Joey's hand tugged at his, but his feet refused to move. He fought the misery, the sudden certainty that Joey and the Slasher and the cave were just a dream and that he was still that little boy he could hear crying in his mind. He turned as if to look around him, but saw nothing. He took a step backward, retreating from the horror, only to come up against a cold stone wall. He closed his eyes and sank to the floor.

"Ash?"

"No." He didn't want her to see him this way, didn't want her to touch him, didn't want her anywhere near him right now.

She knelt in front of him, her hands running over his face, over the dampness of sweat and, if he was honest with himself, perhaps a few tears on his skin.

"It's all right." Her voice whispered over his face, warming it, drying it. Her arms encircled his shoulders and she held him.

Get away from me, dammit.

But his head obeyed when her hands urged it onto her shoulder. His body surrendered to the feel of her warmth, her fingers moving through his hair in soothing rhythm. God, he didn't want her to know....

"I already know." She shifted position, sitting, pulling him with her, holding him with a strength that surprised him. Her arms were silken steel and they wouldn't let go. "There's no locked door here, Ash. And you're not alone. Not anymore."

His head came up and he faced her, not seeing her at all, only feeling her there. He stroked her arm, her shoulder, squeezed it. "I'm sorry."

"You're hurting." Her lips touched his face. "So am I. You don't want to let me in, Ash, but I'm already there."

His breathing had calmed. In her arms, the old terror had evaporated. The little boy inside still cried, but this time someone was listening. He relaxed slightly, leaning back against the wall. He felt her turn to sit tight beside him, her body touching his. She gripped his hand.

"It was your mother who locked you in the little room."

He nodded, though he knew she couldn't see. "She was a whore. I was bad for business."

Her hand clenched. "You were afraid for her."

"I hated her."

"How old were you, Ash?"

He tensed. Bitterness coated the inside of his mouth and his voice came out thick with it. "Four, the first time."

Her head tipped sideways, settling on his shoulder. "Four-year-olds don't know how to hate."

The child inside him cried harder. Ash ignored it, focusing instead on his anger. "This one did."

She shook her head. "I don't think so."

From somewhere deep inside him, the cries became words, pleas. *I just wanted her to love me. Why couldn't she love me?*

Ash went rigid, shaking himself. "Maybe we'd better move on."

But her hands cupped his face and held it close to hers. Her lips touched his, and he tasted her salty tears on them. Her arms crept around his neck. "You're not alone anymore." Her lips moved and she kissed his face, his neck, his ear. "I won't let you be...not ever again."

He snagged her waist and drew her closer, kissing her with an urgency that surprised him. Then he brought her head to his chest and held her there, against his thundering heart. God, he wished he could believe her. It would be so easy to let her in, let her warmth, her love, heal the old wounds.

But he was all too aware that none of it was true. There was no love between them. It was all a farce, one he still didn't understand. And for a moment he wished his pretend amnesia were real, so he could relish this moment, believe in it. It would be easy. It *felt* real.

He pushed her away and got to his feet, gripping her hands and pulling her with him. He shouldn't have talked about his past with her. It made him feel vulnerable, weak. He'd deal with his own problems in his own way. Alone. He would piece together the puzzle of Joey Bradshaw, and he would see the Slasher pay the price. And then he would go his way, resume his search for a life, a family of his own. He would find a woman, one he could build something with, one he could trust. He would have children and give them everything he'd longed for as a child. Everything he'd been denied.

But there would never be love. He hadn't realized that until now. There was a big hole inside him where love should have been. It had never been filled, so there was none there to give.

He cleared his throat and his mind. "Let's go back to the entrance. Maybe the Slasher gave up and left by now."

She stepped nearer, her hands on his shoulders. "Ash, I—"

"No, Joey. No more. It was a brief lapse. I'm fine now."

He thought she nodded. He was glad he couldn't see her face, read whatever was in her eyes, or misread it. He turned the way they'd come, but her hand caught his again.

"There's another exit. This way."

* * *

It was as if he'd slammed a door in her face. Joey wished she could understand why, but she couldn't. She'd felt his thoughts so clearly only moments ago—his anguish, the rush of memories that had engulfed him. But now there was nothing.

She consoled herself that it was good he'd stopped her when he had. She had been about to tell him that she loved him, just to ease his aching heart. Where the impulse had come from, she had no idea. She'd just been overcome with the need to take away his pain, and the words had bubbled up in her throat like some living thing inside her, desperate to escape. She'd let herself get so caught up in wanting to help him that she'd forgotten to protect herself. If she'd blurted out something so blatantly false, he'd have known, or he would find out, as soon as his memory was restored. And then he'd have all the more reason to hate her.

She ignored the recurring urge to hold him close again. She focused on finding the right passages. She knew the cave well, but always before, she'd had a light to guide her. This time all she had was her memory, and it had been a long time. She'd avoided this place and its happy memories after her father had let her down. She hadn't thought she could ever enjoy coming here again...until she'd come with Ash.

He didn't say a word as they walked. His palms were dry, his breathing normal. Maybe she had helped him, then, just a little.

Finally she saw daylight filtering through an opening ahead. She walked slowly, careful not to make a sound. Ash did the same without her warning, just in case the Slasher knew about this cave and was waiting. She honed her senses, opened her mind, sought the prickling sense of danger she feared would come. But she felt only fresh air bathing her face, brilliant sunlight warming it as they drew nearer.

They emerged on a grassy hillside overlooking a farmhouse, a red barn, a cluster of cows. She didn't take her hand from Ash's and he didn't release it until she started down the hill. He stopped her, turned her and then scooped her into his arms. "I couldn't help you in there. Too cramped. But I'll be damned if you're walking on that leg anymore today."

She leaned forward and kissed him. He stared at her for a second, and she saw her own confused feelings mirrored in his dark eyes. Then he started off, carrying her down the hill to the farmhouse.

While Joey spoke to the farmer's wife, Ash used their phone to call the police.

"This proves Joey isn't the Slasher." Ash said it for the fourth time as he paced Radley's office.

"Only if you can be sure the woman you saw *was.*"

"Well, who the hell else would have been slinking through the woods with a knife in her fist?"

Rad's hands came up in front of him. "I didn't say I doubted you, I'm just asking if you're sure."

"I'm sure." Ash stopped pacing and stared at his friend. "What I'm not sure of is how the hell she knew where to find us. You're the only one I told, Rad."

"You saying you think *I* had something—"

"I'm asking if you told anyone else."

Rad shook his head as he rose from his chair. "What do you think, I'm an idiot? Of course I didn't tell..." His words trailed off. He pushed a hand over his graying hair and swore under his breath.

"What?"

Rad sighed. "Bev Issacs. She was in my office when you called, grilling me about that cigarette butt Harris lifted from her ashtray." He grimaced. "Dammit, Ash, I jotted the location down in case I needed to reach you." He turned, searching his desk, moving file folders aside. "The note's gone. She could've taken it."

As he said it, Joey reentered the office. He'd tried to get her to stay off the leg, but she couldn't seem to sit still. Her wide eyes met Ash's. He answered her unspoken question as she handed him a mug of coffee. "There's a chance Bev Issacs knew where we were."

Joey's tongue darted out to moisten her lips. She obviously wanted to say something, but hesitated.

"Go on, Joey. What is it?"

"I think... I think Ted might've known, too. I mentioned this morning that we might go back there." She crossed the room, putting her back to both men, and stared out the window between the white slats of the blinds. "I don't think it was him, though. I really don't. Not Ted."

"I thought you said it was a woman?" Radley's voice conveyed confusion.

"She—the *person*—was wearing a skirt. I never got a look at the face. It could've been a man." Ash stepped up behind Joey, placing his hands on her shoulders. "It would explain a lot. Ted's late-night calls, the things he's been keeping from your sister. And he was in Vegas during that other string of murders."

She whirled to face him, and his stomach tightened when he saw the dampness in her eyes. "It wasn't Ted. And suspecting only the people who could have known where we were is a mistake. There's always a chance we were followed."

"She has a point there, Ash."

Ash heard Rad's words, but kept his eyes on Joey's face. He suddenly understood what she'd meant, in that cave, when she'd said she felt his pain. Because he felt hers now. It would tear her up if Ted turned out to be the Slasher. And it would tear Ash up to see it. He felt close to her, too damn close. As if they were a pair of vines twisting around the same tree, twining together as they grew. Separating two vines so completely entangled would kill them both.

He blinked at the unexpectedness of that thought, and tried to tell himself the vine analogy was overkill. Sure, he was growing fond of her. But he knew they'd go their separate ways in the end, and he knew he wouldn't wither and die because of it. Even if he might wish he could. Damn, there he went again, exaggerating his feelings. What was wrong with him, anyway?

She looked up at him, her eyes so intense he wondered if she'd been reading his mind again. "I want to go home, Ash." She closed her eyes, shook her head slowly. "It's been a long day. I just want it to end."

He nodded, turned her toward the door and slipped an arm around her shoulders, holding her close to his side. It had been a long day. They'd gone back to the lake with the police, answered endless questions, waited restlessly while the area was scoured for evidence. All for nothing. Not a single clue had been left behind. Whoever he or she was, the Slasher was good. Careful. Cunning. Sooner or later, though, there would be a slip. And then the killer would land behind bars. And then...

He stared down at the top of Joey's head. Seemingly sensing his gaze she looked up, met his eyes. And then *what?* he wondered.

The closer the car got to her house, the better Joey felt. She had to put all of this out of her mind, just for one night. She wanted to relax in a steaming bath, drink a glass of wine and spend the night wrapped in Ash's strong arms, feeling safe from the world.

She tensed, though, when Ash drove the car over the graveled driveway and the house came into view. Lights glowed in the windows. Shadows moved behind them. Dread ran in her veins like ice water, and she shot Ash a glance, seeing the same alarm clouding his beautiful face. Then it eased, and he pointed.

"Look. It's Caroline's car. She's back."

Joey glanced in the direction he pointed, seeing her sister's station wagon parked in its usual spot on the paved strip. It could be no one else but Caro. She'd left her car at the airport. But instead of relief, Joey felt an even deeper fear take root inside her. Caro shouldn't be here. She was in danger. God, she'd only been in Florida for a couple of days. Why did she have to come back now?

Ash pulled the car to a stop beside Caro's, and Joey was out like a shot, limping around the house as fast as she could manage, flinging the back door open. "Caro? Caroline! Where are—?"

Her words were forcibly stopped by two small bodies hurling themselves into her arms and hugging the breath out of her. She returned the girls' hugs, but didn't hear their giggling greetings. She focused beyond them, to the foot of the stairs, flooded with relief at seeing Caro there.

She released her pent-up breath all at once, smiling. But the smile died on her lips when the tall, straight form stepped from the bottom stair into her range of vision. Her arms fell limply to her sides, and she gaped.

"Hello, Joey."

Ash was at her side. She felt his strong presence there, felt his eyes on her. But she couldn't look away from the man.

"Isn't it great, Aunt Joey? Grandpa came back with us. He's gonna take us to the zoo and..."

The stream of high-pitched words faded. A dull roar filled Joey's ears instead. Grating her teeth she forced herself to speak. "Hello... Father."

"Joey." He came forward, smiling, stretching out a hand to clasp Ash's. "You must be my son-in-law."

Joey watched Ash's hand gripping her father's, shaking it. "Ash Coye," he said. "Good to meet you, Mr. Brad-shaw." As he spoke, Ash glanced her way.

"Matthew to you," he replied. "I had to come. Had to meet the man who managed to lure my Joey to the altar."

"I am not *your* Joey. I'm not your anything."

Caro bustled her way between them, gathering the girls away from Joey's legs and chattering loudly in an effort to break the tension that filled the room to bursting. "Let's all go upstairs. I made us supper, and if it stays in the oven any longer it'll be dry as a chip. Come on."

Joey opened her mouth to say she was leaving, but clamped it shut before the words escaped. She couldn't leave Caro alone, not when the Slasher was so close, so percep-tive, always seeming to know where she was, what she was doing.

"Go on ahead, girls, and finish setting the table," Caro instructed.

They groaned, but obeyed. When they'd left the room, Joey glared at her sister. "What is he doing here?"

"You can address me directly, Joey. I'm standing right in front of you."

Her gaze shifted to him. He looked older. His skin had lost its tightness and some of its color. His hair was grayer than she remembered. "I have nothing to say to you."

"Well, that's good, because I have a lot to say to you. Maybe you'll be quiet and listen for a change, hmm?"

She shook her head quickly, her hair flying over her face. Ash's arm came around her and squeezed, infusing her with strength when she thought her knees would buckle.

"Come on, Dad," Caro said softly. "Come on upstairs. Just give her a minute." She tugged on their father's arm and, reluctantly, he turned and went with her.

The second they were out of sight, Joey turned into Ash's arms, burying her face against his hard chest. Her arms twined around his neck and she clung to him as if she would never let go, battling tears that fell, anyway.

He held her tightly, nearly crushing her to him. One hand stroked her hair. "It's okay, honey. I'm here, just hold on to me. You can get through this."

"I don't want him here."

"I know."

"Make him leave, Ash. Throw him out, tell him—"

"Baby..." He cupped her face in his palms and tilted it up to his. "*You* have to tell him. Whatever it is that's burning inside you, you have to let it out, say it to his face. And maybe hear whatever it is he feels he has to tell you."

She blinked the tears away. "I don't want to do this. I can't."

One hand left her cheek to brush the hair away from her face. "Sure you can. I'll be here for you. I'll help you."

As she stared into his eyes, Joey saw the pain in their velvet brown depths. Pain for her. And steely strength, as well. If he would stay beside her, hold her close to him, maybe she could get through this night. With Ash at her side, she felt all of a sudden, she could get through anything. Anything at all. My God, how had she let herself fall so hopelessly in love with him?

He lowered his head and caught her lips with his, still cupping her face with one hand, while the other threaded through her hair. He tasted her, sipped from her mouth. A tender kiss, but one packed with more emotion than any they'd shared. He slanted his lips over her face, kissing away her tears, then lifted his head, staring into her eyes.

"I need you, Ash." Her voice was choked, hoarse. The words came of their own volition.

"You've got me, Joey."

She closed her eyes, knowing all too well that she didn't have him. Not really. Not for much longer. But at least for tonight.

Chapter 13

The doors were locked. The gun loaded and within his reach. Brittany and Bethany were finally asleep upstairs, but only after insisting Ash tell them a half-dozen fractured fairy tales. Ash had Beverly Issacs's word, for what it was worth, that a squad car would cruise the neighborhood all night, just in case.

Joey stood stiffly, watching him. Her sister occupied the rocking chair, and Matthew Bradshaw sat in the recliner. Ash took a seat on the sofa, and Joey immediately sat down beside him, her body tight to his. He put an arm around her, bent to kiss her cheek. Why he felt like a lion protecting its cub, he didn't know. He wished he could take every ounce of her pain and suffer it himself. But he couldn't. The best he could do was help her through this, as he'd promised he would. She'd seemed to take strength in that promise. He vowed to live up to it.

"Does Ted know you're back?" Joey's voice was as tense as her body.

Caro shook her head. "I'm going to call him later, before I go to bed."

Joey glanced at Ash, worry in her eyes, then looked back at her sister. "Why don't you wait until tomorrow, Caro?"

"Why?" Caroline stopped rocking, her brows furrowed. "Do you know something, Joey? Is he out meeting some—"

"Of course not!" Joey's eyes widened in surprise. "God, you think I'd keep something like that from you? I just thought you could use tonight to unwind, get your head together. That's all."

Caro still looked skeptical, but she settled back in the chair and began rocking again.

"My God," Matthew Bradshaw said in a gruff voice. "My God, just look what I've done to my daughters." He addressed Ash, and his eyes were brimming. "It's all because of me, you know. They can't trust any man now, because the father they thought was perfect had a flaw."

"A *flaw?*" Joey turned her icy stare on him, and he seemed to shrink back into his seat. "Is that what you call it? You broke our mother's heart, and it's nothing to you but a flaw? She died alone in her room, while you were out doing God knows what with God knows who, and it's a *flaw?*"

Ash squeezed her closer, hearing the tears that choked her voice, but she pulled free and shot to her feet, immediately adjusting her stance to take most of her weight on the good leg, then turning as if to leave the room.

Her father stood, as well, gripped her shoulders and forced her to face him. "Your mother didn't die alone, dammit. She died with her lover right in bed beside her."

Joey slapped him so hard he rocked back on his heels. "How dare you!"

He lifted a hand to his face, running his palm over the red mark she'd left there. "You're going to hear some harsh truths tonight, Joey." He glanced at Caroline, who had gone utterly still, and white as a ghost. "Both of you are. And you're going to sit here and listen to them. After that you never have to see me again, if that's the way you want it. But no one is leaving this room until I've said what I came here to say."

"No. I won't listen to you spew lies about my mother!"

Again she turned from him, and again he caught her shoulders. Roughly. Too roughly. Ash got to his feet and shouldered between them, folding Joey into his arms. Her entire body shook, and he held her tighter. He looked over her, at her father, and saw the man's distress. Matthew spun away, pacing a small circle, pushing his hands through his hair.

"Look, I'm not trying to tarnish her memory. I'm not saying she wasn't the most wonderful woman on this planet, because she was. But, Joey...Caroline, she never loved me. I never loved her. We married because she was pregnant. We were both too young to know anything about love."

Joey turned in Ash's arms, but held them around her waist and kept her back pressed to him. "I don't care why you married her. She was your *wife.* She gave her life to you, and to Caro and me. She didn't deserve..." Her voice trailed off. Her head lowered and a sob wrenched her body.

"We both knew, Joey. Our feelings were out in the open. We decided to stay together, raise you girls in a stable environment. We planned to go our separate ways when you grew up. As time went on, she fell in love with someone else, and so did I. It wasn't a secret, dirty liaison. It was right on the table. When we moved to Florida, we lived separate lives. We only kept up the pretense for the sake of you two girls. Your mother couldn't bring herself to tell you the truth."

"Because it isn't the truth," Joey whispered. "It isn't—"

"It was George Prentiss, wasn't it?" Caroline spoke for the first time, her voice soft, wounded. "He was always coming around, bringing presents for us... and for Mom. Sometimes he'd be there when we came home from school...."

"Uncle George was just a friend! God, Caro, how can you believe this garbage?" Joey's voice rose until she was nearly shouting at her sister.

"Easy, Joey." Ash reached down to close his hands ound her clenched, trembling fists. "Easy. Hold on to me, remember?"

She opened her hands, laced her fingers through his and held on tightly.

"Yes, it was George."

"Liar," Joey spat.

"I don't expect you to take my word for it." He stared at Joey, his eyes filled with pain. "I brought your mother's diary. It's all there, written in her own hand. I think she'd want you both to know the truth now." He shook his head, his shoulders slumping. He looked like a beaten man. "You're adults, women, with families of your own. It's time you understand... and forgive. If you can."

Joey shook her head rapidly. "Get out, damn you. Just go, I don't want to hear any more of this."

He nodded. His feet scuffed the floor as he walked into the kitchen and through the door. Caro ran after him. "Daddy, wait!" Her footsteps pattered down the stairs outside, and their muffled voices floated up from below.

A few minutes later, the back door slammed. Then the sound of an engine came, and Caro's car headlights moved slowly away from the house.

Joey stiffened, then pulled free of Ash's arms and limped to the top of the stairs they'd descended. "Caro?"

Caroline came up slowly, her face tearstained. "He's going to a hotel." She clutched a small satin-bound book in both hands. She bit her lip and handed it to her sister.

Joey stared at it and shook her head slowly from side to side. "It isn't true. None of what he said is true."

Caro pressed the book into Joey's hands. "I don't know what to believe anymore. Was our entire childhood just one big lie?" She closed her eyes and turned toward the stairs, starting up them. "Read it, Joey. I can't."

"No. I won't read it."

Caro stopped, but didn't turn. "You've always been the strong one. I can't do it. You have to." She moved the rest of the way upstairs and disappeared into one of the extra bedrooms, closing the door behind her.

Ash stood in the center of the living room, watching. Joey looked at the diary. She stared hard at its cover, and he knew she was trying to work up the courage to open it. But at last she seemed to decide against it. She crossed the room and set it down on the coffee table. Then she lifted her gaze to meet his.

"What can I do, Joey? What do you need?"

She drew a deep, shuddering breath and let her head tip back until she faced the ceiling before releasing it. When she looked down again, there were fresh tears in her eyes. "Just hold me, Ash." As he moved forward to wrap her in his arms, she went on. "Yes, hold me. The only time I feel right anymore is when you hold me." She melted against him, her bones going limp.

Ash shifted his stance, scooped her up and held her tightly as he mounted the stairs. She wasn't faking the emotions that racked her body. She wasn't faking the tears that burned red trails into her cheeks, or the tremors that passed through her, or the desperation he felt in her arms. She clung to him as if he were the last life preserver on the *Titanic*.

No, he decided as he reached the top of the stairs and turned toward the bedroom, she definitely was not faking any of this. What, then?

He nudged the door open with one foot and carried her inside. Was she really turning to him for support and comfort in the most confusing time of her life? Why, for God's sake? It was almost as if *she* were beginning to believe this phony marriage was for real.

He heeled the door shut, crossed the room and lowered her to the bed as gently as if she were a fragile bird with a broken wing. He caught himself brushing the spun-honey hair away from her cheek, where tears had glued it in place, then stroking the tears away, as well. And even knowing this was all a sham, her feelings for him, and his for her, he leaned over her and pressed his lips to her quivering mouth.

He drew back, gave his head a quick shake. Whatever delusions she was suffering, he was showing symptoms of the same—the way his throat tightened until it hurt to swallow, the way his eyes stung, the way his stomach clenched. He reacted to her pain as if he really was her husband, as if he really was in...*in love with her. God, what a harebrained notion that is!*

He pushed the errant thought aside and went into the bathroom to start a hot bath. He sifted through the cabinet there, sniffing one bottle after another until he found a scent that seemed soothing, then sprinkled the water with perfume. He draped a thin towel over the light fixture on the wall, taking care that the material didn't touch the bulb. The effect was a softer, slightly pink hue rather than the harsh white glare. He drew thicker towels from the shelf and stacked them near the tub.

Without even asking himself why a man who was only passingly fond of a woman would go to so much trouble, Ash slipped out the bathroom's other door and trotted down the stairs to search for wine and glasses. He found both, and returned without pouring, carrying the full bottle of white zinfandel, which he already knew was her favorite wine. He left the bottle and glasses beside the tub, shut the water off and returned to the bedroom.

She lay just as he'd left her, eyes red rimmed and wide, staring at the ceiling, looking shaken and vulnerable. The surge of emotion that flooded him was ridiculous and silly and inexplicable. But that didn't stop him from feeling it, and he decided to stop trying to figure this out and just go with it.

"Joey?"

She blinked, but didn't face him. "I'm all right. I can handle this."

"Never doubted it." He moved around the foot of the bed and sat down close to her.

"Caro was right about that, you know." Her voice was coarse as cherry bark, but no longer wavering or weak. "I am the strong one. I'm the one Mom leaned on when things went bad. And now Caro's doing the same thing, turning to me when she can't turn to Ted."

"You're right." He reached up and began freeing the buttons down her shirt. "But you know something, Joey?"

She shook her head, finally meeting his eyes.

"You have someone to lean on now."

Her lips trembled, turning upward at the corners, but it wasn't quite a smile. "If I lean on you any harder, I'll break your back." She closed her eyes briefly. "I'm not usually like this, you know."

He finished unbuttoning the shirt and moved his hands to the fly of her jeans, deftly releasing the snap, sliding the zipper down. "Like what?"

"Weak. Dependent. Weepy. I usually hate women who act the way I'm acting right now."

He tilted his head to one side, giving that some thought. "Look at it this way, kid. A man wants his woman to lean on him once in a while. Just so he knows she still needs him." He turned away from her, taking her foot in his hands and removing her shoe, then her sock. He repeated the process with the other foot.

She drew a deep breath. "I do, you know."

"Do what?"

"Need you."

He turned fast, catching her gaze in time to see the anxiety in her eyes before she averted them.

"It scares the hell out of me. I hate it, and God knows I never meant for it to happen. But all of a sudden I don't..." She bit her lip and squeezed her eyes closed tightly. The act didn't stop the tears from seeping through to dampen her lashes. She swallowed loudly and rushed on. "I don't know what the hell I'm going to do without you."

"Baby..." A fist gripped his heart as Ash gathered her into his arms, held her to his chest, stroked her hair. The words that leapt into his throat and danced on his tongue were reassurances, promises that she'd never have to be without him. He bit them back, just barely restraining himself from blurting outright lies. Of course she'd have to get along without him. They weren't married. She'd lied and schemed to get him here with her, though he still didn't know why. And no matter how comfortable or how...*right* it felt, it was just a game. They were two grown-ups playing house, and nothing more.

She pretended they were married, he pretended to believe it. He couldn't tell her of his deception—no matter how powerful the urge to do just that had suddenly become—until she told him about hers. He had to know the reason for her lies. She'd started this deception, only she could end it.

He held her close and pushed the blouse down her arms. She remained still, not objecting when he unhooked the bra and stripped that away, as well. He ignored the taut, warm skin of her back beneath his hands, and the gentle curve of her spine, and the soft swell of her breasts pressing to his chest. He'd have to be heartless to try to make love to her now, when she was an emotional basket case. But that was exactly what he would do if he looked down at her naked torso, her peach-colored skin, her dusky-tipped breasts.

Instead, he rose, lifting her into his arms and carrying her to the bathroom. There he lowered her to her feet. "Lose the jeans, fair lady. Your prince hath deduced you be in need of a relaxing bath and some fruit of the vine to ease your weary mind."

She smiled, just a little, then glanced around the bathroom. Ash turned away from her on the pretense of filling the glasses. In truth, he didn't think his chivalrous mood would last two seconds if he had to stand there and watch her slide out of those jeans. He heard the brush of the denim over her legs, her hopping steps as she kicked out of them. He closed his eyes in agony and waited for the gentle lapping of the water to tell him she'd sunk into the tub before he faced her again.

She lay in water to her chin, her knees poking up out of the water, her bandaged thigh just above the surface. Her head rested on the white porcelain; her lashes caressed her cheeks. "Mmm, smells heavenly."

Ash put a glass of wine close to her face, touched it to her cheek. Her eyes opened, then she lifted a dripping hand to take the glass from him. She sipped. Ash's gaze stubbornly fixed itself to her lips, loosely pressed to the rim of the glass, slightly parted as the soft pink liquid flowed through them. She lowered the glass to the side of the tub. Her tongue swept over her lips, sweeping up the traces of wine there. Ash swore under his breath.

"What's wrong?"

He met her gaze head on. Not much sense in lying about it, was there? It must be written all over his face. "I'm an insensitive clod, driven by a one-hundred-eighty-proof libido, and sadly lacking in princely chivalry, no matter how I try to fake it."

She frowned at him. "In English, Your Highness?"

"Okay, in English. I want you, Joey. Here I am, blown away that you'd even think about leaning on me in your hour of need, that you'd trust me to help you through this crisis. And all I can think about is stripping naked and climbing in that tub with you." Her green eyes rounded, but he held up two hands before she could speak. "Don't say it. I'm a rutting buck, a pig. I know."

She looked to be deep in thought for a moment. She took a slow sip of wine, then another, while Ash awaited her condemnation. Then she stood. Graceful as a swan taking flight from the glistening surface of a lake, she rose out of the water. Rivulets of water streamed down her body. Droplets clung to her belly, glistened on her breasts. She reached out, caught the front of his shirt in two hands and pulled him closer. Her lips pressed to his as her hands worked the buttons of his shirt. A second later she pushed the material down over his arms and the shirt pooled at his feet.

"Do me a favor, Ash?"

"Name it." His voice was throaty. His hands skimmed over her wet skin and he found it hard to breathe.

"Leave the mind reading to me. You're no good at it."

"No?"

She shook her head, shoved at his jeans. "No. I want you, too. I want you to hold me and make this crazy world disappear, just for a little while."

Ash kicked away his pants and stepped into the tub with her. Joey's arms slipped around his waist, and her body pressed tight to his. He groaned, bending over her, catching her mouth beneath his and kissing her deeply. His hands slid up and down over her back, tracing its contours, then lower, to cup and squeeze her perfect buttocks, and lower still to the backs of her thighs. He lifted her legs, wrapped them around his waist, and then anchored them atop his hips, slowly lowering himself into the water.

Their lips never parted. He sipped hungrily from her mouth, and she returned every sweep of his tongue with equal fervor. When he was sitting, the hot water surrounding him, he clasped her waist, lifted her slightly and positioned her over his pulsing need. He nudged her open. Her eyes opened, pinioning his. He pulled her down, sheathing himself inside her as all the air rushed out of her lungs. She moved up the length of him and down again, slowly, languorously. His arms wrapped around her waist with room to spare.

He kissed her jaw, her throat. Her head tipped back as he bit and suckled her neck. He pushed her back still farther, and she arched to give him access to her breasts. Those dark peaks strained toward him, silently begging for attention. He laved them with his tongue, going at one after the other like a man possessed. Her body moved faster, harder, taking him more deeply into her with each thrust. He bit her nipples, tugged at them, sucked them mercilessly, until she cried out. Her fingers twining in his hair told him it wasn't too much and urged him on. He obliged her, loving to feel the shivers that raced through her body with every touch of his lips, his teeth. Her pleasure magnified his, and he thought it worked both ways—when he groaned she moved faster. When he shuddered her body trembled in response.

In no time at all he found himself drowning in a sea of sensations, each more intense than the last, each wrapped in a blanket of Joey. Her scent, her feel, her sounds, her taste. He spiraled out of control, catching her mouth beneath his once more, plunging his tongue deep to taste more of her, thrusting it to mimic the movements of their bodies. He was beyond restraint, and he had only a second to wonder if she'd made the journey with him. Then she cried out and bucked, clutching him tighter, her silken dampness convulsing around him, milking him.

He died a little bit as he poured himself into her. What this woman did to him!

As his muscles uncoiled he stretched out, lying back in the tub and pulling her down atop him, her chest pressed to his. He massaged her shoulders, rubbed her back.

"Mmm. Nice."

He smiled, glad he could give her something "nice" to counterbalance all the not-so-nice things in her life right now. "Feel better?"

"Yes." She was utterly relaxed against him, and her voice was drowsy.

"Think you'll be able to sleep now?"

"Umm-hmm."

"Right here in the tub?"

"What?" She lifted her head, but her eyes were heavy lidded.

"The water's getting cold, fair lady."

"I thought frogs liked cold water."

"Not this one."

She settled her head on his chest again. "Well, I guess that proves it. You're no frog."

"Oh, no?" He gripped her tight and held her as he rose. He reached for a towel, wrapped it around her and saw goose bumps rising on her thighs.

"No. You've evolved."

He chuckled as she tucked her head down on his shoulder and closed her eyes. Stark naked and dripping wet, he carried her back to the bedroom, tugging down the covers on the bed. He stood her on wobbly legs and rubbed her vigorously with the towel, then urged her to lie down and pulled the covers over her. "How's the leg?"

"Mmm, just a little sore. No problem." She burrowed deep, hugging the comforter around her shoulders, pushing her head into the pillow. Her eyes closed and she released a long sigh. "Maybe you were a prince all along, and I just couldn't see it."

"I'm no prince, Joey."

Her lips thinned, but she said nothing. Ash used her towel to dry off, then went back to the bathroom to drain the tub and swipe up the water they'd splashed all over the floor. He poured himself some wine, refilled Joey's glass and took them back to the bedroom with him.

She lay very still, and he would have thought her asleep except that her breathing wasn't deep or regular. He set the wine on the nightstand.

"What am I going to do about that damned diary, Ash?"

He shrugged, facing her. Her eyes were open now and searching his. "Read it?"

She licked her lips. "You think?"

"That's what I'd do."

She nodded. "Okay. I'll read it. Only...only not now. I've got enough to deal with right now, with the Slasher, and Caro and Ted breaking up, and this thing with you—"

"Thing with me?"

She averted her face, closing her eyes again. "No, I have too much to deal with now. I'll read it later. When all this is settled."

He wanted to ask what she'd meant by that remark, but realized a second later that he didn't have to. He knew. Hadn't he been wondering about this *thing with her*? This feeling of being too close? Of caring too much? Was he to assume, then, that she was having similar concerns? Maybe she'd never intended to care about him when she'd concocted this insane plot of hers. And maybe now she found herself caring in spite of herself, just as he was.

Right. And maybe I'm spinning straw into gold thanks to an overactive imagination and a case of wishful thinking.

Wishful thinking? Then he did care about her? And he wanted her to care back?

Not. Why would I care for a woman I know is lying to me with every breath she draws? A woman I can't even trust? No way.

He glanced down at her again and knew without a doubt she was sleeping this time. She looked utterly relaxed, peaceful, innocent.

Gorgeous.

Shut up.

He went to the dresser and quietly pulled open the drawer she'd cleared out for him. He found clean jeans and a sweatshirt and pulled them on. He had to go out. Alone. He had to get to the bottom of all of this. He'd never be able to sort out his feelings for Joey until he knew why she'd lied to him. And he knew, instinctively, that he wouldn't know that

until the Slasher was stopped, once and for all. It was time
to start doing some serious digging and he couldn't risk
dragging Joey along. She'd be safe here. He would make
sure of it.

Chapter 14

She knew when he left the room. Not that she'd been feigning sleep. No, she'd really *been* asleep. But she'd drifted off only because of the comforting warmth of his aura. She woke with a chilled start as soon as that warmth left.

What was it? She shook the grogginess of sleep from her mind and focused on what she was feeling. Blackness. Ugly bloodstained soul eclipsing hers. Cold. Violence. Death. She ran a hand over her brow and felt the cold sweat beading there.

God, no!

She lunged naked from the bed, tore clothes from the dresser and slung them on at record speed. She pulled on shoes with no socks and ran from the room, wincing every time she landed on the injured leg, but refusing to slow her pace because of it. Ash was gone. Nowhere in the house; she was sure of it without even looking for him. She turned, raced crookedly down the stairs and skidded to a halt. She looked toward the guest room door.

"Caro," she whispered. Then she glanced down the stairs. "Ash." God, to protect one of them was to leave the other alone, vulnerable.

The sound of a car out front snapped her out of the quandary. She hobbled through the living room to the sliding-glass doors.

The car was Caro's. Her father got out of it and stood there, staring at Joey through the glass. For the first time in recent history, Joey wrenched the broom handle from the tracks, flicked up the lock and tugged the door open.

"Dad. What are you—?"

"Ashville called, asked me to come."

Joey shook her head in bewilderment.

"He said you could be in some kind of danger, Joey. Why on earth didn't you tell me about this? What's been going on in your life that's got you in trouble? What—?"

"Not now." The tone of her voice must have gotten through to him. "Look, I'll explain later. Right now I have to find Ash. He's the one that's in danger, not me. Did he say where—?"

"*He's* in danger?"

"Where is he, Dad?"

Her father stepped forward, ran one hand over her hair as if soothing a child's headache. "You saw it, this danger he's in?"

She nodded hard. Her father had never doubted her being ultrasensitive—psychic. He was the only one who had never doubted it.

"But you're safe? You're sure?"

"Yes, Dad. But I'm not so sure about Caro. I want you to stay here with her. Watch the house. Don't let anyone in. No one, not even the police. My gun is in the nightstand beside my bed. Go and get it, and then stand watch over Caro and the girls."

"You're going to try and find Ashville?"

She nodded. "I have to."

"You love him, Joey?"

She swallowed a huge lump in her throat. "God, yes."

"He said he needed to ask someone some questions. I thought he sounded like he suspected them of something."

One of the people Ash suspected could be the Slasher, she thought grimly. Ted, or Beverly Issacs?

She'd have to check both. She gripped her father's arm, looked him in the eyes. "This is no joke, Dad. Watch out for Caro. Don't let me down...again." She drew him inside and turned to grab her leather jacket from the back of the chair where she'd left it. Then she exited the door he'd just entered. "Lock this behind me."

He did, and turned on the outside light. Joey trotted to the garage, swung one leg over the big bike and painfully kicked it to a start. Thankfully the Harley always started on the first try. With a swing of one foot she got the kickstand up. Finally she notched it into first gear with her toe, released the clutch and gunned the motor. The rear wheel spun as she took off into the night.

The message was simple. "Meet me to talk about the Slasher." Ash had only needed to utter those seven words into her answering machine's recorder before Bev had snatched up the receiver.

"Ash, what is this?"

"You tell me. Screening your calls now, Bev?"

"What have you got on the Slasher?"

"Meet me. We'll talk."

"Where?"

"Someplace quiet. How about the last crime scene?"

"You're one morbid son of a—"

"'Fraid I'm the Slasher, Bev? 'Fraid your throat'll get cut?"

"Try it and I'll break you up in little pieces and feed you to the glow-in-the-dark bass in Onondaga Lake, Coye."

"Funny."

He hung up and then eased Joey's car out of the driveway as quietly as possible. He'd already put in a call to Joey's father, explaining as much as he could and asking him to come and stand watch over the girls while he checked this out. If Bev was guilty, which Ash found himself doubting more and more, then he'd be able to get her to slip up and reveal something. The woman had a temper like nitro and it wouldn't take much to set it off. If she got mad, she'd slip and then he'd know for sure.

Or at least he hoped so. It was worth a shot.

Anyway, he'd made it here, to the old man's house in Central Square. It was empty, ghostly, and the sickening aroma of decay still lingered. It was a simple house, a shoebox kind of a place with the sickly sweet old-man kind of smell on everything—tobacco mingled with liniment mingled with mothballs. It almost overshadowed the scent of death.

He walked back and forth in the living room, past the worn brown sofa and the tilted recliner and the rocker, the magazine rack that spilled over with junk mail, the flooded ashtrays with their stale butts, the half-dozen brown pill bottles huddled together as if for warmth on a folding tray table nearby.

The damned door hadn't been locked. Then again, he saw little worth stealing here. The TV was so old it still had a knob to turn the channels with. No buttons. No remote. Probably had an old-fashioned picture tube shoved into its back. He stiffened as a sound came from behind him.

Slowly he turned and scanned the dim room. He'd only turned on one light, a low-wattage bulb in a big lamp with a yellowed shade. The front door, the one through which he'd entered, was just to his left. But the sound hadn't come from there. It had come from the rear of the house. Maybe from within the house.

He strained his eyes in that direction. A set of steep, narrow stairs ascended into blackness and the second floor. Another black hole led to what must be the kitchen. There would be a back door in there, wouldn't there? And maybe a basement. And the front door hadn't been locked, so why the hell would the back door be? Someone could have come in. Hell, someone could have been here waiting.

The Slasher?

Ash swore the skin around his jugular retracted just a little as he moved slowly forward to investigate that sound. He stopped, going rigid for an instant when someone's fist thumped the wooden door behind him. He spun around. The door swung open and Beverly stepped inside. She pulled a restless hand through her David Bowie haircut, then gave it a shake, as if she was worried the night wind had messed it up. There wasn't enough there to mess.

"I'm glad you came."

"This had better be good, Ash. My last experience in this shack was a little too memorable."

He shrugged and crossed the room toward her, the noise from the kitchen momentarily forgotten. "Have a seat?"

She glanced down at the faded brown couch, then shook her head. "No thanks."

Ash wondered if he'd been tactless. "That isn't where they found the guy, is it?"

"Hell, no. You've seen the Slasher's work."

She was right, he realized. There was no blood anywhere. His curiosity peaked. This was the one crime scene he hadn't taken a good look at. He glanced at her, brows raised.

"The kitchen. You been in there yet?"

He shook his head, the sound he'd thought he heard out there leaping to the front of his mind again.

Bev glanced toward the darkened doorway, her face going tight. "Bloodbath."

"Worse than the others?"

Her gaze came back to his, but it was unfocused, as if she were seeing the crime, instead of him. "He struggled."

Ash closed his eyes, trying to block out the image those two words painted in his mind. He was unsuccessful.

"So what did you want to talk to me about?"

He blinked at the way she shifted gears without warning. It took him just a second to catch up. Then he said, "Vegas."

She stared at him. Hard, as if she was trying to read him. "What *about* Vegas?"

"Come on, Bev. You know what I'm talking about. A string of murders, just like what's happening here. You were a rookie cop with a Vegas beat when they went down."

She averted her eyes, shrugged. "Four murders. I wouldn't call that a string. And they weren't *just* like these. One of the victims was a woman."

"I see you've been giving this some thought."

Her head came up fast, chin jutting. "Damn straight I have, Coye. Wouldn't you? There are similarities, but just as many differences. I've reached the conclusion that we're dealing with two separate killers."

"You're sure?"

She stabbed holes through him with her eyes. "Positive."

He nodded, rubbed his chin. "Because the only other answer is that it's the same lunatic. And if that's the case, we'd have to start wondering about the connection between the Vegas murders and our own. So far you're the only connection I see."

She leaned forward, glaring at him, her eyes narrowing to ice blue slits. "What are you getting at? You saying I have something to do with these killings?"

"Just asking, Bev."

She was on her feet before he finished the sentence. "Damn you to hell, Ashville Coye. You dare even hint at this bull in that rag you call a paper and I'll have you wrapped up in so many lawsuits—"

"Easy, Bev. Come on, you know I wouldn't print anything without facts to back it up. And the *Chronicle* is no rag. Rad wouldn't let anything libelous slip by him."

"You can take Rad Ketchum and his paper and..." She stopped, midsentence. "Is that what that fiasco was all about? That clod you call a reporter sifting through my garbage?"

"It's just a precaution. I'm planning to use a DNA print to rule people out."

"Well, why didn't you just ask? We've already run DNA analysis on the butts found at the crime scenes."

He shrugged.

"You thought I'd get access to the results, didn't you? God, you really think I had something to do with this. I can't believe it."

"Look, I'm just trying to cover all the bases."

"You're trying to cover any base that would take attention away from your cute little wife, Coye."

"Joey's not a suspect. She was with me the last time the Slasher tried anything, remember?"

"Doesn't mean she might not know more than she's saying. She was at the crime scenes, don't forget. You ought to be grilling her, not me."

Ash sighed and shook his head.

"Don't think I'm not aware of the way you've been covering for her, Coye. The times you claimed to be with her while murders were committed, and God alone knows what else. If I can prove it, I'll haul you up on charges."

"Knock yourself out, Bev."

She paced away from him, her strides long, forceful. "So do you have anything useful to tell me, or was this whole meeting just supposed to shake me up?"

"I was hoping *you'd* have something useful to tell *me.*"

"Like what?"

"Like details about those Vegas murders. The things they left out of the official reports. The things that might help me piece this crap together."

She stopped walking, faced him, her expression like chiseled stone. "There *is* no connection between those deaths and these. None. You're barking up the wrong tree, Coye, and I have better things to do than stand here and listen while you do."

She started for the door. Ash lunged after her, gripping her arm. She stopped, but refused to face him. "There is a connection and you know it. If it isn't you, then I have to find out what it is, or this lunatic will go on killing. Is that what you want?"

Her spine was rigid as she twisted her arm from his grasp. "I thought you knew me better. We dated, for God's sake. We were friends. You know, you're obsessed with this case. You were objective before... before *she* came into it. Now it's like nothing else exists. She's involved up to her neck, Ash, and you're scrambling to get her out. But it's not gonna work."

"She's not involved in anything."

"Tell it to a cop with less instincts, pal. She's hiding something, and I'm going to find out what it is before you manage to pin this whole thing on me just to clear her."

He started to argue, but she whirled on him. "Don't deny you're trying to protect her."

"I wasn't going to." He pushed a hand through his hair. "But you can hardly blame me for wanting to look out for my wife."

"I can if she's guilty."

"I *know* she had nothing to do with the murders. I know it as sure as I know my own name, Bev. I wouldn't cover for her if I thought—"

"Hell, Coye, you're so head over heels in love with her you don't know what you're doing. But I'll tell you what you're *not* doing. You're not setting me up to take a fall, just to clear her." She shook her head slowly, turning again toward the door. "Must be nice to have somebody care enough to put their own head on the block for you. Does she know how much risk you're taking for her? Your career could be in the toilet, Ash. Is she aware of that?" She gripped the knob, yanked the door open. "Call me when you get your precious test results back. Then you'll know I'm not moonlighting as a crazed killer and maybe listen to what I have to say."

She stalked out into the night, slamming the door behind her. Ash heard her car start and move away a second later. He paced, rubbing one palm over his nape in a vain effort to ease the knot of tension coiled there. This was like beating his head against a brick wall, and he was beginning to doubt his head could outlast the bricks. There was a kernel of truth to what Bev had said. If Joey turned out to be guilty and it came out that he'd lied for her, his career would be over. He might even end up serving time.

But it was a moot point since she wasn't guilty and had
nothing whatsoever to do with the murders. Nothing.

He stopped pacing, sighed and felt his gaze drawn toward the darkened doorway that must lead to the kitchen.
Well, he was here. He might as well get a firsthand look at
the crime scene, much as that thought disagreed with his
stomach.

He approached the doorway with caution and reached
through it to pat the wall in search of a light switch.

Joey found Ted alone, watching television. She didn't
even bother to knock. As soon as she saw him through the
window, she jumped back on her bike and headed for the
nearest pay phone. There she called Rad Ketchum. The man
had given her his home number when he'd asked her to keep
tabs on Ash for him, and she was glad now that he had.

Rad answered in a sleepy voice, but came alert as soon as
she explained the situation and asked for Beverly Issacs's
home address. Rad recited it, and Joey hung up while he was
still barking questions. Bev's house was only five minutes
away. She skidded into the driveway in under three and a
half.

The lights blazed, but the house was silent. No car sat in
the driveway. Joey walked around the small Cape Cod,
peering through windows, searching for a sign of Ash or
Beverly. Her heart plummeted... and then a tiny red light,
flashing insistently, caught her eye. She did a double take.
The answering machine. It was worth a shot.

She continued around the house until she found an un-
latched window, pushed it up and clambered inside. She
went directly to the machine and depressed the Playback
button....

And heard Bev's recorded message, then Ash's voice, and
then Bev picking up the phone and speaking to him. The

tape had still been running. It had recorded the entire conversation.

Twenty minutes later, Joey lurked outside the small house in Central Square. She'd shut the bike off and coasted down the last stretch of road, parking it behind a huge oak bathed in shadows. No one would notice it there. She saw Beverly go in and crept closer to listen in on the entire encounter.

Something in the center of her chest throbbed when she heard Ash defend her, heard Beverly say he was too in love to know what he was doing. God, she wished it could be true. She knew too well, though, that it wasn't. Ash might be protecting her, but only because he thought she was his wife, and saw it as his duty. When he learned the truth...

At least she knew he wasn't seriously jeopardizing his career by covering for her. She wasn't guilty, and she'd make damned sure no one else ever learned that he'd lied to protect her.

Beverly exited the front door, and Joey ducked lower in the shrubs, their stiff branches scraping her face, to avoid being seen. She breathed the scent of green leaves and night air as she waited. When Bev's car left, she waited some more, thinking Ash would come out a moment later, worrying anew when he didn't.

She slipped out of the shrub and peered through the window into the living room. Ash wasn't there, but a light glowed from another room. Shadows in there moved. She went around the house slowly, peering through one window after another, her fear for him growing. The dark clawed hand that had a grip on her mind tightened. She felt an instinctive panic boiling up inside her and fought to keep herself rational, calm, ready. But her pulse accelerated and her heart throbbed.

Ash stood in the center of a small kitchen, his face twisted into a grimace. One hand rose to cover his nose and mouth, and he turned slowly, examining the room. Joey moved to the next window to see what he was looking at, then finally to the glass panel in the back door.

She drew a breath that caught in her throat. Dark stains marred the floor. Ugly spatters dotted the walls, taking odd, grotesque shapes, even seeming to move....

Wait, that one stain *was* moving. No, not a stain, a shadow! An arm lifting, a slender pointed blade clutched in its fist—

She flung the door open, screaming Ash's name. The wooden door hit a large body just before the blade would have sunk into Ash's throat. There was a thud as the body hit the floor. Joey hurled herself at Ash, knocking him backward, away from that room of death, right through the doorway into the living room. They both toppled to the floor, Joey landing on top of him. Terrified, she scrambled to her feet, spun around and faced the kitchen just as the light flicked off. She saw nothing, only a darker hulk amid the blackness. Joey placed herself squarely between Ash and that darkness.

"The police are on the way, Ash. Are you hurt?"

She heard him get to his feet behind her. She felt his hands on her shoulders, but stiffened her stance, refusing to be moved aside. She shook her head, focusing her concentration on the dark form moving toward them now.

"Come on." Joey spread her arms as if to shield Ash. She was panting, and her heart thudded so hard in her chest that it made her entire body pulse with every beat. "Come on. You want him, you're going to have to go through me. You just better make sure you do a good job, because the minute you touch me, I'll know. I'll know who you are. I almost know now. Touch me and it's gonna be complete. I can feel it. That's why we're so connected, you and I. You're sick and evil, and I'm the one that's going to stop you. I'm the only one who can. So come on, if you think you have time. Come on."

The figure froze in the middle of the dark room. Then a rasping, obviously disguised voice hissed from it. "Another time, bitch. And soon." Then the form moved away, through the back door and into the night.

Ash lunged to go after it, but Joey gripped his upper arm and held on for all she was worth. Her knees buckled. She shook with reaction, every bit of that unexpected steely strength draining from her in a rush.

Ash gathered her to his chest and held her there. He shook his head slowly. "You're insane, you know that?" He held her away from him, searching her face. "You okay?"

She nodded, then stiffened as something warm and wet touched her palm when she slid her hands around his neck. She felt the blood rush to her feet. Dizziness swamped her, and she drew her hand away, staring first at it, then at the red stain on his throat.

"My God! Ash, you're cut!"

He touched his throat, gave his head a shake. "It's just a nick. You pummeled that weirdo with the door just in time." His eyes darkened, and a frown furrowed his brows. "You could have gotten yourself killed, Joey."

"So could you. Are you nuts, coming here alone in the middle of the night to meet a suspect?"

Headlights bounced through the front windows. Tires skidded, and a second later Radley Ketchum surged through the door. "What the—?" He swore a blue streak when he saw the blood on Ash's neck and hurried forward.

"It's nothing, Rad."

"I saw her, Coye. I actually saw her, running down the street. Big woman. Still had the knife in her hand. I thought you'd be dead by the time I got here."

"I would've been if it hadn't been for Joey." He slipped an arm around her and held her closer. "Which way was our Slasher going?"

"East, but she veered off into a backyard and could've changed direction. I called the cops from the cellular."

Ash frowned down at Joey. "I thought you'd already done that."

"I only said that to scare the Slasher away."

Ash nodded, watching Rad rush into the kitchen, flick on the light and run cold water over a clean white hanky he took from his pocket. He returned, and Ash flinched when Rad pressed the cloth to his throat. He yanked it out of the editor's hand and held it to the wound himself. "So what are you doing here, Rad? How'd you know—?"

"I called him." Joey seemed to think it was her turn with the wet cloth. She shoved Ash's hand aside and held the hanky in her own. "I knew you'd gone to meet someone you suspected. I checked Ted's and found him home, so I called Radley to get Beverly Issacs's address."

Ash looked down at her. She kept her gaze on his neck. "And?"

She scrunched her eyebrows together, chewed her lip. "You're not going to like it, but then I didn't much like you slipping out and leaving my father to watch me." She drew a deep breath. "I sort of broke into Beverly's—"

"*Sort of* broke in?"

"Well, the window was unlocked. I listened to the messages on the machine and heard your conversation. That's how I knew to find you here."

Ash shook his head, visibly upset. "And how did you know, Rad?"

"She sounded so upset on the phone, I decided to meet her at Bev's place and see if I could help. But by the time I got there, she was shooting off like a rocket on that Harley of hers.''

"If you followed her, then what took you so long to get here?"

Joey started at the sound of suspicion in Ash's voice. She glanced up at him, worried that he was beginning to mistrust everyone he knew.

"Ease up, Ash. Your lady love here is hell on wheels. She lost me two miles back. I drove around for a while trying to catch sight of her, and then it hit me that I was near this house, so I figured I'd check it out."

Joey lifted the cloth from Ash's neck and shivered. The nick was small, not deep. But right above the jugular. If that blade had cut just a bit deeper...

"Can we just go home? I hate the idea of Caro and the girls there with no one but my father watching over them."

Sirens sounded and grew louder as she finished the sentence. "You can go ahead if you want, Joey." Ash stroked her hair. "I'll stick around and fend off the police and their questions."

She gripped the hand that stroked her hair and held it still. "Dammit, Ash, don't you get it? This bastard is after you. I don't want you out of my sight again, not even for a second."

She bristled when he smiled. "Yeah. My bodyguard, right?"

"This is no laughing matter."

"Who's laughing? You just saved my skin." His smile faded, and his eyes took on a serious gleam. "You did, you know. But if you'd been hurt doing it, I'd never have forgiven you." He pulled her close, surrounding her with his arms. "Dammit, Joey, don't risk so much for me. I don't know what I'd do if anything happened to you."

The police came in, Bev Issacs leading the way. "I heard the address dispatched on the radio in my car before I got five miles away. What happened?"

Joey and Ash exchanged glances, and she knew he was wondering the same thing she was. Had Beverly ever *really* left?

Chapter 15

She was pretty damned pathetic. A killer lurked inside her mind. She felt him invading her again and again, growing stronger with each sortie. She felt his evil, his darkness and his rage. She felt his hatred toward Ash. She battled it with the love she felt for the same man.

She was going to sit in a corner somewhere and go quietly insane.

He could have died last night by the Slasher's blade. God, what if he had? What would she have done if he had?

Quiet. Peace. She needed it in megadoses right now. She still shook all over when she thought of last night. That blade. The killer. So close. That blinding explosion in her mind when she'd stood face-to-face with the embodiment of the shadow of death. When she'd understood, at last, why her fate was entwined with that of a murderer. She had to stop the Slasher. Maybe it was the entire purpose in her having this "gift." Maybe this was what fate had intended by bestowing it. It was a daunting prospect. She wasn't sure she could live up to it.

"You're not relaxing."

Ash's hands massaged her neck and shoulders. His warm breath stirred her hair and his body heat warmed her back. She stared out over the muddy river, her eyes tracing the current and the dapples of orange fire on the water ignited by the rising sun. "Sorry. I'm trying."

"You didn't sleep last night."

"You did," she told him. "I don't know how you could, when you'd just come within an inch of—"

"Don't think about that."

She turned to face him, head tilted up. "Ash, I can't *not* think about it. I almost lost you—"

"But you didn't." He slid his arms around her waist, crossing them at the small of her back and pulling her tight to him. "And you're not going to."

Tears swam in her vision. "Yes, I am. I am, and it's killing me. When you remember . . . when you know . . ."

"Go on." He searched her face, his gaze intense. "When I know what?"

She bit her lip and closed her eyes, willing herself to screw up enough courage to be honest with him for once, even as she realized she couldn't. She couldn't let him storm out of her life. Not yet. Not until he was safe from the wrath of the Slasher. Maybe he'd hate her in the end, but it was worth that price to save his life.

Damn, but fate was asking a lot of her.

"I know there's something you've been keeping from me, Joey. Something big, important."

She opened her eyes and let his probe them as she battled inwardly with her urge to be honest and her need to protect him.

"Tell me, Joey. Trust me."

His melted-chocolate eyes were darker than she'd ever seen them. She felt trapped in their depths and felt them pulling her deeper. Like quicksand. She could drown in those eyes and not regret it. God, how she loved him. And it went against everything she believed to love a man this much and still lie to him. Maybe he would understand. Maybe he would find a way to forgive.

"Ash...I'm not really—"

She broke off as her name was shouted. Blinking away her surprise at how close she'd just come to ruining everything, she turned to see Ted Dryer loping down the lawn toward the river. For just an instant, she'd thought it was her father. The tall, long-limbed build, the straight-backed stance. She had never realized how much Ted resembled her dad. Maybe that was why Caro had chosen him.

She heard Ash's frustrated sigh, but kept her eyes on Ted as he drew to a stop on the dock in front of her. He was not in a good mood.

"Caro up yet?"

Joey frowned. How could he know Caro was here? Dad had taken her car back to his hotel last night, so Ted couldn't have seen it parked out front. "Ted, I don't—"

"You've always been a lousy liar, Joey. So don't bother. Your father called me last night. I know Caro and the girls are here."

"She was still sleeping last time I checked, Ted." Ash stepped off the dock, one arm slung around Joey's shoulder to propel her along beside him, and to support some of her weight. "Come on up to the house and have some coffee. Brit and Beth will have her awake any time now, if they don't already."

Joey planted her feet and glared up at Ash, then turned her gaze on Ted. "Look, if my sister wants to see you, she'll let you know."

Ted shook his head. "Not this time, Joey. I have to see her. We've got to talk this out, her and I." He opened his mouth to say more, then snapped it shut again. "How is she? Did she read the diary yet?"

Joey frowned. "I can't believe that bastard told you..."

"What, Joey? The precious family secret? I'm family, too, don't forget."

Ash's arm tightened on her shoulder. "He had a right to know, honey. What's going on between Caro and your father is having a direct impact on Ted and Caro's marriage. You can't deny that."

She tugged free. "The only thing hurting Ted's marriage to my sister is Ted." She whirled to face him, her breaths coming faster in her anger. "Sneaking out nights, lying about where you were going, spending huge sums of money on God knows what, mysterious phone calls and meetings at all hours. You think she's an idiot? You think she doesn't know what you've been up to?"

"The only thing I've been *up* to, is looking out for my wife's hellion sister!" He gripped her shoulders as her jaw dropped. "Will you quit condemning me and—"

"Looking out for me? What in hell is that supposed to mean? Dammit, Ted, don't spin me some fairy tale. I trusted you. I loved you like a brother, for God's sake, and you let me down. You let my sister down. You broke both our hearts when you were unfaithful."

He only gaped, as if searching for words. But it was Ash's deep voice that broke the strained silence. "Just like your father did, right, Joey?"

She closed her eyes at the pain of those arrowlike words hitting home. Then she opened them slowly and met Ted's tortured stare.

"Joey...I was afraid it was you. I couldn't tell Caro. If she hadn't believed me she'd have hated me for thinking it, and if she *had* believed me it would have killed her. God knows I couldn't go to the police. I wanted to protect you from them, get you some help..."

Joey puckered her face and shook her head. "What help? What are you talking about?"

"The murders. Joey, you've been so obsessed with them, and since the beginning you've been ... different. Strange, preoccupied. I knew your feelings for your father."

She felt her eyes widen in horror. "You thought *I* was the Slasher?"

He looked at the ground between them. "Not at first. At first I just wanted to know why you were so involved in the crimes. But once I hired the P.I. and began hearing his reports..." He shook his head. "There were the cigarette butts, the way you were seen at the crime scenes...and then this thing with Ash. Hell, Joey, what was I supposed to think?"

"You hired a private investigator?"

Ted nodded. "That's where the money went. Those were the secret meetings and odd phone calls. I just didn't want Caro to know."

Joey felt she'd been hit with a hammer. She couldn't even justify feeling angry with Ted for suspecting her. Hadn't she been on the verge of suspecting *he* was the Slasher? She lowered her head, released all her breath in a rush. "God, you're an idiot, Ted." When she looked at him again she asked, "So do you still think I'm a crazed murderess?"

"My P.I. says the Slasher has made two attempts on Ash, both while you were with him. I guess you're exonerated."

"Your faith in me is astounding." She turned, and the three of them began walking again, toward the back door. "So what if your P.I. had found out I *was* the Slasher, Ted? What were you going to do then?"

Ted's brow furrowed. "I have a stack of information on various mental hospitals in the shop."

"Oh."

When they walked inside, Ted was assaulted by his daughters, still in their matching purple nightgowns with a well-known dinosaur on the front. They leapt into his arms and he caught them with practiced ease, one on each side. He kissed them both, then his gaze moved past them to Caro. She stood at the foot of the stairs in her regulation sweats, her long wavy hair pulled into a ponytail.

He closed his eyes. "I've missed you, Caro."

She nodded. "Me, too."

"We need to talk."

Ash heaved a sigh of relief when the four of them left for an overnight getaway. God, the look of bliss on Caro's face after she and Ted had spent an hour talking alone had almost had Ash choking back tears. He no longer suspected Ted had anything to do with the murders. Partly due to instinct, but mainly because he had proof. While Caro and Joey were packing the girls' things upstairs, Ash had had a heart-to-heart with Ted. Not only had Ted produced the name of the P.I. he'd hired, but he had also shown Ash some of the reports he'd had from the man. It was obvious the P.I. *had* been investigating the Slasher killings and *had* been trying to find evidence of Joey's involvement, or lack thereof. Ted would hardly hire someone to find out if Joey was the Slasher, if he were the Slasher himself.

Cross one more suspect off the list, he thought glumly. He hated to think Beverly Issacs was a killer. But it was looking more and more like that was the case.

At least Caroline and the girls would be out of harm's way tonight and tomorrow. They'd all packed into the wagon to head up north to a popular theme park, where the girls could raise hell to their hearts' content, and Ted would have time to romance his wife.

The lucky bastard.

Ash looked to the sofa, where Joey had collapsed as if exhausted. She sat there now, and her gaze kept straying to that diary on the coffee table.

"There's time now," he said softly. "You can read it if you want."

She met his gaze, shook her head. "I don't know if I can."

"I'll leave, give you some privacy—"

"No. If you go, I know I won't be strong enough to do it."

"Then..."

"Read it with me?"

Ash tilted his head slightly.

"Sit beside me, and hold me close, and read it with me, Ash."

There was so much in her eyes. Pain, fear and something else, reaching out to him with a magnetic pull. It was some sticky, invisible substance that seemed to want to meld him to her—soul to soul, pain to pain. It was an intensely private thing she was asking him to share. And he couldn't have refused her even if he'd wanted to.

He sat beside her, and she curled close to him. He put an arm around her shoulders, and she pressed her head into the crook beneath his chin. She lifted a hand, reaching for the little book, but the hand stopped in midair and began to tremble.

He kissed the top of her head and picked up the diary. He opened it to the first entry and held it low, so they both could read.

* * *

Clouds roiled outside, dark black masses blotted out the sun, and thunder reverberated in the distance. Joey sobbed as she hadn't done since she was a child. Violent, racking, uncontrollable spasms that tried to snap her diaphragm in two. And Ash held her, tighter all the time. He kissed her. He made love to her with tender caresses and gentle touches and seemed to absorb part of her pain into himself. And later he bathed her face with a cool cloth.

Her life had been a lie. Everything she'd ever believed about her parents, her family, had been make-believe. They'd never been in love. They'd both had someone else. They'd only remained together for their daughters, and neither could bring themselves to tell the truth.

Her father had, last night. She hadn't believed him then. She still didn't want to believe any of this, but it was unavoidable now. All the proof she'd needed had been shown to her, in her mother's own hand.

"You okay, Joey?"

He was pulling a big, soft brush through her hair, his strokes soothing her aching head as he worked. God, he was going to a lot of trouble to make her feel better.

She'd worshiped her parents once. Then she'd grieved for her mother and despised her father. And now . . . now . . .

"I don't know how to feel about him, Ash."

"Give it some time. It'll come to you. I promise."

She shook her head. "I don't know."

"It will. You're still reeling from the shock. In a day or two that will fade, and you'll know how to deal with this."

She closed her eyes as he pulled the brush through her hair. Then he set the brush aside and replaced it with his fingers. "I couldn't have done this without you. You took away the pain, Ash, and I wish . . ."

He moved around in front of her, knelt down and stared up into her eyes. "You wish?"

"I wish I could do the same for you. I wish I could take away the hurt your mother caused." She saw his face tighten, but she caught it between her palms gently and she lowered her head to kiss him. "If I could go back in time, I would. I'd be with you in that closet every time. And I'd hold you, love you, until the door opened again."

She saw his eyes widen in wonder, just before the telephone shrilled and broke the fragile bond she'd felt forming between them. Ash rose, averting his gaze. He reached for the phone as Joey searched her mind for some way to heal his oldest, deepest wound.

He spoke softly, then hung up. "Ted," he told her, his eyes still not quite meeting hers.

"Problem?"

"They're worried about Felix. He was outside when they left and it's going to storm. We've been elected to drive over there, find the cat and put him in. Ted says you have a key."

She nodded, glancing toward the darkness beyond the window. "We'd better hurry. It's going to pour any minute."

Her prediction proved all too accurate. Ash drove Joey's car through the deluge, wipers swashing back and forth in a frantic attempt to clear the windshield. She hoped it would let up a little by the time they got to Caro's house, but it rained all the harder as they pulled to a stop in the driveway, huge droplets ricocheting off the car's hood like tiny explosions.

After exchanging one long do-or-die glance, they both leapt out of the car and went in opposite directions, calling "Kitty, kitty" at the tops of their lungs just to be heard over the rain.

Joey finally heard an answering pathetic yowl and followed the sound. Felix sat in the tree house, on the back lawn, peering down at her and crying over and over.

"Ash, he's out here!"

Ash joined her. Joey glanced at him, the way his hair was plastered to his head, the rivulets of water running down his nose. She laughed. He lifted his arms from his sides in a helpless gesture, then squinted at her. "Don't knock it, Princess, you're pretty soggy yourself." He hugged her hard, gave her a long, wet kiss, then strode purposefully toward the tree and mounted the ladder. "If this doesn't elevate me to prince status, then nothing will."

He climbed the tree, picked up Felix and then struggled to hold on to the frightened eighteen-pound cat all the way back down. They ran around the house again, and Joey quickly unlocked the door.

Inside, Ash put the cat down. He looked down at his dripping wet clothes, and at the puddles forming around their feet. "Now what?"

Felix tilted his head up and yowled plaintively.

"We'll have to borrow something of Caro and Ted's to wear home. They won't mind. Especially since we saved Felix from a fate worse than death for them."

"You sure?"

She nodded, reached down to scoop up the cat and led the way up the stairs. She pointed Ash toward the bedroom, while she carried Felix into the bathroom to rub him down with a towel. A few minutes later, Ash joined her, wearing a pair of Ted's jeans and a sweater. He reached for another towel and rubbed his hair dry.

"Hurry and change, Joey."

"Felix could catch pneumonia."

"So could you."

Their eyes met, and Joey's hands stilled on the cat. Felix twisted from her grip and jumped gracefully to the floor, his fur sticking up in odd patterns, a black patch laying one way, a white patch another, some sticking straight up. Ash swallowed and cleared his throat. "Might as well hang out here until the rain stops, hmm?"

Joey nodded. "Looks like it might be awhile."

"Yeah. I'd better let Rad know where to reach us."

"There's a phone in the kitchen. Why don't you see if you can scare up a hot drink while you're at it. Caro usually has cocoa mix in the cupboard."

"Okay." Ash started to turn away. Then he looked back at her. There was a longing in his eyes, a glow of something she didn't recognize. "Joey, I..." He bit his lip, then shook his head. "Later. Change now, your lips are turning blue."

I love you. That was what she'd thought he was going to say. *Joey, I love you.* So was that her psychic receptor picking up on a phrase that was practically screaming from his mind? Or was it wishful thinking rearing its persistent head yet again? She watched him go, then shivered and hurried into Caro's bedroom to find some dry clothes.

It didn't take long. She pulled out a pair of warm, comfy gray sweats and a matching sweatshirt. She found some thick socks and even borrowed a pair of tennis shoes from Caro's closet. Brushing her hair and wielding the blow-dryer, she took out most of the moisture.

As she worked she realized that she hadn't been hurting over the diary's revelations. It seemed the shock had been what rocked her at first, and now the knowledge seemed to be settling in her mind and in her heart, rather than eating away at them. She glanced toward the phone and thought about calling her father at the hotel. At least just to tell him she'd read the diary. She recalled the pain in his face when she'd spoken to him, called him a liar. She'd branded him a cheat, a heartless cad. She'd been wrong. She was still angry, or perhaps just hurt, that her parents had lied to her. But she'd convicted an innocent man of the wrong crime. Didn't he deserve this? Just one, brief call?

Ash ought to be finished with the phone by now. She reached for it, still undecided, but when she brought it to her ear, she heard voices. Ash's and Rad's. She shook her head and started to replace the receiver.

"Then she's still lying to you," Rad grumbled.

Joey frowned at the earpiece and slowly pressed the phone back to her ear.

"She almost told me the truth today, Rad. I know she wants to. It's only a matter of time—"

"You don't have time, pal. Maybe you ought to just tell her you know. Tell her the damned amnesia was a ruse all along, and that you know she's lying about the marriage. Force her to come clean."

"Rad, I can't—"

"We're running into a brick wall, Ash. We have to know what she's up to, why she made up this sham marriage and what she knows about the Slasher...."

The receiver fell from her suddenly numb hand and clattered to the floor. She heard a male voice ask, "What was that?" but ignored it. She turned, stricken, and sank onto the bed, staring into space, seeing nothing, feeling her heart shred to bits.

She heard Ash swear, then silence buzzed from the fallen receiver. Hurried footsteps on the stairs came next. He stood in the doorway, and she knew he was staring at her, at the receiver on the floor, at her again.

"Joey?"

She didn't look at him. She couldn't, or she'd break down. "You knew. You knew all along."

"Joey, it isn't—"

"Didn't you?"

He was silent for a long moment. "Yes."

"And yet you deceived me. You never had amnesia."

"*I* deceived *you*? Joey, you told me you were my *wife.*"

"And you pretended to believe me. Why?"

He came closer, reached out to touch her face, but she ducked away and he let his hand fall to his side. "Because I needed to find out what you were up to. I thought it might have something to do with the murders, and I had to know for sure."

She nodded stiffly. "For a story. You turned me inside out for a story."

"Joey, you're twisting this all out of shape. *You're* the one who started this deception, not *me*. You going to tell me you had a better reason than I did?"

Finally she lifted her chin and met his eyes. The tears in her own prevented her from reading whatever emotions might be there. "I know that bastard is going to kill my sister. I saw it. She was lying on the floor, facedown, the back of her sweatshirt covered in blood, the ends of her beautiful hair tinged crimson. That dagger on the floor near her. The Slasher standing over her. And I saw you. *You* are the victim just before Caro. The Slasher will try to kill you before he does her. I had to do something. I had to break the chain, and I sensed I had to break it with you."

His eyes widened and he searched her face. "You had a vision? You came up with this whole crazy scheme to keep your sister alive?"

"At first. But almost as soon as I met you it became just as important to me to keep you alive, Ash. *You* made me feel that way. You let me think...and all the time... God, I made love to you, Ash! How could you let me do that when you knew, when you were only pretending?"

"Joey, no. I wasn't—"

"You let me fall in love with you! Damn you. Damn you, Ash!" She got to her feet and started for the door.

"Wait!"

She froze, but didn't turn to face him.

"You ... you *love* me?"

Her spine stiffened. God, he'd played her well, acting as if he cared when in truth ... Tears streamed over her face, but she wouldn't let him see. "*Loved*, Ash. Past tense." She paused only long enough to tear the fake ring from her finger and throw it to the floor before she raced down the stairs and out the front door, never looking back. She went through the rain to the car, started the motor and took off, spinning the tires on the wet pavement, fishtailing before lurching forward.

Chapter 16

Ash picked up the simple gold band, stared at it and pushed a hand through his hair in frustration. Dammit to hell, she was a freaking lunatic! Angry at him for lying to her when she'd told a whopper as big as his, or bigger. Blaming him for letting her fall in love.

In love.

My God, she loved him. He stood stock-still in the bedroom and let that information seep into his bones, into his heart. He felt something stir deep inside. That old longing. That little boy he'd tried to lock away, the one that yearned for love more than for air or warmth or even light. The deep pit inside him wasn't so empty anymore. And it shook Ash to realize that it hadn't been for some time. Because even though she hadn't vocalized it, Joey had been steadily filling it up with her words, her touch, her presence. God, her kisses, her body, her very breaths, had all been filling that well inside him. It wasn't empty at all anymore. It was filled to bursting; *he* was filled to bursting. No wonder he'd had such confusing emotions about Joey. He loved the woman right back.

He heard the car pull away. He couldn't lose her. Not now. He had to make her understand why he'd done what he had. But how?

He started for the stairway to go after her. Then he realized he couldn't do that. She'd left him without wheels. Think! Hell, he couldn't let her go on another minute believing what she'd just accused him of—that none of this had meant a thing to him, that he'd been playing a role all along. He hadn't been doing that any more than she had.

He paced some more, then stopped at the telephone still on the floor. He'd call her. He'd talk her into coming back, or just tell her what he had to tell her on the phone. He'd make her listen. God, he was only just beginning to realize why she meant so much to him. She'd done what he'd believed could never be done. She'd healed that child inside him. She'd given him the ability to love. He had to tell her that.

Her phone rang endlessly, but no one answered. Frustrated, he slammed the receiver down. Okay, she just hadn't had time to get home yet. He'd give her five minutes. Five minutes, no more. Then he'd call again. And if she still didn't pick up, he'd get to her if he had to crawl. And in the meantime, he'd ponder this some more, decide how best to explain this to her, what to say. It would have to be perfect. She was angry.

He paced the bedroom floor, rehearsing lines, tucking the ring into his pocket.

When he heard the car in the driveway, he stiffened. She was back. His heart skidded to a halt in his chest when he realized it would be now or never. He'd have to make her understand or...

His heart sank when someone else appeared in the doorway instead of Joey. "Damn. What are you doing here?"

"Anonymous caller says the Slasher will strike again tonight. Wanted to check up on you. Everything all right?"

"Nothing's all right."

The person frowned, then shrugged. "So where's the little woman?"

"Her house." Ash thrust his hands into the jeans pockets and turned slowly, head low. "She's mad enough to kill..." His words faded as something heavy and hard came smashing down onto his skull. He sank to the floor, and just before darkness descended, he realized what he should have noticed right off. The person was wearing black leather gloves, with two little buttons....

Joey paced. Then she cried. Then she paced some more. It was nothing. Ash felt nothing for her. He was hard-nosed, stubborn, ready to do anything necessary to get this story. He'd used her all along. God, he'd used her own lie against her, even slept with her. While she'd been losing herself to him, heart and soul, he'd probably been laughing at how far she'd go to carry off her charade. But she hadn't made love to him to convince him the marriage was real. She'd done it because she loved him. She loved him ... still.

She groaned deep in her throat and realized this was going to hurt for a long, long time. Then she stilled as grim laughter filled her mind. Not her own. Nothing this evil could come from her.

The Slasher.

The maniac prowled somewhere out there tonight, enveloped in darkness, somewhere out there sheltered by the storm itself.

Her vision! God, how could she have left Ash alone when she knew he could be next? What if it was too late? What if that blade had already ripped across the tight skin of his throat? She ran to the phone, yanked up the receiver. She'd call, just to make sure he was okay. Then she'd get back to him. She'd...

No dial tone. The phone was dead.

Okay. It doesn't mean anything. Think! Think of the vision. Try and see the area around Ash, when he's lying on the floor. Could it be Caro's house? Could that be where it happens?

She strained to conjure the vision in her mind, but instead of Ash's body on the floor, she saw Caro's. She lay facedown, on a brown sculpted carpet. It could have been the carpet in Joey's living room. Her long, multicolored waves were loose and spread over her back. The ends had soaked some of the blood from the back of the gray sweatshirt and—

Joey went perfectly still and her heart seemed to trip to a stop in her chest. The sweatshirt in the vision... She glanced down at herself. It was the one she was wearing right now. Again she sought details in the image she'd foreseen. It could be her, not Caro. Their hair was alike. She'd only assumed she saw her sister in the vision because of the signature clothing the woman on the floor wore. But the face hadn't been visible. And Joey was wearing those exact clothes right now.

And the phone was dead.

Her heart began functioning again, hammering so hard against her ribs that her body shook with the percussions. She had to get to Ash. The killer would hit him before her. She was certain of that. And she might already be too late.

She turned toward the door. Thunder rattled the windows and lightning flashed for an instant. A dark silhouette was framed beyond the curtains of the sliding-glass door. Not Ash, but a large woman, wearing a skirt.

The Slasher was here already. Finished with Ash. It was Joey's turn now.

"God, please, no," she whispered, limping slowly on trembling legs toward the stairs. "Please don't let Ash be dead. Please." Maybe he was still alive. Maybe, if she could get help to him in time, he could survive. He'd been lying utterly still in the vision, but that didn't have to mean he was dead. It didn't... it couldn't.

She found the stairs and climbed them. She walked softly, trying not to make even the tiniest sound, into her bedroom, to the nightstand. Carefully she opened the drawer, pulled out the gun.

She extracted the clip, made sure it held all the bullets it could hold, then slipped it inside again.

Glass shattered downstairs. She clapped a hand to her mouth to keep from screaming and tiptoed fast to the bedroom door, closing it and turning the lock. She retreated to the far side of the room and huddled in the corner, gun ready.

Footsteps sounded on the stairs. Heavy ones. Then they sounded in the hall. They stopped.

Joey trembled from head to toe as she waited for the knob to jiggle, or for the door to splinter beneath a heavy blow. But nothing came.

She waited longer, and still nothing. Not a sound, or a step, or anything at all. What was happening? Maybe the killer had given up, or left to search somewhere else. She had to find a way to get to Ash. She couldn't huddle in this corner all night while he might be bleeding to death at her sister's house. She had to help him.

Slowly, silently, she crept back to the door, the gun held in a two-fisted, white-knuckled grip. She moved closer and closer, ears straining to hear a sound, or movement. She opened her mind and tried to hone in on the evil presence that had invaded her home, her very being. But she found nothing there. She bent low, pressing her ear to the door.

It smashed open suddenly, cracking the side of her head and sending her sprawling. The gun skittered across the floor and under the bed. The door hit the wall behind it. Joey shook her head to clear it and scrambled to her feet.

The Slasher stood in the doorway, his masculine face grotesquely made up with rouge and shadow and mascara, now running from the rain outside. He even had on lipstick. The damp, blond wig was slightly lopsided. The rain-spattered dress was big and still straining at the seams against broad shoulders and a wide, flat chest. There was a thin layer of dark, curling hairs on muscled arms that ended in fine black gloves of kid leather, with those two tiny buttons she knew so well. And clutched in one of those gloved hands was the double-edged dagger, its jeweled handle glinting in the dim room. The face beneath the garish facade was one she recognized, but still it took a moment to sink in.

Radley. Radley Ketchum.

Ash fought his way to consciousness, a single, blood-chilling phrase ringing over and over again in his mind. "Where is the little woman?"

Joey. The bastard was after Joey, and he'd blurted out where she was. Home. Alone.

Rad. God, he couldn't believe it was Rad. Ash struggled to roll over, then pulled himself into a sitting position. His head was screaming. He was dizzy. He reached for the phone on the nightstand and brought it to his ear, dialing quickly. He asked the cop who answered at the station to put him through to Beverly, then waited until he heard her voice.

"Bev...it's Ash."

"You don't sound too good. Been drinking?"

He could have yelled at her for that. His voice was slurred, but not from alcohol. "The Slasher...it's Radley."

Silence.

"You hear me? It's Radley. He's on his way to Joey's house right now, and she's there alone. Hurry." He slammed the phone down as she began shouting questions. Then he picked it up again and punched Joey's number. It rang endlessly, but no one answered.

His heart was rapidly turning into a lump of stone in his chest. Either she'd changed her mind and was on her way back, or the storm had knocked the phones out...or he was too late.

He got to his feet, still unsteady, staggered down the stairs and out into the rain. The car was gone, but in front of the shop beside the house, Ted's pickup sat waiting. Ash loped crookedly to it, yanking open the door.

No keys.

Panic was trying to set in, but Ash fought it. He had to get to Joey, and he would, if he had to steal a neighbor's car.

He ran to the shop's door, peered through the glass. Yes. The little key rack had one set dangling from it. Ash made a fist and drove it through the window.

"Why?" Her entire body quaked in fear as she saw the insanity in Rad Ketchum's eyes. This was not the man she'd met, the man she'd known. "God, Radley, why?"

"I have to." He spoke softly, almost kindly. "You won't get out of my mind. I can *feel* you there. You said it yourself, you're the one who'll destroy me. But I can't let it happen. Not until I kill *him.*"

He advanced. She backed up a step. "Kill who? Ash?"

"I didn't want to hurt him."

"But you did, didn't you? Did you kill him? Is Ash dead?" The backs of her legs hit the bed, and she began edging sideways, toward its foot.

"It's him. Martin. My foster father. He hates me, you know."

"No. I didn't know that." She didn't want to hear it, either. All she wanted to hear right now was that Ash wasn't dead, or dying. But Radley went on.

"There were others there. My younger sister. Other *girls*. But Martin never hurt them. It was only me." He glanced at the dagger in his hand and seemed to remember his mission. He focused on Joey again. "I can't let you stop me until he's dead."

She recalled the psychiatrist's words, that the killer might be executing the same person over and over again by killing men. But there had been one female victim in Vegas. She watched him come closer and wanted to distract him again. Maybe if she kept him talking. "You don't just kill Martin. You killed a woman in Las Vegas. You want to kill me."

He stopped, blinking twice. "I had to kill her. She saw me. And you ... you won't get out of my mind."

She shook her head rapidly. "I'm trying. Really I am."

"No! Every time you look at me I *feel* those eyes like little drills, digging holes in my brain, trying to find all my secrets. You're a witch!"

Bad subject, she decided. She was almost to the bathroom door now. Distract him, she thought. Distract him and then run. "Why do you wear a dress, Radley? To make the police think the killer is a woman?"

His eyes narrowed as if he thought her stupid. "I *told* you. Martin doesn't hurt the girls. I'm safe this way. And by the time he recognizes me, it's too late." The last three words were accompanied by a slow, evil smile. Radley's eyes got a faraway look, and Joey imagined he was remembering one of the murders and getting great pleasure from it. "And then I cut him, and then I watch him die," he whispered.

Chills raced up her spine and over her nape. Her hand inched toward the door that led to the bathroom. He took another step toward her. His gaze caught the movement of her hand and he lashed out with the blade. She shoved the door open and ducked through it, slamming it behind her just in time. She sprinted across the bathroom, through its other door into the hall and down the stairs. She ran straight through the living room to the sliding-glass doors, shaking hard, her thigh screaming, her blood pounding in her temples, the echo of her pulse deafening in her ears. She bent low and tore the broom handle out of the track, then flicked the lock up, grasping the handle to pull the door open.

He grabbed her from behind and spun her around so hard her head snapped back as if her neck were made of rubber. One hand caught her hair cruelly, tipping her head to expose her neck. The other lifted, clutching the dagger.

She brought her knee up for all she was worth, heard the forced expulsion of air from his lungs and then the thud of the dagger falling to the carpet. He doubled over. She dropped to her knees, eyes never leaving Radley, hands patting the floor. Her hand closed on the chilled handle.

Touching the weapon caused myriad faces to appear in her mind, and an instant later she realized they were the faces of his victims. Innocent, frightened, sad faces. She reached behind her for the door. Radley straightened and took a step toward her. She swung the blade in a wide arc, right to left, and felt the resistance of the skin of his chest as she swung again.

Radley dropped to his knees in front of her, blood spreading over the front of the dress. But he was still conscious, and she couldn't turn her back to try to make it through the door. She darted past him, running for the stairs, hoping to make it to the back door. But before she even reached the kitchen, she felt his arms come around her from behind in a brutal bear hug. He tackled her, knocking her to the carpet, squeezing the breath from her body, crushing her ribs, his weight adding to the burn in her thigh. She felt the wound tear, felt it bleed.

He came down on top of her back, and she could feel the warmth of his blood soaking into her shirt. She swung back with the dagger, her arm twisted so awkwardly it was painful. The blade sank into his side, and when he jerked instinctively away from the pain, she wrenched herself out from beneath him, scrambling to her feet.

Horror like nothing she'd ever known surrounded her, pummeling her senses, and hysteria tried to take over. She fought it, taking a step back, waiting for a chance. Her stomach lurched as he made it up to his knees, reached down and jerked the blood-slick dagger from his side. He looked down at the blade, then his eyes rolled and he fell forward.

She screamed and jerked away still farther, but her back met the wall. Her teeth clattered against each other. The hairs on her nape tingled with static electricity and fear. Her knees vibrated and kept threatening to give out.

But Radley didn't move. He lay motionless, blood steadily seeping into the carpet beneath him. Trembling so violently her muscles felt as if they'd tear free of the bone, Joey bent low, reached out. Slowly, slowly, her hand inched toward the still bloody one that held the dagger. She touched its slippery tip, gripped its blade and pulled it from its owner's grasp.

He didn't move. He was dead. She'd killed him. He wasn't moving. Why was she still so terrified?

She lifted one foot to step past him, to move toward the door. Then she lifted the other. One more step and she would be beyond his reach. She made her legs move. He was behind her now. The door was only a few feet away.

A warm, sticky hand closed around her ankle with crushing force. She fell forward at the sudden tug on her ankle, cracking her head on the corner of a table before she hit the floor, facedown. She felt the knife fly from her hand, saw it land on the carpet, leaving the outline of its shape, drawn in blood, on the pile.

He was getting up on all fours. He was dragging himself forward. She had to move! She lifted her head, though it screamed in agony when she moved it. The blade lay on the floor ahead of her, and she stretched her arm to reach for it. But her fingers fell short of their goal, and then her mind slowly sank into the depths of a black quagmire.

Through the sliding-glass door, Ash witnessed a nightmare. Joey was lying on the floor, facedown. Her back was covered in blood. A dagger lay near her still hand and it, too, was coated in sticky red moistness. She wasn't moving.

Rad stood, hunched over, a grotesque image with smeared makeup and bloody hands and hairy arms extending from the sleeves of a dress. As he straightened, the blond wig toppled to the floor. He stared at Joey and took a step forward.

Ash leapt for the door, knowing it would be locked, intending to kick it in if necessary. But when he jerked on the handle, it slid open. He hurled himself at Radley, smashing him in the face twice, before the big man tottered backward and crashed to the floor like a felled redwood.

Ash dropped to his knees beside him, noticing for the first time the blood pulsing from his side and wondering if it had been his punches or this wound that had brought the man down. The flow of blood stopped. Ash frowned and reached for Rad's throat. There was no pulse.

Agony twisting inside him, he whirled toward Joey, and it hit him that what he was seeing was precisely the image she'd described to him. Except that she'd thought the woman on the floor, her back coated in blood, was Caro. The truth was too much to take. She had foreseen her own murder. Not her sister's.

"God, Joey, don't die on me. Not now."

He bent to lift the sweatshirt away from her back, hoping he could stop the bleeding and keep her alive until help arrived. Already he heard the sirens in the distance. He bent low, squinting in the poor light to see how bad her injuries were, but he saw only a coating of blood. No cuts. No slashes. No punctures. Not even a scratch.

Frowning hard, he caught her shoulders and gently rolled her onto her back. "Joey? Joey, baby, can you hear me?" His eyes scanned her throat and found it smooth and untouched. Her forehead was gashed open and blood trickled over one side of her face, but it wasn't a mortal wound.

The sirens grew piercing, and then the flashing lights came through the still-open glass door, bathing Joey in color. "Joey?"

Her eyes opened. She blinked. "Ash?"

"You're okay..."

"He didn't kill you," she muttered. "He didn't kill you." Tears coursed down her face as he gathered her to him. Her arms tightened around his neck and she clung to him, sobbing softly, words tumbling from her lips the way the tears fell from her eyes. Rapidly. Without order or will. "I would have died if you had. I love you, Ash. I do. I don't care about my parents or the lies we've told each other or anything else. Just you. I'll never lie to you again, Ash. It tore me apart to lie to you. I hated it. But you're alive. You're alive and I love you. I love you."

Her tears made it tough to understand all the words, but Ash knew exactly what she was saying. He still couldn't believe she was all right. He'd thought her dead when he'd first seen her lying there, so still. He stood, scooping her up into his arms as the room filled with cops and an ambulance pulled into the driveway. He ignored the shouted questions, the restraining hands on his arm, and carried her outside, toward the rescue vehicle and the paramedics spilling out of it.

He bent over her, kissing her again and again as he carried her to the ambulance. Then he lowered her to the stretcher the men had just pulled from the back of it and fell to his knees beside it.

"You'll have to get out of the way, sir," one of the medics began.

"I'm not going anywhere except with my wife." He saw her eyes widen at his words, and he reached into his pocket, pulling out the ring she'd thrown at him before. He caught her left hand in his and slipped it on to her finger. "I want you to keep wearing this, Joey."

She frowned at him, ignoring the hands that fastened safety straps across her waist and took her pulse and probed at her injured forehead. "Ash?"

"Just until I have a chance to buy you a real one." He pushed her hair off her face and kissed her lips softly. "I love you, you know. I'm not letting you go. You said you were my wife, and I'm holding you to it, lady."

Another vehicle came bounding up the driveway and skidded to a stop. Matthew Bradshaw, looking frantic, leapt out and ran toward the ambulance. "What's happened? Where's Joey? What's—? My God!" He spotted her on the stretcher and raced toward her, stopping across from Ash, on her opposite side. Ash had never seen anyone so pale, or terrified.

"She's all right. Just a bump on the head," Ash assured him. "She's gonna be fine."

Matthew leaned over her. "Are you?"

She nodded, lifted a hand and closed it around her father's. "I am," she told him firmly. With her other hand she clasped Ash's, her eyes brimming with love as she stared into his. "We all are."

*   *   *   *   *

ETERNAL LOVE
by Maggie Shayne

Fans of Maggie Shayne's bestselling Wings in the Night miniseries have heard the whispers about the one known as Damien. And now the most feared and revered of his kind has his own story in TWILIGHT ILLUSIONS (SS #47), the latest in this darkly romantic, sensual series.

As he risks everything for a mortal woman, characters from the previous books risk their very existence to help. For they know the secrets of eternal life—and the hunger for eternal love....

Don't miss TWILIGHT ILLUSIONS by Maggie Shayne, available in January, only from Silhouette Shadows

MILLION DOLLAR SWEEPSTAKES (III)

INTIMATE MOMENTS®
™ *Silhouette*®

COMING NEXT MONTH

NIGHT SHIFT, NIGHT SHADOW, NIGHTSHADE...
Now Nora Roberts brings you the latest
in her *Night Tales* series

NIGHT SMOKE
Intimate Moments #595

The fire was under control when American Hero
Ryan Piasecki got there. But he was an arson
inspector, so the end of the fire was the
beginning of his job. He scanned the crowd,
looking for that one face that might give him a
clue, a lead. Then he saw her.

She was beautiful, elegant, cool—an exotic
flower amid the ashes. She was an unlikely
candidate as an arsonist, but as a woman...

As a woman she probably wouldn't even give
him the time of day.

**Look for Ryan Piasecki and Natalie Fletcher's
story in NIGHT SMOKE, coming in October to
your favorite retail outlet. It's hot!**

NIGHT94

"HOORAY FOR HOLLYWOOD" SWEEPSTAKES

HERE'S HOW THE SWEEPSTAKES WORKS

OFFICIAL RULES — NO PURCHASE NECESSARY

To enter, complete an Official Entry Form or hand print on a 3" x 5" card the words "HOORAY FOR HOLLYWOOD", your name and address and mail your entry in the pre-addressed envelope (if provided) or to: "Hooray for Hollywood" Sweepstakes, P.O. Box 9076, Buffalo, NY 14269-9076 or "Hooray for Hollywood" Sweepstakes, P.O. Box 637, Fort Erie, Ontario L2A 5X3. Entries must be sent via First Class Mail and be received no later than 12/31/94. No liability is assumed for lost, late or misdirected mail.

Winners will be selected in random drawings to be conducted no later than January 31, 1995 from all eligible entries received.

Grand Prize: A 7-day/6-night trip for 2 to Los Angeles, CA including round trip air transportation from commercial airport nearest winner's residence, accommodations at the Regent Beverly Wilshire Hotel, free rental car, and $1,000 spending money. (Approximate prize value which will vary dependent upon winner's residence: $5,400.00 U.S.); 500 Second Prizes: A pair of "Hollywood Star" sunglasses (prize value: $9.95 U.S. each). Winner selection is under the supervision of D.L. Blair, Inc., an independent judging organization, whose decisions are final. Grand Prize travelers must sign and return a release of liability prior to traveling. Trip must be taken by 2/1/96 and is subject to airline schedules and accommodations availability.

Sweepstakes offer is open to residents of the U.S. (except Puerto Rico) and Canada who are 18 years of age or older, except employees and immediate family members of Harlequin Enterprises, Ltd., its affiliates, subsidiaries, and all agencies, entities or persons connected with the use, marketing or conduct of this sweepstakes. All federal, state, provincial, municipal and local laws apply. Offer void wherever prohibited by law. Taxes and/or duties are the sole responsibility of the winners. Any litigation within the province of Quebec respecting the conduct and awarding of prizes may be submitted to the Regie des loteries et courses du Quebec. All prizes will be awarded; winners will be notified by mail. No substitution of prizes are permitted. Odds of winning are dependent upon the number of eligible entries received.

Potential grand prize winner must sign and return an Affidavit of Eligibility within 30 days of notification. In the event of non-compliance within this time period, prize may be awarded to an alternate winner. Prize notification returned as undeliverable may result in the awarding of prize to an alternate winner. By acceptance of their prize, winners consent to use of their names, photographs, or likenesses for purpose of advertising, trade and promotion on behalf of Harlequin Enterprises, Ltd., without further compensation unless prohibited by law. A Canadian winner must correctly answer an arithmetical skill-testing question in order to be awarded the prize.

For a list of winners (available after 2/28/95), send a separate stamped, self-addressed envelope to: Hooray for Hollywood Sweepstakes 3252 Winners, P.O. Box 4200, Blair, NE 68009.

CBSRLS

OFFICIAL ENTRY COUPON

"Hooray for Hollywood"
SWEEPSTAKES!

Yes, I'd love to win the Grand Prize — a vacation in Hollywood —
or one of 500 pairs of "sunglasses of the stars"! Please enter me
in the sweepstakes!

This entry must be received by December 31, 1994.
Winners will be notified by January 31, 1995.

Name _____

Address _____ Apt. _____

City _____

State/Prov. _____ Zip/Postal Code _____

Daytime phone number _____
(area code)

Mail all entries to: Hooray for Hollywood Sweepstakes,
P.O. Box 9076, Buffalo, NY 14269-9076.
In Canada, mail to: Hooray for Hollywood Sweepstakes,
P.O. Box 637, Fort Erie, ON L2A 5X3.

KCH

OFFICIAL ENTRY COUPON

"Hooray for Hollywood"
SWEEPSTAKES!

Yes, I'd love to win the Grand Prize — a vacation in Hollywood —
or one of 500 pairs of "sunglasses of the stars"! Please enter me
in the sweepstakes!

This entry must be received by December 31, 1994.
Winners will be notified by January 31, 1995.

Name _____

Address _____ Apt. _____

City _____

State/Prov. _____ Zip/Postal Code _____

Daytime phone number _____
(area code)

Mail all entries to: Hooray for Hollywood Sweepstakes,
P.O. Box 9076, Buffalo, NY 14269-9076.
In Canada, mail to: Hooray for Hollywood Sweepstakes,
P.O. Box 637, Fort Erie, ON L2A 5X3.

KCH